THE
BABY-SITTER

Books I and II

D0681280

THE
BABY-SITTER
Books I and II

R.L. STINE

SCHOLASTIC INC.

New York Toronto London Auckland Sydney
Mexico City New Delhi Hong Kong Buenos Aires

The Baby-sitter, ISBN 0-590-44236-8
Copyright © 1989 by Robert L. Stine

The Baby-sitter II, ISBN 0-590-44332-1
Copyright © 1991 by Robert L. Stine

ISBN 0-7607-4925-6

12 11 10 9 8 7 6 5 4 3 2   4 5 6 7 8/0

Printed in the U.S.A.   01

First Compilation printing, September 2003

Contents

The Baby-sitter   1

The Baby-sitter II   171

THE BABY-SITTER

Chapter 1

Jenny stared at her reflection in the dark window glass as the bus squealed around a corner and headed up North Road. Dark houses and trees rushed past in the night. She examined her face in the window, her round, black eyes catching a sparkle from a streetlight and reflecting it back. She liked the way she looked in the glass, so smooth, so cool, so calm.

The bus slowed for a stop sign. What was that animal darting through the hedges? Was it a deer? No. Just a rock. Don't start seeing things, Jenny, she told herself, laughing at her vivid imagination. She was always trying to make the world more interesting than it was.

"Hey — I don't think you've heard a word I'm saying!" Laura's voice broke into her thoughts.

Jenny turned quickly from the window and smiled guiltily at her friend beside her on the bus seat. Laura had been talking nonstop, mostly about boys, as usual, and Jenny, lost in her own thoughts, had practically forgotten she was there. "Sorry. Guess I'm just nervous. It was nice of you to ride partway with me."

"I know," Laura said. "So what are you nervous about? It isn't like you haven't baby-sat before."

"I don't know. I guess it's just new people, a strange house, a strange neighborhood. There's a lot I could worry about if I really put my mind to it." That was supposed to be a joke, but Laura didn't laugh. They'd been friends so long, they didn't have to laugh at each other's jokes.

Jenny glanced at her watch. It was already seven-ten. She didn't want to be late on her first night. The bus hit a deep pothole, and both girls nearly bounced off the plastic bus seat. Jenny leaned forward to retrieve her book bag, which had tumbled onto the floor.

"Maybe the kid's a monster," Jenny said, somehow feeling that she had to justify her nervousness. "Maybe the parents are weird. Maybe they belong to some sort of secret cult and when I find out about it, they keep me locked up in the basement for the rest of my life so I can't tell anyone. Maybe the house is haunted. There's the ghost of a young girl trapped in the attic, and I accidentally let her out, and she inhabits my body and I'm not the same person anymore."

"Possible. Very possible," Laura said thoughtfully. She was used to Jenny's wild imagination. She didn't even bother being sarcastic about it anymore. What was the point? There was no way to stop Jenny from dreaming up the crazy things she did.

2

"Hey — isn't that Bob Tanner?" Laura cried, pointing out the window.

"Where?"

"That guy, raking the leaves in the dark!" Laura reached past Jenny and struggled to pull up the bus window. It was stuck, and she only managed to raise it an inch. "Hey, Bob! Bob! Hi!" she shouted through the narrow opening.

Jenny looked to the front of the bus to see if the other three passengers were staring at them. They were.

"Hey, Bob! Look up! Hi! Bob!" Why did Laura always have to embarrass her?

Because she was Laura. She didn't care about what other people thought. She always did what she felt like. Jenny wished she could be more like that, less thoughtful, less timid, more impulsive. She thought that since they spent so much time together, maybe some of Laura's boldness would rub off on her. But it didn't seem to.

Sometimes Jenny wished she could look like Laura, too. Laura was so tiny, so light, so perfect. She was the shortest girl in the sophomore class, but that was certainly no handicap because she was also the most beautiful. She had cheekbones like a model, and curly, straw-colored hair that fell down to her shoulders like a waterfall. She had sky-blue eyes and creamy white skin, and a tiny, red, heart-shaped mouth.

Needless to say, Laura was very popular. She could go out with a different guy every night of the week if she wanted — and she usually wanted!

Jenny felt terribly plain next to Laura. She was of average height, which made her nearly a head taller than Laura, but her figure was still extremely boyish. She had dark brown hair which she wore in stylish, long bangs that fell over her left eye, the hairstyle copied from a model she had seen in *Mademoiselle*, large, serious eyes, a long, straight nose (that her mother said was her best feature!), and lips that always seemed to be pouting.

"You shouldn't put yourself down. You look just like that actress Demi Moore," Laura had told her one day.

"Don't be ridiculous," Jenny had said, and then rushed home to look in the mirror and see if Laura was right. "Laura's totally nuts!" she told herself. But she was secretly pleased.

"Hi, Bob! Over here!"

The boy looked up as the bus started to move again. It wasn't Bob Tanner. He didn't look anything like Bob Tanner.

Laura slumped down low in the seat and laughed. "That's okay. I don't even like Bob Tanner. He's a creep."

"What? Why's he a creep?" Jenny asked, glancing at her watch. Seven-fifteen.

"He thinks he's cool just because he's so tall." Laura was always accusing people of thinking they were cool just because they were tall. "Hey — are you going to go out with Chuck?"

The question caught Jenny off guard. She'd been thinking about Chuck a lot, but she hadn't been able to decide anything. "Oh, I don't know. He's such a goof."

"He's funny," Laura said.

"He's a total nut case," Jenny agreed.

"Did you see him in the lunchroom today when he put the hardboiled egg slices over his eyes? He was a riot."

"If I went out with him, he'd probably embarrass me to death," Jenny said, feeling embarrassed just thinking about Chuck and how he was always goofing on things.

"Did you see him dissecting that rubber chicken in biology?" Laura went on, ignoring Jenny's negative attitude. "I thought Mr. Holstrom was going to have a fit!"

"The worst was the day we had the substitute teacher in McNally's class," Jenny said, shaking her head. "Chuck convinced the poor woman that he was deaf, and then he kept talking to her in this dreadful, phony sign language. We were all on the floor. She didn't know what was going on! I felt so sorry for her."

Chuck had only been at Harrison High for a few weeks, but already he was a legendary class clown. When he had come up to Jenny at her locker after school and asked if she'd like to go out sometime, she was startled. She hadn't ever really talked to him except to say hi in the halls or at the beginning of history class. She had put him off, saying she was very busy studying.

Why had she been so reluctant? Because she was reluctant about everything? Because she liked to think about things first, to imagine what they would be like before she actually did them?

Because she preferred imagining things to actually doing them?

No. She was just a cautious person, that's all.

Besides, why should she go out with such a goof? He'd probably spend the whole night showing off and trying to be funny. How boring.

"I don't know. If he asks me again, I might go out with him," she told Laura.

She glanced at her watch again, shook her head impatiently, and stared out the window at a lawn blanketed with shifting, tumbling brown leaves. The tall oaks and maples that bordered the yard were nearly bare. Winter was only a few weeks away.

"So you're going to baby-sit for these people twice a week?" Laura asked.

"Yep. Thursdays and Saturdays."

"How'd you get this job, anyway?"

"It was an accident, really," Jenny replied. "I was at the mall last Saturday with my cousin Melanie. We were just hanging out, not shopping or anything. Then I saw this little boy. He was hard to miss. He had the most amazing blond hair. It was almost pure white, and very straight and shiny. He looked like the kind of kid you see only in TV commercials.

"He was by himself, playing near the fountain, and his toy tank fell into the water. He started to climb in after it.

"I shouted for him to stop. He didn't seem to be with anyone. And he wasn't paying any attention to my shouts. He got up on the ledge over the fountain and was about to jump in after his tank. I ran as fast as I could. That fountain's pretty deep. I grabbed him by the shoulders, picked him up, and pulled him away.

"He was pretty upset with me for stopping him. But he got over it as soon as I pulled his tank out of the water for him. He was the cutest kid I've ever seen, big blue eyes, so big they didn't look real, round cheeks, and that amazing blond hair.

"He thanked me and told me his name was Donny. I asked him where his mom and dad were, and he just shrugged. He didn't seem to care. He told me he was six, but he seemed very sophisticated for six."

"Kids are sophisticated these days," Laura said. "My nephew Eddie is only four, and he's already into girls."

"Well, he seemed just like a little adult to me," Jenny continued. "He was so cute. Melanie had to leave, but I wanted to stay with him until his parents found him. He and I sat down by the fountain and had a nice talk, mostly about toys. I think he wanted to tell me every toy he had at home and every toy he wanted for Christmas."

"So then Donny's parents came?"

"Yeah. A few minutes later. And did they look relieved to see him! It turned out they'd been searching for him for nearly twenty minutes. They were frantic, and he didn't even look up when they came. He just wanted to keep talking with me.

"Mr. Hagen introduced himself and his wife. Then he said, 'Well, you and Donny really seem to have hit it off.' Then Donny asked if he could bring me home with him!

"We all laughed. Then Mr. Hagen said that actually they *were* looking for a baby-sitter, someone to come and stay with Donny every Thursday and Saturday night. He asked if I might be interested in the job.

"Well, of course I started to say no."

"Why?" Laura asked.

"I don't know. Because I always say no when I'm asked something the first time, I guess. I like time to think things over. But Donny started begging me to say yes. He was so cute. And I knew Mom and I could really use the money. The Hagens seemed like okay people. So I said yes, I'd give it a try.

"Then Donny started leaping up and down for joy and almost fell into the fountain again!"

"Oh, no!" Laura suddenly jumped up. "My stop!" She lurched toward the front of the bus. "Hey, stop! Please! My stop!"

The bus driver slammed on the brakes. Laura saved herself from flying the rest of the way by grabbing a pole. She turned back to Jenny. " 'Bye! Call me later. Good luck!" And she hopped down the steps and out the door.

The bus pulled away. Jenny looked nervously at her watch. Seven twenty-five. No way she'd be there on time at seven-thirty. She stared into the dark glass and watched the houses glide by. It was a long ride from her house across town to the Old Village where the Hagens lived. She'd have to remember to leave earlier on Saturday night. If she was going to make this trip twice a week, she had to get the timing right.

A few minutes later, the bus pulled into Millertown Road and Jenny, still staring at her dark reflection in the window glass, nearly missed her stop. Suddenly realizing where she was, she pulled the bell cord and ran up to the front door just as the driver was about to pull away.

Bad start, she told herself, stepping down into the cool night air. She squinted up at the street signs, which were partially covered by low-hanging tree branches. Then, following the Hagens' directions, she turned right and headed down Edgetown Lane.

Three blocks to go, she told herself. She started jogging. She was about ten minutes late. The houses she passed were old and very large, mostly Colonial style, with wide, landscaped lawns and majestic old trees that bowed in the wind, as if watching her pass by.

The blocks were long. The houses gave way to woods. A small black dog came running up from behind her, yapping and sniffing at her sneakers as she ran. "Go home, dog. Go home," she said, already out of breath, a sense of dread growing from the pit of her stomach, slowing her steps, making her legs feel as if they weighed a thousand pounds. Yipping excitedly, the dog gave a last snap, just missing her ankle, and turned back into the woods.

She crossed the empty street. The Hagens'

house should be in the next block. She slowed to a walk and tried to catch her breath. On the corner stood a low ranch-style house, completely dark, the hedge ragged and overgrown, the leaves still unraked. That wasn't it.

The wind picked up. Jenny pulled up the collar of her jean jacket and adjusted her backpack. She passed by a narrow lot of tangled trees and low brambles. Just past the lot, a mailbox on a pole jutted out into the street. Jenny was relieved to see the name HAGEN painted on its side.

She looked up the long driveway to the house. A porch light was on, casting pale white light against the dark, mottled shingles. The house was enormous, a rambling old Victorian. Even at first glance, it seemed rundown. A loose shutter banged loudly against an upstairs window. Another shutter had fallen at an angle and was hanging by only one hinge. A window at the far end of the house had been broken, the hole filled in with balled-up newspapers.

Oh, great. The house is right out of a horror movie, Jenny thought. There's probably green slime pouring out of the walls!

She looked at her watch. Fifteen minutes late. She didn't have time to be worrying about broken windows or green slime. She ran up the drive, the crunch of her sneakers on the gravel the only sound except for the wind.

She stepped into the white light of the porch, straightened her hair, pulling the long bangs down over her left eye, adjusted her backpack, cleared her throat, prepared a smile to greet the Hagens with, and rang the doorbell.

The bell didn't work. So she knocked, having to bang with all her strength to make a sound against the hard, thick wood. She heard footsteps inside.

Okay, kiddo, she told herself. Break a leg.

Chapter 2

"Come in, Jenny. Come in. We were just starting to worry about you." Mr. Hagen pushed open the storm door and stepped aside so that Jenny could enter the narrow front hallway. "Getting chilly out there. Is that jacket warm enough? Did you have trouble finding the place?"

"No. Sorry I'm late. The bus — "

"Let me take your jacket," he interrupted, pulling at the sleeve before she could remove her backpack. "The coat closet door is jammed shut, so I'll put it in our bedroom closet upstairs. Okay? As you can see, the house needs a bit of work. We just moved in a few months ago. The house was built before the Civil War — can you believe it? Well, I can. It looks as if no one did any work on it since then! Ha ha!"

Jenny laughed politely and struggled to get the jean jacket off.

Didn't he ever take a breath? He seemed terribly nervous, not at all like at the mall the weekend before.

Mr. Hagen was a big man, so tall he had to stoop in the low entranceway. He was built wide with big shoulders and powerful-looking hands. He was good-looking in a square-jawed, old-fashioned kind of way. He was wearing a charcoal-gray suit which was snug against his broad chest. His dark hair was cut short, almost a crew cut, and thinning just a bit in front. His eyes were small and steel-gray, and never seemed to stop darting about. His cheeks and ears were red, whether from excitement, or nervousness, or just their natural hue, Jenny couldn't tell.

As he hurried off to take her jacket upstairs, Jenny noticed that he walked with a slight limp. She didn't remember that from the mall, either. But of course she had only seen the Hagens for a few minutes there by the fountain.

"Oh, hi, Jenny. Where is Mike off to?" Mrs. Hagen walked quickly into the hallway, her rimless glasses catching the overhead light and reflecting it so that her small face seemed to radiate light. She was tall and thin, sort of homey, down-to-earth-looking, Jenny thought, with short, curly brown hair and those rimless glasses that hid her large, brown eyes. She wore a simple white peasant blouse and a dark wraparound skirt, clothes that made her look older than she was.

"He took my jacket upstairs. Sorry, I'm late. The bus — "

"Oh, that's okay. We have plenty of time. Don't pay any attention to Mike. He's always nervous on the nights we go out. No. Change that. He's always nervous. Period. But you'll get used to him."

"I heard that!" Mr. Hagen called from the top of the stairway.

"Where's Donny?" Jenny asked, picking her backpack up off the floor.

"He's in the den watching a tape. *Ghostbusters*, I think. He's seen it six hundred times. He says it's awesome." She laughed. "It's funny how all of the trendy words and phrases, you know, words like awesome, drift down to the six-year-olds about two years after they've gone out of style. I keep waiting for Donny to tell me that some movie is real groovy, but that word hasn't caught up with him yet. Or maybe it passed him by. I was a linguistics major, believe it or not. So I'm very interested in words and how they travel."

"Really," Jenny said. Then she felt like a jerk. Really? Was that the best she could do? Really??

"Hey, Donny — look who's here," Mrs. Hagen called.

Jenny followed her through the large, cluttered living room. The living room furniture seemed as ramshackle and rundown as the rest of the house. The sofa cushions didn't exactly match, and a large, peach-colored, overstuffed armchair had one arm that appeared to be held in place with masking tape.

"Don't mind the furniture," Mrs. Hagen said, catching the surprised look on Jenny's face. "We inherited it with the house. We're redoing the whole room as soon as Mike gets established at his new job." She continued to the den and motioned for Jenny to follow her in. "Donny, look who's here to stay with you."

Donny was lying on his stomach on the carpet in front of the TV. He didn't look up. "Quiet," he said. "This is a good part. Venkman is gonna get it."

"Donny, don't be rude," Mrs. Hagen said. "You can at least look up from the TV for one second and say hi to Jenny."

"Hi," Donny said without looking away from the screen.

"I guess the romance is over. How quickly they forget," Jenny said with mock sadness.

Mrs. Hagen laughed. "He's impossible," she said.

"No, I'm not," Donny muttered, engrossed in Venkman's battle against the slimy green ghost.

"We're going to be late," Mr. Hagen said impatiently, bursting into the den and shoving his wife's coat at her. "Donny, you have to go to bed when the movie's over."

"Aw, Dad. I didn't have any time to play. Can't I stay up just a little?"

"Well . . . maybe a little. But you have to listen to what Jenny tells you." Mr. Hagen turned to Jenny. His ears and cheeks were bright scarlet. "I'm sorry I didn't have a chance to show you around. I'm sure you won't have any trouble. Donny can give you the grand tour after his movie."

"I'll be fine," Jenny said, looking at Donny.

"We won't be too late," Mr. Hagen continued, talking rapidly. "I left the number where we can be reached in the kitchen. Call if you have any problem at all. Donny can show you how to operate the VCR if you want to watch a tape or something. We're not expecting any phone calls, but in case — "

"Really, Mike," Mrs. Hagen scolded, "I'm sure Jenny has baby-sat before — haven't you, dear?"

"Yes, of course," Jenny said, giving them her most confident smile.

"Here comes a good part," Donny shouted over several loud, explosive blasts from the movie soundtrack. "Awesome! Awesome!"

"Well, if you have any problems at all, the number is on the pad by the phone in the kitchen," Mr. Hagen continued undaunted. "Donny will show you where the kitchen is. And by all means, be sure to keep all the doors locked. Did you read in the paper about the attacks on baby-sitters in this town?" He shook his head sadly and sighed. "Some world we live in."

"I saw it on the news," Jenny said softly. Some creep in a ski mask was breaking into homes and beating up baby-sitters. So far, there had been two attacks. Both baby-sitters had had to be hospitalized.

After she saw the news stories, Jenny decided not to take the job with the Hagens. Her imagination ran wild and she pictured hideous, horrifying scenes. But then she forced herself to think about it clearly. What were the chances the attacker would choose the Hagen house way over on the far end of town? One in ten thousand? No — one in a million!

If I keep the doors locked, I'll be perfectly safe, she told herself. And, besides, she really needed the money. . . .

"Mike, why on earth did you have to bring that up? Are you trying to make Jenny nervous on her first night? Come on. You've said more than enough. Move on out." Mrs. Hagen gave Jenny a conspiratorial wink and shoved her husband hard from behind. He didn't budge. It was like trying to move a tank.

"Good night, Donny. Be good," both parents called as they headed to the front door.

Donny didn't reply.

Jenny slipped into a soft, white leather armchair against the wall. "You're sitting awfully close," she told Donny. His face was only a few inches from the screen.

"I'm allowed," he said. He watched the movie for a while. Jenny watched him. She just couldn't get over his beautiful blond hair. It was so smooth and wonderfully-shaped like a perfect golden bowl, so shiny, so fine.

"Do you like *Ghostbusters*?" he asked.

"I haven't seen it for a few years," she told him.

The front door slammed. The Hagens had left.

Donny turned away from the TV screen and actually looked at Jenny for the first time. "Did they leave?" he asked, looking concerned.

"Yes," she told him. "They just left."

"Good," he said. "Can I have a candy bar?"

Getting Donny to bed wasn't as hard as Jenny had predicted. He was a very lively, active kid, and when he finally got tired he just suddenly crashed, his energy all used up, barely enough strength left to keep his eyelids up.

Jenny took him up to his room and tucked him in. "See you on Saturday night," she whispered, running her hand tenderly through his amazing hair.

He was nearly asleep before she turned out the light and crept out of the room.

The carpet on the stairs was worn right through to the wood in several places. The stairs creaked beneath her feet as she descended to the living room.

What a creepy old place. Why did people think it was neat to live in 200-year-old houses? When I have my own home, Jenny decided, it's going to be sparkling and brand new.

She stopped in the living room to look around. Everything smelled so musty. The floor creaked as she walked. A tall, mahogany grandfather's clock in the corner ticked, then tocked, loudly, insistently.

I'd go nuts if I had to listen to that all day, Jenny thought.

She suddenly imagined the original owners of the house, sitting by the fire, listening to the tick-tocking of the big clock. The ghostly pale woman was dressed in black except for a white bonnet on her head and a gray wool shawl over her shoulders. She sat knitting another gray wool shawl. The man was also dressed in black. He had a long, white beard and mustache. He stood by the fireplace, staring at an enormous, dripping red hog being roasted on a spit in the fireplace. "Just think," he said softly, "more than a hundred years from now, that clock of ours is going to drive whoever's in this house bananas!"

BAAAAM!

A loud banging noise made Jenny jump. Her fantasy old-time couple vanished. What was *that*?

Then she remembered the loose shutter on the front of the house. She walked to the window, pushed back the heavy, crushed-velvet drapes, and looked out.

The darkness seemed thick enough to touch. Swaying trees were black shadows against the black sky. The house appeared to be surrounded by woods. She couldn't see another house, another car, another sign of human life. Her eyes adjusted to the darkness outside, but there was only more darkness to see.

She shivered. It was drafty by the window. One of the panes was cracked, and cold air was seeping in all around the window frame.

Somewhere not too far away an animal howled. Was it a dog? Please, she thought, let it be a dog. The shutter banged again, harder this time. Again, she jumped.

She stepped back and rearranged the heavy drapes. Tick Tock. Tick TOCK. The annoying clock seemed to grow louder. She heard a soft cracking sound above her head. The house groaned and shifted as the winds picked up outside.

Take it easy, she told herself. All old houses make weird sounds. She was sorry she had put Donny to bed. The noises weren't so loud or frightening when he was around. When she was playing with him, she didn't have time to think about where she was, all alone in this creepy, old house surrounded by nothing but dark woods.

She looked up at the wall above the mantel. A hideous moose head, its fur caked with dust and mold, seemed to glare down at her. The grandfather's clock chimed loudly, nine o'clock, tick TOCK, tick TOCK, its pendulum swinging quickly back and forth, clicking the time away.

Jenny decided to check out the kitchen. She turned toward the hall — and something grabbed her leg.

Chapter 3

She screamed.

The ghost of the lady in the gray shawl had her by the leg.

Now she was going to carry Jenny into the clock, where she would live forever, listening for all of eternity to the tick TOCK tick TOCK along with the other spirits of this old house.

She looked down.

It wasn't a ghost. It was a ginger-colored cat. The cat pawed her again, softer this time, then rubbed its back against her jeans leg, mewing loudly.

Jenny's heart was still pounding.

Why didn't they tell me they had a cat?

She reached down to pet it, but it ran away, tucking itself under a large sofa.

She felt foolish screaming like that. She wasn't the screaming type. She took a deep breath and held it, a trick that usually worked when she wanted to calm herself.

Had her scream disturbed Donny?

She ran up the creaking stairs and tiptoed into his room. He was still sleeping peacefully. He looked even more angelic when he slept. She was tempted to wake him up, tell him he could come downstairs and play until his parents came home.

No, Jenny. You've got to show them you're responsible.

She heard the animal howls again, closer this time, louder and longer. They seemed to be coming from the backyard. She crept over to Donny's window, pushed back the curtains, and looked down.

A spotlight on the side of the garage cast a narrow triangle of yellow light over the gravel driveway, a low woodpile, and the tall grass of the yard. Shadows from the trees danced over the grass, which leaned first this way, then that in the swirling wind.

The howling had stopped.

Jenny replaced the curtains, took one more look at Donny, then walked quickly downstairs. She found the kitchen, the last room off the long, back hallway, and turned on all the lights. It was the only modern room in the house, bright yellow and orange linoleum tile on the floor, newly painted white wooden cabinets, new appliances, even a microwave.

I guess this is the only room they've been able to redo, Jenny told herself. She found a Coke in the refrigerator and a bag of nacho chips on the counter. Maybe I'll just stay in the kitchen all night, she thought. It's so much less creepy in here.

But the kitchen stools were uncomfortable, and she had left her backpack in the den. And she realized that from way in the back of the house she wouldn't be able to hear Donny if he called from upstairs. So she carried her snack back down the long hallway, through the living room with its creaking floors and annoying clock, and back to the den.

Well, what shall I do now? she asked herself, dropping back down into the big white leather chair. I can't just sit around and listen to the wind howl and the shutters bang, and think about how creepy it is here.

She picked up the newspaper from the table next to the chair and scanned the front page. "Oh!" A headline made her gasp. *THIRD BABY-SITTER ATTACK HAS POLICE ON ALERT*. She tossed the paper down without reading the story.

Then she remembered that before leaving the house she had grabbed a book to read. But what was it? She searched in her pack and pulled it out. Oh, great. A Stephen King novel. Good choice, Jenny. That'll really cheer you up!

She stuffed the book back into her pack and got up. Should she switch on the TV? No. She couldn't sit still. She decided to explore the living room for a while.

She was walking past the soot-stained, marble fireplace in front of the sofa with the cushions that didn't match when she heard the first footstep.

She stopped.

She wasn't sure she had heard it.

Yes. Another. This time she was sure. It was a footstep. A soft footstep.

The cat again?

No. The cat was curled up in a chair by the window.

She listened. Silence now. So silent except for her breathing, except for the pounding of her heart, except for the ticking of the clock.

So, she had imagined it.

Another ghost, another creature of her imagination.

"Stop it, Jenny," she said aloud. "Stop imagining things. It's scary enough here without you trying to scare yourself."

Another footstep.

This one louder.

This one closer.

Someone was in the house. Someone was walking quietly . . . slowly . . . deliberately.

She spun around and looked back to the den. Could she get there in time? Could she lock herself in the den? Could she call the police? Would they get to the house in time?

Another footstep.

She turned back to face the front hallway.

The footsteps were coming from the stairs.

She froze. She felt completely paralyzed, paralyzed by fear. So this is what it's like, she thought. So this is what it's like to be frightened to death.

An image flashed into her mind. She was driving home with her mom late at night. They were

24

in the old Pontiac. She must have been five or six. They pulled into the driveway. A rabbit was standing at the top of the drive. Caught in the headlights, it froze. The poor creature became paralyzed, a statue of fear. It stood there staring into the headlights as the car came closer and closer. It didn't move a muscle until Jenny's mom turned the headlights off. Then it bounded away, its long ears standing straight up in the air.

Another footstep on the stairs.

Jenny was the rabbit now, frozen in front of the fireplace.

She wanted to move. She wanted to run. She wanted to scream.

But her fear held her in a tight grip.

"Who — " She finally managed to make a sound. "Who's there?"

Silence.

Another footstep.

"Who's there?" she called.

Chapter 4

"Who's there?"

Donny stepped into the hallway. His cheeks were flushed from sleep. He had red leather slippers on his feet. One pajama leg had hitched up over his knee. "I woke up. I'm thirsty."

Jenny took a deep breath. Her knees felt weak. She grabbed onto the mantel to steady herself. She didn't want Donny to see that she had been afraid.

She felt like laughing. Then she felt like crying. Then she felt like running up and hugging him.

What an idiot she had been! Footsteps. Of *course* there were footsteps on the stairs. How could Donny come down the stairs without making footsteps? How could she have forgotten that she wasn't alone in the house?

He stared at her from the entranceway to the living room. "I'm thirsty," he repeated. His voice was hoarse from sleep. He had a very devilish look on his face.

She walked over to him and smoothed her hand through his hair. "You shouldn't sneak down the stairs."

"I didn't sneak. I walked. Slowly. I didn't know where you were. I didn't want to scare you."

Didn't want to scare her?!

She squeezed his shoulder playfully. He giggled. "Are you *sure* you didn't want to scare me?" she asked.

"Well . . . maybe a little." He giggled some more.

"Are you the kind of guy who likes scaring his baby-sitters?" she asked, starting to feel a little more normal.

"Maybe."

They headed toward the kitchen, her hand on his pajama shoulder. He felt so warm, like a little stove.

"Well, I'm glad to see you," she said. What an understatement! "What do you want to drink? Apple juice?"

"No. I brushed my teeth tonight."

"So?"

"So, apple juice tastes funny after you brush your teeth. I want milk."

"Okay. Milk, it is."

In the kitchen, he climbed up on one of the stools while she poured out his glass of milk. He drank it quickly in three long gulps, then wiped the milk mustache off his upper lip with the sleeve of his pajamas.

"Want to play a game or something?" he asked.

"Get serious. You get right back up to bed," she told him. "Did your other baby-sitters play games with you late at night?"

"Maybe," he said, the devilish grin reappearing.

"Tell the truth, Donny," Jenny said with mock sternness.

"Well . . . no," he admitted sheepishly. Then he quickly added, "I'll only go back to bed if you'll tuck me in again."

"Okay. That's a deal," Jenny agreed.

It took a long time to tuck him in. First he insisted on showing her all of his stuffed animals and telling her their names. When she finally got him into bed and under the covers, he said, "Kiss me good night."

She bent down and kissed him on the forehead. "Good night."

"Now tell me a story," he demanded.

"What?"

"Tell me a story. I can't go to sleep without a story."

"But, Donny, that wasn't the deal. The deal was for me to tuck you in."

"Now the deal is for you to tell me a story," he insisted. She saw that he was a tough bargainer. There was probably no use in arguing with him.

"What kind of stories do you like?" she asked,

sighing resignedly and settling down at the foot of his narrow, stuffed animal-cluttered bed.

"Scary stories."

Of course.

"Okay. Let me think." She didn't have to think too long. She was good at thinking up stories. It was one of the real advantages of having a wild imagination.

"This is a story about a little boy who liked to scare his baby-sitter," she began.

Donny laughed. "I like it," he said, sitting up.

"If you don't lie down and try to sleep, I won't finish it," Jenny threatened. He plopped back onto his pillow. "This little boy was about your age, about your height, just about your weight. In fact, he looked just like you." She scooted up closer to him so she could whisper the story.

"And this little boy had a very mischievous personality. He liked playing tricks on his baby-sitter and scaring her to death. He would sneak down the stairs as quietly as he could just to frighten her. He would make loud noises and jump out at her from dark doorways and run into the room and leap onto her shoulders from behind when she thought he was sound asleep.

"One night, he scared his baby-sitter so badly, her hair turned white. And one night, he scared his baby-sitter so badly, her eyes popped out, and he had to find them and push them back in for her. And one night, he scared his baby-sitter so badly, she jumped right out of her skin — and it took her hours to put it back on."

Donny thought this was hilarious. He laughed

until he had tears in his eyes. He made Jenny tell that part again. And then again.

"So one night the little boy's baby-sitter decided to get even. She decided that it was her turn to scare the little boy."

Jenny scooted even closer so she could whisper as quietly as possible. "She thought and thought about how to scare the little boy. Should she dress up in a gorilla costume and pop out of his clothes closet? No. Not scary enough. Should she invite a monster to come in and chase the little boy around the house? No. Not scary enough. Should she take off her skin again and dance around in her bones? No. Not scary enough."

Jenny leaned down very close to Donny's ear and softly whispered the conclusion to her story. "And then the baby-sitter finally got an idea. She finally thought of the scariest trick of all. Very quietly, she crept into the little boy's bedroom. Very quietly, she leaned down over his bed where he was about to fall asleep. And very quietly, quiet as a mouse, almost silently, almost as silent as a soft breeze, almost so silently you couldn't hear her, she shouted, '*BOOOOOOOOOOO!*' "

Jenny shouted the word *boo* at the top of her lungs.

The story received the proper reaction. Donny leaped up in surprise and nearly fell out of bed. Then he laughed uproariously. "Tell it again," he insisted when he had finally stopped laughing.

Pleased with her success, Jenny headed to the bedroom door. "No. Go to sleep now."

"Come on, Jenny. Tell it again."

"No. Next time. I'll be back on Saturday night. I'll tell it to you then. Only I'll make it scarier."

He made her promise three times that she wouldn't forget. Then he finally settled down to go to sleep.

Jenny was smiling as she started down the stairs. "That was a good story," she told herself. "I'm going to be good at this job." The thought gave her special pleasure. Her mother was always accusing her of being irresponsible, of living in a world of daydreams and not being able to handle anything real. But her mother was wrong. Jenny was proving that.

Her smile faded when she heard the loud knock on the front door. She stopped on the bottom step and grabbed the bannister. She could feel the fear grip her body, the same fear she had felt in the living room when she had heard the quiet footsteps.

The knock was repeated, harder this time.

Who could it be?

It was too early for the Hagens to be home. And they wouldn't knock.

Could she see out? No. The door was solid wood, no window or peephole.

Whoever was out there pounded again, three hard raps, then three more.

It sounds like a burglar, Jenny thought. A picture of a guy in a black-and-purple striped sweater, wearing a black mask over his eyes, carrying a bag of burglar tools flashed into her mind.

No. It's not a burglar. A burglar wouldn't knock.

Unless it was a very cautious burglar, and he was checking to make sure no one was home before breaking in. So if I don't answer the door, he'll think no one is home, and he'll —

It's the baby-sitter attacker, the one in the papers.

No. Don't be stupid. How would he know there's a baby-sitter here tonight? It's my first night on the job.

It's the police. A truck carrying toxic waste turned over outside, and they have to evacuate the neighborhood immediately. If I don't answer the door, I'll breathe the toxic fumes and be turned into a drooling mutant. . . .

Three more hard raps on the door.

Jenny pressed her cheek against the door. The wood felt surprisingly cold. "Who is it?"

No reply.

She could hear the wind roaring outside the door.

"Who is it?" she repeated. She didn't want to shout too loudly for fear of waking up Donny.

"Who is it? Who's there?"

She pressed her ear against the door again. The wind was howling too loudly to hear anything else.

"I'd better open the door," she told herself. She looked for a chain to attach so that an intruder couldn't just push his way in. But there was none.

Three more knocks.

She took a deep breath and pulled the door open a crack.

"Oh." The cry escaped her lips before she could stop it.

The white porch light revealed a short but powerfully built man. Despite the cold and gusting winds, he was wearing only an oversized, red plaid lumberjack shirt. His eyebrows caught Jenny's attention first. They were bushy and black, as wide as caterpillars. He had thick black hair slicked down with some kind of grease and brushed straight back so that it looked more like a helmet than hair.

His nose was bent and leaned to the left. It looked as if it had been broken several times, or maybe removed and put back on wrong. He had a stubble of black beard on his cheeks, and an unlit stub of a cigar tucked between his teeth. He reeked of the aroma of cigars. It must have been soaked into his shirt and jeans.

He looked as startled to see Jenny as she was to see him. "Who are *you*?" he asked, his voice surprisingly deep but gravelly. Somehow he was able to speak and still keep the cigar butt clamped between his teeth.

"I — I'm the baby-sitter," Jenny said, struggling to remember exactly who she was. "Who are you?"

He looked at her suspiciously. He didn't seem to hear her question. "Everything okay in there?"

"Yes," she said, squeezing the doorknob until her hand hurt. "Can I help you with something?"

Dumb question, but what else should she say?

"No. Uh . . . I'm sorry. I'm Willers. I'm the neighbor."

"Oh. The neighbor." Jenny started to feel a little relieved. But then she thought, maybe he's lying, and her fear returned.

"I thought Mike and Mary were home." He chewed on the cigar butt and looked her up and down.

"Uh . . . no. They're out tonight. They go out on Thursday nights."

Why did I tell him that? How stupid! Now he knows that I'll be alone here with Donny every Thursday night. Stupid, stupid, stupid.

"I'm sorry to disturb you this time of night. I thought I saw a prowler out back." He pointed a stubby finger toward the woods on the right. "Did you happen to hear anything?"

"No. Not a thing."

Was he really the neighbor? Did he really hear a prowler? Was *he* the prowler?

"I thought I saw someone. There's been a prowler in the neighborhood." He removed the tiny cigar butt from his teeth and jammed it into his shirt pocket. "Mind if I come in and look around?"

"Yes. I mean no. I don't think so. I mean, I don't know you. I don't think the Hagens would. . . . I mean, everything's okay. I didn't hear anything."

He squinted at her suspiciously, his thick, black eyebrows folding above his eyes like upside-down V's. "You sure?"

"Yes. Positive. It was nice of you to be concerned, though. Thank you."

She started to close the door. He took a step forward.

Her heart jumped up to her throat.

Was he going to try to push his way in? What was he going to do?

Why was he staring at her like that?

"If you hear anything, I'll be nearby," he said, backing down. He looked into her eyes. "I'm always nearby."

Was that a threat?

Why did he stare at her like that when he said it?

Or was she just imagining that he meant more than he said?

"Good night," she said. She closed the door quickly, slamming it hard without realizing it, and locked it. Then she slumped down on the first step and buried her head in her arms, trying to catch her breath.

"YAAAAAIIII!"

She screamed when she felt the hand on her shoulder.

"Sorry. I didn't mean to scare you," Donny said. "I'm thirsty again."

Chapter 5

"So did you mmpfell the mmmpphh about the nmmmmphh?"

"What? I can't understand you, Laura."

Laura held up a finger, signalling for Jenny to wait a second while she finished swallowing. "I had a mouthful of pizza. Sorry. What I said was, did you tell the father about the neighbor?"

"Tell Mr. Hagen? No. He's much too nervous already. I didn't want to make him more nervous. Besides, what's to tell? The neighbor came over to make sure everything was okay. Big deal."

"But, Jenny, you said you thought — "

"But that's my problem, don't you see? I'm always thinking too much, thinking crazy things. So the neighbor was a little shifty-looking. Lots of neighbors are shifty-looking. It doesn't mean they're going to break into the house and cut you up in little pieces or anything."

"Mmmmphhh wwwmmmmphh," Laura replied.

"Huh?"

They were sitting in the back booth at the Pizza Oven. It was three-thirty on Friday afternoon, and the small restaurant was usually filled with Harrison High students by now. But for some reason only a few kids were there today. Jenny and Laura liked the back booth despite the torn seat cushions and the fact that it was directly across from the restroom, because from there they could see who was in all the other booths and who came in the door, without being easily seen themselves.

"Do you think this is real cheese?" Laura pulled a long strand of it with two fingers. It stretched for about two feet before it tore.

"I don't know. Of course. What else would it be?"

"I saw on TV where some pizza places were using fake cheese. You know, artificial cheese, all chemicals and stuff."

"It tastes like cheese. A little," Jenny said, taking a large bite for scientific purposes. "Why do you always have such upsetting news? I mean, if you can't believe in pizza, what can you believe in?"

"I'd like to believe in *him*," Laura said, dropping her pizza slice to stare at a tall boy with wavy blond hair, wearing tight-fitting 501s and a leather bomber jacket. "Who is he? Look at that smile. He looks like he just walked off a movie set."

"Never seen him," Jenny said, concentrating on her pizza. She'd been starving all day. "What's with you and Eugene?"

"Who?"

"Laura — stop staring at him like that."

"You think I'm being too obvious?"

"Well . . . the staring part isn't so bad," Jenny told her, "but the drooling is not very subtle. I asked you about Eugene."

"I think I'm going to break up with him."

"What?"

"Well, I think I have to. You'll never guess who asked me out."

"Who?"

"Promise you won't laugh."

"What? Okay, Laura. I promise. I mean, I'll try. Who?"

"Bob Tanner."

"You're joking!"

"Stop laughing!"

"But you said he was too tall — "

"Well, he sort of stooped over when he asked me out."

"But I thought you and Eugene were — "

"Finished. It just got stale, know what I mean? We were only going out together because we couldn't think of anything else to do."

They've been going together for two weeks, Jenny thought. And it got stale?

But she didn't say what she was thinking. Laura was so beautiful, she really could have any boy she wanted. But Jenny thought it was kind of sad that Laura wanted them all. At the end of summer, Laura had broken up with Rick Danielson. That had lasted nearly three months, a long time for Laura. Since then, she'd gone out with at least three other guys. Now Eugene was about to be dumped.

I'd settle for just one guy, Jenny thought, one serious guy. Again, she felt plain and boring compared to Laura. Why couldn't she stare at boys the way Laura did, or touch their shoulders all the time the way Laura did, or act real kittenish and sexy and not get embarrassed about it?

She took another bite of pizza. It had no taste at all. Maybe the Pizza Oven did use artificial cheese. Yeccch.

"So, are you keeping this job?" Laura asked. The blond boy in the bomber jacket had walked out with a tall, black-haired girl, so Laura's attention returned to Jenny.

"I guess so. Sure," Jenny said. "They're paying me five dollars an hour since it's so far away from my house. I can really use the money. I'll actually be able to buy people Christmas presents this year. And I can help Mom out a little."

"But you said the place was creepy, and you were scared to death, what with the weird neighbor and everything."

"It was all in my mind, Laura. It was all just me. I got terrified because I heard footsteps, and they turned out to be Donny's footsteps. There wasn't anything to really be afraid of. The neighbor was perfectly fine, too. If I hadn't already been in such a state, he wouldn't have frightened me at all. I frightened myself, that's all. Next time I'll be cool."

"And the kid isn't a monster?"

"No. He's adorable. I think he likes scaring

the baby-sitter, though. It's sort of a game with him. I'm going to have to talk to him about that. But he's fine, just fine. His father is a bit of a basket case, though."

Laura took a long sip of her Coke. "What do you mean?"

"He's just such a worrier. I guess those news stories about the attacks on baby-sitters have gotten him upset, or something. I don't know. He drove me home, and all the way back he kept asking me, 'Did it go okay? Was everything okay? Was Donny okay?' He must've asked me two dozen times."

"Maybe he was just nervous because it was your first night."

"Yeah, maybe. Maybe he'll calm down. He's very devoted to Donny. It's easy to see that. And his wife is really nice. She just makes jokes about how nervous Mr. Hagen is and what a worrier he is. I guess she's used to it."

"Well . . . it's rough, giving up all your Saturday nights," Laura said, looking toward the front as a group of Harrison kids came in, laughing loudly and shoving each other through the door.

"Not really," Jenny said. "Not for me." She didn't mean to sound quite as gloomy as she did. She looked away.

"Did you save me any pepperoni?" a boy's voice said, nearby.

Jenny and Laura both cried out. Where was the voice coming from?

Suddenly Chuck, a wide grin on his freckled

face, pulled himself up from under their table. He looked very pleased that he had startled them both. He stopped about halfway up and rested his chin on the tabletop.

"Chuck! What were you doing down there?" Laura shrieked.

"Nothing. Just looking up your dress. Ha ha!" His grin grew wider. His blue eyes actually seemed to light up, as if the electricity had just been turned on.

"You idiot!" Laura cried. "Hey — I'm not wearing a dress."

"Then I don't know *what* I was doing down there," Chuck said.

"How long were you down there?" Jenny asked, appalled at the thought that he may have been eavesdropping on their conversation, trying to remember if they'd said anything really embarrassing.

"Since Tuesday, I think." He pulled himself up and squeezed in beside Jenny. "No — don't move," he told her. He put his arm around her shoulder. "I'm comfortable like this." He beamed at her, four hundred perfect white teeth in her face.

"Glad one of us is," Jenny said sarcastically. She took his hand with both of hers and lifted it off her shoulder. He had large hands, she noticed. He was a big guy. Big shoulders, powerful-looking arms. He looked like a football lineman, or a wrestler.

He grabbed up the rest of the pizza on her plate, a tiny sliver, mostly crust. "Our first pizza together," he said, holding it up as if it were a prize. "I'm going to rush home and paste this in my memory book." He stuffed it into his jeans pocket. "I have a very messy memory book."

"Your mother must love to wash your jeans," Jenny said.

"I live with my dad. I wash my own jeans," Chuck said, surprising Jenny by saying something serious.

"I've got to get home," Laura said, starting to climb out of the narrow booth.

"Oh, no," Jenny protested. "You're not leaving me here with him, are you?" She meant it as a joke, sort of. She hoped it came across that way. She looked at Chuck. He didn't seem hurt. Maybe he was used to having girls say that about him.

"I thought she'd never leave," he said loudly, ignoring Jenny's plea and ignoring the fact that Laura hadn't left yet. He put his heavy arm back around Jenny's shoulder.

"Really. I've got to get home," Laura repeated, still not standing up.

"It's been real," Chuck said. "Real gross. Ha ha!"

Jenny laughed. Laura gave her a surprised look. "You think that's funny? It's pitiful."

"It's kind of funny," Jenny said.

Chuck pulled the pizza crust from his pocket and ate it.

"Later," Laura said. She stood up, pulled on her maroon-and-white Harrison High sweatshirt, gave Jenny a meaningful look, and headed to the door.

Jenny looked down at the red Formica table. Should she try having a conversation with Chuck, or should she make an excuse and leave, too? Was it possible to really talk to him, or would he just make nonstop jokes the whole time?

How was she going to get his arm off her shoulder? It weighed at least a ton!

"Could you scoot over to the other side?" she asked, deciding to try to talk with him for a short while.

"You want me to stay?" He looked very surprised. He scratched his curly blond hair, and pulled himself around to the other side of the booth so that he was now facing her.

"When did you move to Harrison?" Jenny asked. It was a test question to see if he could be serious.

"My dad and I came here from Mars a little more than a month ago."

Uh oh. He was flunking the test.

"And what kind of spaceship did you fly in?" Jenny asked, rolling her eyes. "Did you come to defeat our planet, or on a peace mission, or what?"

"No, really," he insisted. "We came from Mars. It's just north of Pittsburgh. In Pennsylvania."

"You're putting me on, right?"

He laughed. He had a dimple in his right cheek when he laughed. With the curly blond hair and all the freckles on his face, he looked like Huck Finn. Jenny decided he was kind of cute. But also kind of goofy-looking.

He raised his right hand. "I swear. I come from Mars. You can look it up on any map. It's near Frisco."

"Near San Francisco?"

"No. Near Frisco. Frisco, Pennsylvania." He raised his hand again. "No joke. I'll swear on my mother's grave."

"Your mother's dead?"

"Well . . . no."

They both laughed.

"I still think you're putting me on," Jenny said.

"I'll bring you a map of Pennsylvania. I'll prove it to you. It's a real tiny town. It's on the old Baltimore and Ohio railroad line. There's not much there. The name is the only interesting thing about the place."

"There must be something wrong with me. I'm starting to believe you," Jenny said.

Chuck just smiled back at her.

The waitress interrupted to ask if they wanted anything else. Chuck ordered a pepperoni pizza. "That should be enough for me. Can I get you anything?" he joked.

"Make it two," Jenny joked.

The waitress wrote it down on her pad and disappeared.

"Hey, wait — " Jenny called after her, but the waitress couldn't hear over the raucous shouting and laughing from the kids in the front booth. "Wow. She thought I was serious," Jenny said to Chuck.

"So did I," he grinned.

"The joke's on you," Jenny grinned back. "I don't have any money. Ha ha!"

Chuck leaped out of the booth and went running up to the front counter. "Cancel that pizza! Hey — cancel the pizza!" On his way back, he stopped at the front booth to talk to the kids from Harrison.

He's amazing, Jenny told herself. Only in school a couple of weeks, and he knows everybody! Or at least, everyone seems to know who he is. She couldn't hear what Chuck was saying, but she could hear a lot of laughing coming from the booth. He was making jokes, as usual.

When he squeezed himself back into their booth, she was surprised to see that he had a serious look on his face. "Are you busy Saturday night?" he asked, not looking at her, looking down at the red Formica table instead.

"Yes," she replied.

"That's good. Because so am I!" He exploded in laughter. It sounded forced to Jenny.

He's really disappointed, she thought. And he's covering it up by making a joke. She realized that she had just learned something important about him.

"Were you really asking me out?" she asked, a bold question for her. But she really wanted to know.

He looked down again. "Yeah."

"Well, I'd like to go out with you sometime," she said, surprised that she could say these things, that she could talk so easily to him, "but

I have a job. I baby-sit on Thursday and Saturday nights."

"Then how about Saturday morning?" he asked, brightening. "We could get up early and go watch cars being washed at the Kwik Wash. We could pretend it was one of those beach movies."

Jenny laughed. "I don't think so."

"I've got a better idea." He was tapping the table with his big hands, nervous, his brain in high gear. "I'll come by on Saturday night when you're baby-sitting."

"No. Bad idea," Jenny said quickly.

"Was that a yes?"

"No. It was a no."

He cupped his ear with one hand. "What? I can't hear. You said yes?"

"No. I said no," she shouted, even though she knew he could hear perfectly well.

"What time should I come by?"

"I said no. I don't want you to do that."

"Please — don't beg. I'll come. Nine o'clock too late?"

"Chuck — " She hated the peevish tone in her voice, but she couldn't help it. He was really being annoying. "Don't you know when to stop?"

"No. When? That's what I'm asking. When should I stop by?"

She got up angrily. "You're not funny."

"Who's being funny? I'm serious."

Was he deliberately trying to drive her away?

She had really enjoyed talking with him. And she was beginning to feel really attracted to him.

She thought she had been able to get past his constant joking and fooling around. But now he was deliberately being obnoxious. Why was he trying to make her angry? Because she had rejected him?

"I've got to go," she said quickly, gathering up her down jacket and backpack.

"Well, when you've gotta go, you've gotta go," he said with a shrug. "Hey — what about your pizza?"

"Put it in your memory book," she said and, pleased that she was able to think of a good parting line, turned and walked quickly from the restaurant.

Chapter 6

"Sorry I'm late," Jenny said, tossing down her backpack and pulling off her jacket. "The bus had a flat tire. Do you believe it? We were stranded. They had to call out another bus. The driver wouldn't change the tire. It's against union rules." She realized she was chattering a mile a minute, but she felt terrible being late two nights in a row.

"You should leave a little earlier," Mr. Hagen said, pulling nervously on his tie.

"It's okay," Mrs. Hagen said, giving her husband a quick frown. "You know we have plenty of time." She handed Jenny's jacket to him. He started for the coat closet, remembered the door was jammed, then jogged up the stairs to put it in the bedroom closet.

"Don't pay any attention to him," Mrs. Hagen whispered confidentially, bringing her face close to Jenny's ear. Jenny could smell her perfume. It smelled just like her mother's. "He's been very nervous. That's why I decided to get him out a couple of nights a week."

"I see," Jenny said, feeling foolish. She couldn't think of anything else to say. What was she *supposed* to say?

"I think it's the new job and the new house and everything," Mrs. Hagen continued in a low voice, looking up to the top of the stairs to make sure Mr. Hagen wasn't returning. "He's really a very sweet man, but lately he just seems to get excited about things. He worries so much more than he used to."

Jenny started to say "I see" again, but decided just to nod her head.

"I try to keep things smooth for him," Mrs. Hagen whispered. "If little things go wrong in the house while you're here, I'd really appreciate your not troubling him about them. You know what I mean."

"Sure," Jenny said. She felt flattered that Mrs. Hagen talked to her as an adult, confided in her that way.

Mr. Hagen reappeared on the stairs, and his wife quickly put a forced smile on her face. "Try to get Donny down a little early tonight," he said, picking up his gray wool overcoat from where it was draped over the bannister. "He's been looking a little pale today. He may be coming down with something."

"He looks perfectly fine to me," Mrs. Hagen said lightly. "He is naturally pale, you know, Mike."

"Not that pale," Mr. Hagen insisted. "The number where we'll be is on the pad in the kitchen."

"She knows. She knows," his wife said, pulling him by the hand. "See you later, Jenny. It shouldn't be too late. We're going to a very boring party."

"Be sure to keep the doors locked and the curtains pulled," Mr. Hagen warned as they stepped out the front door. Jenny locked the door behind them and went to look for Donny.

She found him in the den, playing with a pile of small action figures, space warriors of some kind. He dropped the figures in his hands when he saw her come in. "Let's play hide-and-seek," he said.

"Don't you say hi?" she asked, pretending to be hurt.

"Hi," he said. "Let's play hide-and-seek."

"I really don't want to," she said, stretching. "I'm kind of tired tonight. Why don't we just settle down together in the big chair and watch a tape or something?"

"I don't want to," Donny said stubbornly, sticking out his lower lip to show he planned to stick to his guns.

"Let's see if you can go an entire night without saying 'I don't want to,' " she said, sitting down on the edge of the chair cushion.

"I don't want to," he said.

I asked for that, she thought.

"I want to play hide-and-seek," he insisted,

grabbing her hand and trying to pull her up off the chair.

"Stop pulling me. I said I don't want to. I want to watch TV." She realized she was sounding as petulant as he was.

"Well, why don't we compromise?" he suggested. Suddenly he was the grown-up.

"Compromise? That's a good word." She laughed. He looked so serious.

"I learned it in school, of course," he said, talking to her as if she were six.

"Okay. What's your compromise?"

"We play hide-and-seek for just a little while!"

They both laughed. He knew he was being funny. And he knew it was impossible to say no to him. He was just too clever, too charming, too cute.

She ruffled his hair. It felt soft as feathers. "Okay. A little while," she said. "Go hide. I'll be it. But don't make it too hard, okay?"

He was already out of the room. "Count to a hundred!" he yelled from somewhere down the back hall.

Jenny counted silently to herself for a short while and then stopped. This house with its endless rooms cluttered with antique furniture, dark, empty hallways, deep closets, and dozens of hidden nooks and crannies was a great place to play hide-and-seek. Especially if you were the one who was hiding.

Why did she feel so nervous? Because she'd much rather keep Donny in sight, much rather know where he was? She was the adult here, she realized. She couldn't get into the game the way she would if she were a kid. She had to be responsible.

Did that explain her feeling of dread? Or was it something else?

She had to learn to say no to Donny, she decided. Here she was, playing this game she didn't want to play at all, just because she couldn't ever say no to him.

"Here I come, ready or not!" she shouted.

She walked quickly through the living room first, keeping her eyes low, looking under chairs and tables, even though she knew he was most likely in another room. "Here I come!" she repeated loudly, hoping he would reply somehow and give himself away.

Hearing the sound of a car out on the street, she stopped. She stood by the mantel, listening, waiting to see if the car stopped or passed by. It passed by. "Okay, I'm going to find you now!" she shouted.

She stepped into the back hallway. What was that? A giggle coming from a room she had never explored?

She entered the dark room, and her hand fumbled against the wall until she found the light switch. When she pushed it, an old, Tiffany-style lamp in a corner cast dim, orange light over the room.

Where was she? It appeared to be an extra sitting room. It was hard to tell exactly because all of the furniture — what appeared to be tall armchairs and two high-backed, facing sofas — was covered with bedsheets. A thick layer of dust had settled over everything in the room. A massive tangle of cobwebs covered the one working lamp, so thick they blocked much of the light and cast eerie shadows on the maroon wallpaper.

It looked just like a room in a haunted house movie. Jenny pictured the sheets rising up off the chairs and floating after her.

"Donny, are you hiding in here?" she called, her voice a little shaky.

A sheet over one of the tall armchairs looked a little lumpy. Had he crawled under the filthy cover to hide inside the chair?

She crept closer to the chair. Everything smelled musty and mildewed. The dust was so thick, she felt she couldn't breathe. "Are you here?" she cried.

No reply.

She crept closer.

She reached for the bottom of the sheet. She pulled it up quickly, sending a flurry of dust into the air.

No Donny.

She coughed, choking on the dry dust. "I'm getting out of here," she said aloud, and turned and walked quickly from the silent room, flicking the light switch and returning it to darkness as she left.

Still coughing, she headed into the pantry. The

shelves at floor level, she remembered, were empty. Perfect hiding places.

What was that creaking sound in the kitchen? Was that Donny? She stopped and listened. No. Maybe it wasn't coming from the kitchen. Maybe she had heard the creaking of her own shoes over the soft hallway floorboards.

She heard it again. Not footsteps. But a creaking sound. She passed by the pantry, peeked quickly into the laundry room. "Gotcha!" she yelled, running to look behind the washer-dryer. But he wasn't there.

She turned and walked to the kitchen. "Okay, Donny, here I come. I know you're in here," she called from the doorway.

Silence.

Then the creaking sound again, this time behind her.

Was it just the house groaning and creaking? The old house had dozens of different sounds that it made, all of them frightening, all of them mysterious and unexplainable.

She stopped to listen.

Was someone walking in the front hallway?

On an impulse, she turned from the kitchen and ran at full speed to the front hallway.

No. No one there.

Back to the kitchen, feeling chilled, her stomach rumbling, wishing she hadn't agreed to this game, wishing she could end it NOW! She pulled open a low cabinet door. "Gotcha!"

But he wasn't inside.

"Donny — can we quit now? I give!"

Silence.

"Can you hear me? I really don't want to play anymore."

Silence.

The creaking sound again, followed by the click of some appliance turning on.

"Donny?"

She ducked down to search under the kitchen table. Not there. She pulled open the cleaning supply closet. Not there.

"I give! You're too good a hider! I give!"

Silence.

More silence.

What if something had happened to him? What if he had picked a dangerous place to hide and had gotten himself trapped somewhere? What if he had fallen and hit his head and was lying unconscious in the basement and —

STOP!

"Donny — I give! You can come out now!"

Maybe he wasn't in the kitchen after all. Maybe he just couldn't hear her.

She was about to leave the kitchen when the door to the narrow ironing board closet flew open.

"YAAAAAIIIIII!"

She screamed in fright and tumbled to the floor as a figure came flying out at her from the tiny closet, just ahead of the ironing board, which swung down to the floor with a deafening *clang*.

"DONNY!" she cried. "You scared me to death!!"

He jumped on top of her. He was laughing and crying out triumphantly at the same time. He thought it was hilarious.

"Get off! Get off me! You really scared me!"

But her protests made him laugh even harder.

Finally he stopped laughing and helped pull her to her feet. "Your turn to hide," he said.

"Oh, no!" she cried. "The game is over."

"Scaredy cat. Chicken."

"Don't call names, Donny. It's your bedtime."

It took another forty-five minutes to get him tucked into bed. He was so excited from his hide-and-seek triumph, he couldn't calm down. She had to read three books to him, play with his stuffed animals for a while, give him a bowl of corn flakes, and bring him three glasses of apple juice before he finally caved in and agreed to try to sleep.

Feeling totally wiped out, and still a little shaky from the fright he had given her, she started down the stairs. She had brought a lot of homework, but she knew she wasn't going to look at it. She was just going to veg out in front of the tube.

She was halfway down the stairs when the phone rang. Where was the nearest phone? In the kitchen? No. The den. She ran across the living room and got to the phone on the desk in the den by the fourth ring.

It was an old-fashioned, black dial phone. She was surprised by how heavy the receiver was as she lifted it to her ear. "Hello?" She was out of breath from scrambling to the phone.

Silence.

"Hello?"

She couldn't hear anything. Maybe this old phone didn't work.

Then she heard it. Soft breathing on the other end.

Someone was definitely on the line.

"Hello?" Her voice sounded funny, high-pitched, tight. She struggled to catch her breath.

She heard the breathing, a little louder.

"Hagen residence," she said. "Who's calling?"

The breathing became louder.

Was someone trying to scare her?

"Hello? Hello?"

More loud breathing. Whoever it was was sort of groaning into the phone now.

What is going on here? she asked herself, feeling the fear begin to grow in the pit of her stomach.

Suddenly she had an idea.

A crazy idea. A stupid idea. An idea only someone with her crazy imagination would have.

Of course, she told herself, there's no way this is who I think it is on the other end of the line. But I've just got to make sure.

"Hello? What do you want?" she repeated.

The loud breathing continued.

Jenny gently placed the receiver down on the green felt blotter on the desktop. Then she ran as quickly and as silently as she could, out of the den, across the living room, up the stairs.

Of course this was insane. Truly insane.

No way. No way the breather could be him. Of all the silly ideas!

But when she got to the top landing, turned, and burst into Donny's room, there he was standing by his low, white desk, the telephone held tightly to his ear.

Chapter 7

"Donny!" Jenny screamed.

He looked up, startled. His blue eyes grew wide and he seemed to go chalk-white instantly.

She grabbed the phone from his hand roughly and held it up to her ear. There was nothing but a dial tone.

"Donny — why??"

His face twisted into a frightened frown. He looked as if he were about to cry. "You . . . scared . . . me."

"What were you doing on the phone?"

"Listening." Tears formed in his eyes, big, round ones. He rubbed them away with his little, white hands.

"Listening? What do you mean?" She looked at the phone. It had buttons for two separate lines. The phone had probably been left by the previous owner of the house. Donny could have called her on this phone.

"Just listening," he bawled. "Why did you scare me like that, Jenny?" He walked over and buried his face in her side so she wouldn't see him crying.

She had a sudden pang of guilt. "I'm sorry," she said softly, patting his head. "Don't cry. I'm sorry. Why did you call me? Were you trying to scare me?"

"No," he said, the sound muffled because his head was pressed against her waist.

"No, you weren't trying to scare me?"

"No, I didn't call."

"What? What do you mean?"

"I didn't call. Somebody else called. I was asleep. The ringing woke me up. So I picked it up to listen. But no one was talking. Then you jumped in and scared me." He started to cry loudly, pressing his head against her.

Jenny felt terrible. Was he telling the truth?

Of course he was. How could she have suspected a six-year-old child? How could she have suspected Donny? Once again, her stupid imagination had gotten her into trouble.

She hugged him and apologized and did her best to comfort him. Then she led him back to his bed and tucked him in. "Now tell me the story," he said.

"No, Donny. It's way too late. And I really don't think I could tell it right now."

"But you promised!" he whined. He was so tired, he could barely keep his eyes open. "You promised and you forgot."

"Next time I'll tell it twice," she said, smoothing the feathery blond hair off his forehead. "I just can't tonight, Donny. I'm sorry. I'm really sorry."

He was too sleepy to protest any more. She tiptoed out of the room, feeling guilty, feeling like a monster, telling herself she'd never suspect him of anything ever again.

It hadn't even sounded like a child's breathing. What had made her think it was Donny in the first place?

And the furious way she had leaped at him and grabbed the phone out of his hand! She'd never forgive herself.

I was just scared, that's all, she argued with herself.

Don't make excuses, Jenny. You wanted the caller to be a six-year-old because then you wouldn't have to be afraid, then you'd be in control.

But he looked so guilty when I walked into his room. The way he went pale like that, as if he knew he'd just been caught doing something terrible.

She didn't have any more time to argue with herself. As she reached the bottom of the stairs, she hung up the phone. It rang almost immediately.

The sound sent a chill down her back. She stood frozen in the front hallway, her eyes closed, wishing it away, wishing it to stop.

But it rang again. And again. I'm just not going to answer it, she told herself. But then she realized the ringing would wake up Donny again.

And what if it wasn't the breather calling back? What if it was a call for Mr. or Mrs. Hagen?

She took a deep breath, ran to the den, and picked up the phone. "Hello?"

Silence.

"Hello?"

"Hi, Babes."

The voice was a hoarse whisper.

"Who is this?" Jenny demanded.

"Hi, Babes. Are you all alone?" She couldn't tell if it was a man or a boy.

"What do you want?" She tried not to sound frightened, but she couldn't help it.

"Are you all alone in that big house? Well, don't worry. Company's coming."

"Listen, you — "

She heard a soft click at the other end.

Chapter 8

Jenny stared at the heavy receiver in her hand and listened to the drone of the dial tone until her heart stopped pounding. Her hand was trembling. Her throat felt tight and dry.

Someone was trying to scare her — and was doing a pretty good job of it!

Someone knew she was there. Someone knew she was alone.

Someone knew her.

Or did they?

Everyone knew about weirdos who got their kicks by making sick phone calls to strangers. Maybe this was some creep picking phone numbers at random, some guy going through the phone book, seeing who he could upset, who he could get a reaction from.

Or maybe it was a kid. Some guy from school, trying to be funny.

Trying to be funny?

Chuck?

Would Chuck do something like that?

No. Of course not. He was a joker, a goof. Everything he did was good-natured. Or was it? She didn't really know Chuck that well. Actually, she didn't know Chuck at all.

She suddenly remembered their conversation at the Pizza Oven, how Chuck's mood had suddenly changed after she told him she couldn't go out with him on Saturday night. He hadn't seemed so good-natured then. In fact, he was downright obnoxious. It was as if he had turned against her, as if he had tried to make her angry.

But perhaps he was just disappointed, just hurt that she had turned him down, and that she hadn't wanted him to drop by the Hagens' when she was baby-sitting.

That didn't mean he was capable of making those frightening calls. That didn't mean he would do such a disgusting, sick thing.

She refused to believe it was Chuck.

But then, who? Someone nearby? Someone in the neighborhood? Someone who had been watching the house, had seen her arrive, had seen the Hagens leave?

Was there someone out there who really was preparing to harm her?

"Are you all alone?" he had whispered. *"Are you all alone in that big house?"*

He knew where she was. He knew she was alone.

"Don't worry — company's coming!"

"Company's coming!"

When? Tonight?

The neighbor!

What was his name? Willers. Willers would know she was there. Willers would know she was alone.

Of course.

That gravelly voice. That hoarse whisper.

Willers was so creepy, the way he stared at her, the way he looked her up and down.

It had to be Willers.

She grabbed the phone to call the police. Then she took her hand away.

She had never called the police before. She had only seen it done in movies and on TV. People in real life didn't call the police, did they?

They did if they were frightened. They did if someone was threatening them, someone who lived right next door.

But would they believe her? What would they say?

"Oh, Jenny," she imagined the policeman's bored reply, "we all know about your wild imagination. These calls are all in your mind. Please don't bother us. We have real work to do."

Even if they believed her, what would they do? They probably had dozens of weird calls reported every night. What could they do about it? Send someone out to hold her hand until the Hagens returned home?

"Are you all alone? Don't worry, company's coming!"

I don't care, she thought. I'm calling the police.

She reached for the phone again, and as she did, it seemed to explode in her hand.

"YAAAAIII!" she screamed and jumped a mile in the air.

But it wasn't exploding. It was only ringing. Again.

"Oh, no," she said aloud. "Please — leave me alone."

Her hand reached out and gripped the receiver, but she didn't pick it up. She could feel each ring vibrating up her arm. Finally she picked it up just to stop the noise.

"Hello?" Her voice sounded strange to her, high and frightened.

"Hi, Jenny. Just wanted to see how you're doing."

"Mr. Hagen?"

"Right. Everything okay? I guess you were far from the phone. It rang so many times, I was a little worried."

"I . . . uh . . . was in the bathroom. Sorry."

Was that the best excuse she could think of? It didn't matter. It was good enough.

She was very relieved to hear his voice.

"Donny okay? Did you get him to bed early?"

"Well . . . pretty early. He's fine. No problem."

"Sometimes he takes advantage of his sitters and stays up really late. He looks like an angel, but he can be a real devil."

Did he really mean that? Was Donny really capable of being evil?

Of course not. Have you lost your mind entirely, Jenny? Just calm down. Take a deep breath and calm yourself down.

"No. He was no trouble. Really." Mr. Hagen

certainly is a nervous parent, she thought. She looked at her watch. He'd only been away two and a half hours. Why was he calling?

"Is he sleeping okay? Sometimes he throws off his covers and then he gets cold in the middle of the night."

"I checked him once. He was fine," she said. "I'll go up and check again."

"Good. Sounds like everything is under control. We won't be too late. Another hour or two. You have the number here, right?"

"Yes. I have it."

Should she tell him about the calls? She was so tempted to tell him! But no. She held herself back. He's so nervous, he'd probably call out the FBI, the CIA, and the National Guard! she told herself. And Mrs. Hagen asked me not to upset him.

"Okay, Jenny. 'Bye. Hope you don't mind my checking in like this."

"No. I'm glad. I mean . . . it's okay. Everything's fine."

"Good. Help yourself to anything in the kitchen. And keep the doors locked."

Don't worry. "Yes, I will. Thanks."

Finally he hung up. Despite her fear, Jenny had to smile. Mr. Hagen looked so big and macho, but he was such a Nervous Nellie. He was sweet, though. It was sweet the way he worried about Donny.

She realized she felt better after talking with him. She decided she wouldn't call the police after all. They would probably only take down the information and then forget about it. What else could they do?

She felt edgy, restless. She paced back and forth in the living room for a while, but the creaking floor and the ticking of the grandfather's clock made her even more nervous. She went back to the den and pulled her government textbook from her backpack. But there was no way she could concentrate on the separation of powers tonight.

She shoved the book back into the backpack, paced back and forth in the small den for a few minutes, then decided to get a Coke in the kitchen. Crossing the living room again, a framed photograph on an end table by the worn sofa caught her eye. It was a color portrait of Donny. She had never noticed it before.

She walked to the end table and picked up the photo to examine it more closely. "He must have been only two or three when this was taken," she thought. Then her mouth dropped open in surprise.

The child in the photo looked a lot like Donny, had the same blue eyes, the same white-blond hair — but it wasn't Donny. For one thing, this child had a pink ribbon in its hair. And was wearing a green corduroy jumper. This child was a girl.

Jenny stared at the photo. The child was so beautiful, it was hard to take her eyes off her. "Donny has a sister," Jenny told herself. "But where?"

Then she realized what the horrible truth must be.

"Donny *had* a sister."

She dropped the photograph onto the desk and looked away. She couldn't bear to look at it any longer.

This explained a lot. It certainly explained why Mr. Hagen was so nervous and worried about Donny. The poor man. The poor family. It probably also explained why Mr. Hagen had changed jobs, why they had moved to this neighborhood on the far edge of town.

The room suddenly seemed stuffy and hot. Jenny went to the window and pulled back the heavy, crushed-velvet drapes. She peered out through the frost-stained glass.

It was cool by the window. The cold wind seeped in through the cracked glass. Outside, the wind swirled, whistling loudly, shaking the leafless trees, making them clatter like dry, brittle skeletons.

The moon was full, a gold coin in a pink-gray sky. On the radio, they had said it could snow. The pink sky meant that snow clouds hovered above. The strange lighting gave the ground an unreal look, made everything clearer and brighter than real life.

What was that in the front yard? Jenny squinted through the glass.

Were they squirrels? The squirrels seemed to be holding paws. There were four or five of them, dancing in a circle, holding onto each other, twirling faster and faster, first in one direction, then the other.

No.

That's not right.

Jenny realized they weren't squirrels. They were leaves, blowing round and round in the swirling winds.

Stop doing that, girl, she scolded herself. They'll lock you up if you keep seeing things.

She squinted again, trying to make the leaves turn back into squirrels. It was such a wonderful, comical scene. But the wind had changed. The leaves had blown away. She couldn't bring it back.

She had a sudden chill. The face of the little girl in the picture, Donny's sister, floated back into her mind. She tried to blink it away.

Taking a step back, she started to pull the drapes into place. But something else outside caught her eye.

Was there a car parked at the curb in front of the house?

No. It was probably a tree stump. She started to scold herself again for seeing what wasn't there. But no matter how hard she squinted, she couldn't make the small, black car turn into a tree stump.

It was a car. She wasn't imagining it.

And that shadow in the front seat. . . .

The shadow moved.

There was a man sitting in the car.

Why? What was he doing there? Was he

watching her? Was he waiting for . . . for what??

"Don't worry, company's coming!"

"Company's coming!"

Jenny yanked the drapes shut and went one more time to make sure the doors were locked.

Chapter 9

"Here. Put some more syrup on those."

Mrs. Jeffers leaned over Jenny and poured the thick, brown syrup onto the stack of pancakes.

"Don't, Mom. Stop!" Jenny pushed her mother's arm away. They had the same argument every Sunday morning. "That's too much. You want me to weigh three hundred pounds?"

"No, I don't," Mrs. Jeffers sat down across from Jenny at the small kitchen table. "But I would like you to put a little meat on those bones."

"Mom, really," Jenny said, a mouthful of soft, warm pancakes making it hard to talk. She swallowed. Delicious! "I'm going to be skinny like you my whole life. Skinny and flat-chested. It's hereditary."

Her mother smiled. She never laughed. "You don't have to blame me for everything." She raised a hand to brush a wisp of hair from over her eye. Jenny was surprised to see that she had a few gray hairs. She had never noticed them before.

Suddenly her mother looked very tired to her. Maybe she'd looked that way for a long time. Jenny realized she seldom really looked at her mother at all. She wondered if her mother looked this sad and tired down at the office, too. A picture flashed into her mind of her mother at the law office where she worked, laughing and joking with the other legal secretaries, running around energetically, suddenly tap dancing on the top of a desk, leaping off it into the arms of one of the lawyers.

"More orange juice?" her mother asked, yawning.

"Mom, I still have a full glass."

"Oh. Sorry." Mrs. Jeffers took a small bite of the single pancake on her plate. "Chilly in here, isn't it?" She pulled her cotton robe around her tighter. "When did you get in last night?"

"Late. About one, I guess."

"Mr. Hagen drove you home?"

"Yes. He's such a worrier. He'd never let me take the bus home."

"I should hope not." The wisp of hair fell down over her eye again. This time, she left it there. She took another nibble of the pancake. "I'm glad he's a worrier. I worry, too. They live so far away. And with these awful news stories. . . ."

"Yeah, I know." Jenny didn't feel like telling her there was more to worry about than just the distance.

"How come you're not eating?"

"Mom, I am, too. You piled on a dozen pancakes here. I'm not Arnold Schwarzenegger, you know!" She didn't mean to sound so shrill. She was very tired, she realized.

"Okay, okay."

They ate in silence for a few minutes. Then Jenny looked up to see that her mother had a strange smile on her face. "What's that smile for?" she asked, wiping syrup off her upper lip with her napkin.

"You've been keeping something from me, haven't you."

What? Did she know about what happened at the Hagens? About the frightening phone calls? No. If that's what she meant, she wouldn't be smiling like that.

"Come on, Jenny, 'fess up. You know it isn't nice to keep secrets from your loving mother."

Jenny laughed. It wasn't like her mother to tease her like this. She usually just said what she meant. "What are you talking about?"

"You know. I'm talking about Chuck."

"Chuck?!"

"Don't act so dumb. That's his name, right? Chuck Quinn?"

"Yes. I know a guy named Chuck Quinn, but — "

"You're blushing." Her mother's smile grew wider.

"I am not," Jenny insisted. "Stop teasing me, Mother. I really don't like it. What about Chuck? Did he call you?"

"You didn't tell me there was a boy interested in you. Did he stop by when you were baby-sitting last night? I really don't approve of that."

"No, he didn't," Jenny said, her mind spinning. "Did Chuck call you? Did he?"

"Yes." Her mother seemed surprised by Jenny's reaction. "He called last night. About seven-thirty. He said he needed your phone number and address. You know, at the Hagens. I was a little reluctant to give it to him, but he seemed very polite, and he said you had given it to him already, but he had lost it."

"That's not true," Jenny said.

"Uh-oh. Did I do something wrong?" Her mother tightened her hands into little fists, the way she always did when she was upset.

"No. You didn't do anything wrong." No point in getting her mother all worked up, Jenny thought.

"He didn't call you?"

"No."

Maybe he did. Jenny had a heavy feeling in the pit of her stomach, and she knew it wasn't from the pancakes.

Maybe he did.

Chuck got the phone number from my mom. Then he called and tried to frighten me with his disgusting breathing and horrible threats.

She had a feeling all along that it had been Chuck. There was obviously something wrong with him. He was dangerous. He was out of control. He had seemed out of control to her in

75

school, always joking, always trying to trick the teachers, always trying to be the center of attention.

Everyone thought he was so funny. But he wasn't funny. He was sick.

Her mother thought it was cute that a boy was interested in her. If only she knew why he was interested. He was only interested in making her his victim!

And now he not only had the Hagens' phone number; he had the address, too.

That must have been him, sitting in that little car in front of the house. Waiting there, waiting for me, his victim, to come out, waiting for me to —

No. Wait.

There she went again, letting her imagination run wild. She realized she was being terribly unfair, jumping to conclusions that might not be true. That couldn't be true!

Just because Chuck had the phone number didn't mean that he was the one who had called — did it?

She had no right to accuse him.

She should give him the benefit of the doubt, right? He didn't seem like such a bad guy, after all. In fact, he was kind of sweet. He was funny. He was a class clown. He wasn't evil.

Or was he?

"You look terribly worried. If I did anything wrong. . . ." Mrs. Jeffers interrupted Jenny's confused thoughts.

Jenny forced a smile. "No. I'm sorry, Mom. I

was thinking about something else. I'm really tired, that's all. Everything's fine. Chuck's really a nice boy. He's new. He just moved to Harrison a few weeks ago."

"You do look tired," her mother said.

"What would you think if I quit my baby-sitting job?" Jenny asked suddenly. The idea popped into her head, and she said it. She regretted it immediately as soon as she saw the disappointed look on her mother's face.

"Is it really too much for you?"

"Well, no. . . ."

"Then I really think you should stick with it, Jen. It's such a bad habit, not sticking with things. You just started, you know. You'll get used to the routine."

"I know, but — "

"And we really can use the money you're making. The Hagens are so generous. Christmas will be here before you know it, and — "

"You're right, Mom. It was a stupid idea. I don't know why I said it."

I do know why I said it, Jenny thought as she carried her breakfast dishes to the sink. I said it because I want to run away. Mom's right. I always try to run away from everything. Well, this time I'm going to surprise everyone — including myself. I'm not going to run away, not from the baby-sitting job, and not from Chuck.

"See you later, Mom. I'm meeting Laura at the mall." She gave her mom a quick kiss on the forehead and headed out the kitchen door.

"Don't worry so much about things," her

mother called after her. "Everything will be fine."

I hope you're right, Jenny thought, searching the coat closet for her down jacket. I sure hope you're right.

"It couldn't be Chuck," Laura said. "He's a teddy bear!"

"Yeah, you're right," Jenny said.

"How could you accuse someone with that little boy face and those freckles? No way!" Laura continued. She picked up a pack of bright magenta press-on fingernails. "What do you think? You just press these on, and instant cool!"

"Instant weird, you mean," Jenny said, grabbing the package from Laura's hand and examining the nails carefully. "Really gross."

"I thought I'd surprise Bob Tanner tonight with something a little different."

"Get real. You wouldn't wear these things, would you?"

Laura shrugged. "I guess not." They walked out of Cosmetics Plus, past Earring World. "Maybe I'll go in and get my nose pierced."

"You can't," Jenny said, pulling her past the store. "You need a parent's permission if you're under eighteen."

"How do you know?"

"Ellen Sappers tried to get her ears pierced in three stores a few weeks ago, and they wouldn't do it without a note from her mother."

"Did she get the note?"

"No way. Ellen said that if her mother approved of it, she didn't want to do it."

"Let's go into Sock City," Jenny said. "I like to look at socks."

"You're definitely in a weird mood," Laura said, following her into the narrow store.

"So did you really break up with Eugene?"

"Look at these, Jenny. Who would wear socks with little pink pigs on them?"

"I have a pair just like those. Did you break up with Eugene?"

"Kind of."

"What do you mean?"

"I mean I stood him up."

"You just didn't show up for your date last night?"

"I thought it was kinder than telling him I'm sick of him. I didn't really want to hurt him."

"Laura, I don't believe you!"

Laura grabbed Jenny's arm. "You won't believe this, either! Look who's here!"

Jenny looked to where her friend was gesturing. There was Chuck, rummaging through a basket of sweat socks in the back of the store.

"Quick, Laura — move. Let's get out of here before he sees us." She shoved Laura toward the door.

"Too late," Laura said.

"Hi!" Chuck dropped the socks in his hand, and came jogging over. "We've got to stop meeting like this." He grinned at Jenny, a goofy Huck Finn grin.

"What are *you* doing here?" Laura asked.

"Hey, I wear socks, you know. I have a right to come in here, too."

Laura laughed. "I didn't mean it like that."

Jenny backed away without realizing it. She really didn't want to talk to Chuck. She needed time to think, time to figure out what she felt about him.

"How was the baby-sitting?" he asked her, picking up the pig socks and examining them. "Everything go okay?"

He's not looking me in the eye, Jenny realized. He's pretending to look closely at the socks instead. He *can't* look me in the eye.

"It was okay," she said quickly.

"I like these socks," Chuck said, waving them in front of him. "They'll look nice with my polka-dot 501s!"

Laura laughed. Jenny smiled briefly. He still wasn't looking at her.

"Are you guilty, Chuck?" she wanted to ask. "Are you feeling a little guilty about the calls you made last night?"

Finally he turned to her with a serious look on his face. He put a big hand on the shoulder of her jacket. "Listen, Jenny . . . uh . . . I want to apologize."

She stared back at him. She couldn't speak. Was he really going to admit it? How could he admit doing such a horrible thing?

"Apologize?" she finally managed to say.

"Should I leave?" Laura asked, grinning, looking as if leaving was the last thing on her mind.

"Apologize for what?" Jenny asked, ignoring Laura, keeping her voice low and steady.

"For being so obnoxious Friday afternoon. At the Pizza Oven. I really shouldn't have given you such a hard time about not wanting me to come by while you were baby-sitting."

"Oh. I mean . . . that's okay."

"Oh? It *is* okay? Great! I'll be there Thursday night!"

All three of them laughed.

Chuck pulled one of the pig socks down over his hand and made a hand puppet out of it. "Hi, girls," he made the sock say in a high, squeaky voice. "Want a sock in the nose?"

The store manager, a short, bald man with a sour expression, cleared his throat and shook his head at Chuck.

"We socks can all talk, but he won't let us!" Chuck made the sock say. "That's because he's a heel!"

"Are you buying those socks?" the manager barked.

"Do you take Confederate money?" Chuck asked, reaching for his wallet.

The manager just scowled.

"Then we're leaving!" Chuck told him. "It doesn't fit, anyway. It's tight around the knuckles." He pulled off the sock and dropped it back onto the shelf. "Let's go, girls."

The three of them held their breaths until they were several yards from the store. Then they burst out laughing.

"Hey — look what's at the theater!" Chuck

cried, pointing at the sign in front of the mall movie theater. "A clay animation festival! Neat! Come on — let's go!"

"What? We can't!" Jenny protested.

"Why not?" Chuck looked surprised.

"Well . . . uh . . . I don't know!" Jenny couldn't think of any reasons.

"I can't," Laura said, looking at her pink-and-black Swatch. "I promised my mom I'd be home. But you two go on without me." She gave Jenny a meaningful look.

"Laura — "

"Okay. Come on, Jenny," Chuck said eagerly. "I'll even treat."

"No, I — " Jenny looked imploringly at Laura for some help, but Laura was ignoring her plea.

"Have a great time," Laura said. She obviously thought Jenny and Chuck would make a great couple and was doing her best to see that they became a couple despite Jenny's misgivings.

She really likes bullying people, Jenny thought. Do all short people like to push people around?

Of course, Laura wouldn't see it that way. Laura would see it as only trying to help. She gave Jenny and Chuck a wave and, looking very pleased with herself, headed past the fountain and toward the exit.

"Come on. It just started," Chuck said, taking Jenny's hand. He smiled at her, and blushed.

He's actually very shy, she realized. Maybe that's why he wasn't looking me in the eye before.

"Okay," she said, and hurried with him up to the window of the box office.

"Two," he told the girl behind the glass.

Jenny smiled. She liked being part of a two. And she liked being with Chuck.

If only she knew the answer to one question. . . . Was he the one? Was he the one who called to frighten her the night before?

Chapter 10

"Tell me another story."

"No. Come on, Donny. I've already told you a really long one. It's time for you to go to sleep. Look at the clock on your dresser. It says nine-thirty."

"So?"

"So, it's bedtime."

Jenny had played three games of Chutes & Ladders with him and an endless card game called Uno, and now she was sitting on the edge of his bed, trying to coax him to go to sleep.

"A short story. Very short?"

"No deals. Bedtime is bedtime. Give me a break. I need some time to myself."

"No!" He made an angry face and tossed a stuffed bear across the room.

Jenny nearly laughed. It was funny to see someone who looked so angelic trying to act bad.

He heaved another stuffed animal across the room. It hit the wall and slid to the floor. "Are you gonna tell me another story or not?" he demanded, sticking out his lower lip like a tough guy.

"Not," Jenny said, beginning to lose patience. She knew he was just testing her, seeing how far he could push her around.

"You know, I know some bad words," he said. It wasn't a threat. It was a secret he was sharing with her. "Want to hear some?" He gave her a conspiratorial smile.

"Not tonight," she said wearily. "Please. It's getting really late. Don't make me get angry."

He climbed beside her on the bed and sat real close. She could feel the heat radiating off his thin body. He was always as warm as a furnace. "What do you do when you get angry?" He was testing her now.

She had to smile. "When I get angry, I . . . turn into a WEREWOLF!" She roared at him like an angry beast.

He laughed. "Okay. Get angry. I want to see."

She jumped up from the bed and leaned over him, putting her hands on his tiny shoulders. "You wouldn't like it if I got all hairy and grew fangs."

"Sure, I would. Do it. Do it!" He pulled away from her, stood up, and began jumping up and down, using his bed as a trampoline.

It took another half an hour to get him tucked in. He was going out of his way to be difficult, but it was so hard to get angry at someone that cute. Girls had better watch out for him in a few years! Jenny told herself, walking down the stairs.

She entered the den and picked up her backpack. She had come better prepared tonight with things to keep her entertained and keep her mind off the creepiness of the old house and how alone she was. Slipping her Walkman over her ears, she shuffled through the tapes she had brought, pushed a new Bangles cassette in, and turned up the volume. Then she pulled out her government textbook and searched for the pages she had to read.

The loud music made it easier to study. It shut out the rest of the world and forced her to concentrate harder on the words. At least, that was Jenny's theory.

Suddenly she pulled off the headphones and listened.

Was that Donny calling?

Was the phone ringing?

No. The house was silent except for the constant clicking of the grandfather clock in the living room.

Maybe the Walkman was a bad idea, she decided. Donny was still awake upstairs. He might call her for some reason, and she wouldn't be able to hear him. He might come to the edge of the stairs when she didn't respond to his calls. He might start down the stairs. He might fall.

He might fall and — stop! Stop dreaming up fresh worries!

She clicked off the Walkman, folded up the headphones, and replaced it in her backpack. I'm on duty, she reminded herself. I've got to remember, got to stay alert, got to stay at attention, like a soldier on guard duty.

And what was the penalty for a soldier who fell asleep on guard duty? Instant death! Hadn't she seen that in some movie? Or did she make it up?

She tried reading more about separation of powers in her government book, but it was hard to concentrate without the music. Suddenly feeling thirsty, she turned the textbook over and placed it on the table, climbed out of the low leather chair, and walked to the kitchen.

All of the lights were on in the living room, making it a lot brighter and less depressing than on the other nights. It was a still night outside, and so the shutter didn't bang and the wind didn't howl, and in general the atmosphere was a lot less threatening.

"If only I could do something about that awful clock," she told herself. For a brief moment, she was tempted to go over to it, grab the pendulum, and hold onto it until she had stopped the ticking forever.

She walked into the kitchen, switched on the lights, and headed to the refrigerator for a Coke. She found herself suddenly thinking about Chuck. They had had such a nice time together on Sunday. He really was a lot of fun to be with, not at all goofy and hard to talk to, the way she had imagined. He was very funny and entertaining, his mind was so quick, but he could also stop the jokes when he wanted to. During those times he was shy, and Jenny thought, even cuter.

He had come over to her house to study on Tuesday night. Jenny's mom had thought he was really terrific, too. Sure, he did some pretty gross things with a bunch of bananas he found on their kitchen table — but he wouldn't be Chuck if he didn't clown around some of the time.

If only . . . if only there weren't that one question she had about him, nagging at the back of her mind, keeping her from really being able to feel close to Chuck. If only she knew. . . .

She almost asked him once during their study date, almost asked him point-blank if he had made those frightening calls. But she stopped. She couldn't. If he said yes, it would ruin everything. And if he said no — then *she* would have ruined everything. He would never forgive her for accusing him. He'd have every right never to speak to her again.

And so she had pushed it out of her mind. At least she had tried to. And she found herself liking him more and more.

She snapped open the Coke and took a sip from the can. When the phone rang, she thought it must be Chuck. She had told him in school that afternoon that he could call.

She picked up the receiver of the kitchen wall phone and said brightly, "Hello. Hagen residence."

"Hi, Babes."

The gruff, whispered voice.

She gasped. Her bright mood vanished, replaced by the cold dread she had felt on Saturday night. She could feel her muscles grow tense. Her heart began to pound. She gripped the bright red phone receiver so tightly her hand began to ache.

"Hi, Babes. Are you all alone?"

She didn't say anything.

She wanted to shout, to scream at this creep, to slam the phone down as hard as she could. But she didn't say anything, and she didn't move. It was as if the whispered words had paralyzed her, frozen her with their menace.

"Don't be sad. I'll be there soon. Then the fun will really begin."

Was it Chuck?

She couldn't tell. It might be. No. It couldn't be.

"I'm . . . calling the police," she finally managed to say. She didn't recognize her high, tight voice. It was as if someone else was speaking, as if this was happening to someone else.

"See you soon, Babes."

There was a CLICK at the other end.

She stood there for a long while, receiver pressed to her ear, listening to the steady hum of the dial tone. The sound was soothing somehow. It meant that the whispered threats were over.

Jenny jammed the receiver back onto the wall, then ran to the back door and made sure it was locked.

Now what?

Now what?

She was pacing back and forth the length of the kitchen without realizing it. She picked up the can of Coke, took a long swig to moisten her achingly dry throat, then carried the can with her as she paced.

Now what?

Now what?

Her hands were ice-cold. Her muscles all felt tight and knotted. She heard a car door slam somewhere down the street.

"I'll be there soon. Then the fun will really begin."

She stopped pacing and listened.

Silence.

She knew what she had to do. She picked up the phone and pushed O. After three rings, a husky woman's voice said, "Operator."

"Please. Put me through to the police." It was all unreal. None of this was happening. What was she going to say? What were *they* going to say?

"Do you want the town police or the village police?"

"What? Oh. I don't know. I mean — "

"Are you in Harrison, or are you in the village?" The woman was trying to be helpful. But her calm, steady tone was driving Jenny crazy. Didn't she realize that Jenny was frightened? Why couldn't she sound frightened and upset, too?

"I — I'm not sure. I'm in the Old Village. Edgetown Lane. Off Millertown."

"Then you probably want the village police."

Probably?? "Oh. Thank you."

"You can dial them directly. The number is 066-1919."

"What? Dial them? Can't you — What was the number again?"

The operator repeated the number, then clicked off.

Jenny pushed the number, got it wrong the first time, then pushed it again.

"Village police, Officer Mertz."

"Hello, Mr. Mertz. I mean — Officer — "

"Can I help you?"

"I — I want to report some calls."

"You want to make some calls?"

"No. I've been getting these calls." Calm down, Jenny. Calm down. You're not going to make any sense at all if you don't lower your voice and speak more clearly, more slowly.

"Is this a matter for the phone company?"

"No. I'm sorry. I've been getting these calls, threatening calls."

"Someone is threatening you?"

"Yes. On the phone. Whispering."

"Where are you calling from?"

"Edgetown Lane. 142 Edgetown. Off Miller-town."

"Your name?"

"I'm Jenny Jeffers. But I don't live here. I mean, it's not my house. I'm the baby-sitter."

"Have you heard any strange sounds in the house or outside? Seen any unfamiliar cars? Any sign of anyone outside?"

"Yes. I don't know. I mean, no. Not tonight. Just the calls."

"I see." He seemed to be writing everything down. "Do you think this could be a friend of yours, maybe someone from school, someone pulling a prank?"

"I don't know. I don't think so. Are you going to send someone out to investigate?"

"Investigate what? We can't investigate phone calls."

"Oh. I guess you're right. I just — "

"Is there someone you could call to come stay with you? Someone you trust?"

"Well . . . no. My mother isn't home tonight. Uh . . . I could call a girlfriend, maybe."

"It might help make you feel better. Chances are, it's just a phone creep. These guys never go outdoors. They stay in, making charming threats, getting their kicks by frightening people. But they seldom show up at the door."

"That's good."

"Normally, I'd tell you not to worry. But because of the baby-sitter attacks, we have to take this seriously. I'm going to give you a different phone number. This is the number of Lieutenant Ferris from the town police. This type of thing is sort of his department." He gave Jenny Lieutenant Ferris's phone number. She wrote it down quickly on a sheet of paper towel she tore off the rack over the sink.

"Got it," she said. "I should call him — "

"If you get any more threats. Or if you hear anything unusual, or see anything unusual. Just call that number. Ferris will be there. He's the man who can help you. But as I say, these phone creeps seldom leave their princess phones."

"Thanks, officer. Thanks for your help."

"Just doing my job."

Jenny replaced the receiver and stood staring at the number she had written on the paper towel. Then she folded it carefully and pushed it into her jeans pocket.

She was feeling a little better. At least, her heart had stopped pounding like a bass drum and her neck muscles weren't so tense and tight. She took a long swig of the Coke and started toward the den with it.

Passing the stairs in the front hallway, she suddenly remembered Donny. She turned and headed up the stairs to check on him. She tiptoed into his room to find him sleeping lightly with his eyes open. He looked as if he were staring right at her, even though he was asleep.

How do kids do that? she wondered. It looks so strange.

She was starting to feel a lot more normal as she headed back down the stairs. Calling the police had helped a lot. That officer had been so calm and reassuring. And it made her feel good to have a special phone number to call in an emergency.

"These guys never go out," the policeman had told her. "They never show up at your door."

She was halfway across the living room when she heard the loud knocking.

She jumped. Her heart seemed to skip a beat.

No, she thought. That's the loose shutter banging against the house.

But it couldn't be. There was no wind.

She heard it again. Four hard raps. Someone was knocking on the front door.

She ran to the door. "Who's there?" she called. No reply.

If only there were a chain on the door. If only there were a peephole.

Four loud knocks.

"Who is it?"

Silence.

An idea flashed into her head. The living room window. Maybe she could see the front porch from the living room window. Maybe she could see who it was from there.

Three more knocks.

She ran into the living room, tripping over a tear in the worn carpet. She fell, hitting her left knee hard. Pain throbbed up her leg. She pulled herself to her feet. She hobbled the rest of the way. Her knee throbbed, but it was okay.

She pulled back the heavy drapes. Light from the porch light cast a yellow glow over the front yard.

Suddenly someone leaped up on the other side of the glass, as if being shot up from under the ground.

"YAAAAAIII!"

The scream ripped from Jenny's throat as she saw the hideous, deformed figure staring back at her, his twisted face pressed menacingly against the windowpane.

Chapter 11

No. This has to be a nightmare, Jenny thought.

This person — this creature — can't be real.

Then she realized it was a mask. It was someone in a monster mask, with enormous rubber fangs, huge bloodshot eyes that popped out two inches from their bloody sockets, and long tangles of red vinyl hair that shot straight up in the air.

"Don't worry. Company's coming."

"I'll be there soon. Then the fun will really begin."

Jenny reached into her jeans pocket for the piece of paper with the policeman's number on it. Where had she put it? She had written the number on a paper towel and put it — Here it is.

But would she have time to call?

Would the police be able to get there in time before this creep . . . before he. . . .

He pulled off the mask.

"CHUCK!!" Jenny screamed. "Chuck — how could you?? Why??"

"Gotcha! he called through the window glass. He tossed the hideous mask high in the air and, laughing like a lunatic, leaped up after it. Then he did a cartwheel on the grass. Still laughing jubilantly over his triumphant joke, he walked back to the window and pressed his nose against the glass.

Jenny's terror quickly turned to fury. She slammed the drapes shut and strode angrily to the front door, her hands still shaking as she turned the lock and pulled open the door.

Chuck was waiting for her on the porch, grinning like he'd just won the World Series of Practical Jokes, turning the disgusting mask over and over in his hands. "I *knew* you'd come to the window," he laughed. "You should've seen your face!"

"Go away, you dork!" Jenny screamed. "Get lost! I mean it!"

He didn't seem to hear her. Or maybe he didn't realize she was completely serious. "I gotcha. I really gotcha. Whoa! That was incredible!"

"You're not funny. You're sick! You scared me to death." She started to slam the door, but he shoved his foot into the opening.

She felt a stab of renewed fear. He had moved so quickly, so deftly to block the door, as if he had done it before. She had the sudden realization that maybe he had come to harm her. Maybe he was the whispered voice on the phone. Maybe he truly was dangerous.

She didn't really know him, after all.

No one did.

"Move away, Chuck. I don't want to see you. I'm — "

"You look cute when you're scared."

Was he trying to make her more scared?

"Go away! I really mean it. I'm furious at you. You're not funny. Stop smiling at me like that!"

The smile faded slowly. "Come on, Jenny — "

"No."

"It's cold out here. Just let me come in for a few minutes."

"No. Go away."

He gave her a pleading, little-boy look. "Please? I'll let you try on the mask!" More high-pitched laughing. He really thought he was a riot.

"I'm serious, Chuck. Move your foot. I don't want to see you. You had no right to scare me like that."

He finally began to realize that she meant what she said. He let the mask fall to the porch floor and shrugged. "Sorry."

"Apology not accepted," she said, pushing on the door. "Good night."

"You're right, Jenny. It was stupid. I don't know what I was thinking of. I just wanted to surprise you, I guess."

"Surprise me?! Well, you did a great job, Ace!"

A cold burst of wind caught them both by surprise. They heard a crash somewhere down the street, a garbage can being knocked over, the lid rattling down the street.

"I'm really freezing, Jenny," he wrapped his arms around himself. She saw for the first time that he had no coat, only a gray sweatshirt. He looked really cold, and really apologetic. And really cute, hugging himself like that, his eyes pleading with her like a little boy begging for a cookie. "Can't I come in?"

"I guess. Just for a second. Hurry." She backed away, and he eagerly stepped into the narrow hallway, shivering, still hugging himself.

"You can't stay long. The Hagens may be home soon. Mr. Hagen is so nervous. He'd kill me if he found a boy here with me."

He followed her into the living room. "Wow! What a dump!"

"They're planning to redo it all. They just moved in."

"This room is huge. Great place to party!"

She spun around angrily. "Stop talking like that. This is my job."

He looked hurt. "Sorry. I'm sorry. Sorry. Sorry. Sorry."

She started to say something, but she heard footsteps running down the stairs. Donny, in his G.I. Joe pajamas, burst into the room, one cheek bright red from where he'd been sleeping on it. "Who's he?" he demanded, pointing at Chuck.

"He's my friend Chuck," Jenny said quickly, giving Chuck an annoyed look. She really didn't want Donny to know she'd had a visitor. Donny was certain to tell his parents.

"Hi, Donny," Chuck said, giving him a big, friendly grin.

"How'd you know my name?" Donny asked suspiciously.

"Just took a lucky guess," Chuck said, still grinning.

Donny thought that was funny.

"Donny, what are you doing up?" Jenny demanded.

Donny ignored her question. He pointed to the mask in Chuck's hand. "What's that?"

"A monster mask." Chuck held it up so he could see it. "Want to try it on?"

"Yeah!" Donny's eyes lit up.

"No, Chuck. Donny's got to go back to bed," Jenny insisted.

"Aw, come on," Donny whined, grabbing for the mask.

"Aw, come on," Chuck repeated, sounding just like him. "It'll only take a second. And then Donny promises to go right back upstairs, don't you, pal?"

"Maybe," Donny said cautiously. He stood still while Chuck pulled the grotesque rubber mask down over his head. "How do I look?"

Both Jenny and Chuck burst out laughing. He looked so ridiculous, that gigantic head on such a skinny little body.

"Let me see! Let me see!" Donny yelled. He went running to the full-length mirror in the front hallway.

"Don't run!" Jenny called after him. Too late. Unable to see through the mask, he tripped over the sofa and fell hard against a mahogany end table. "Are you okay?" Jenny went running after him, giving Chuck a dirty look for causing all this trouble.

"I'm okay," Donny said, pulling himself up quickly and hurrying to the mirror.

"Kids are made of rubber," Chuck said to Jenny. "How do you look?" he called to Donny.

"Scary," Donny called back. "I'm a monster, and I'm going to eat you!" He came charging back into the living room, his arms outstretched.

"No! Don't eat me! Don't eat me!" Chuck ducked behind the couch. Then when Donny got near, he rolled over the couch, tumbled across the floor and hid behind one of the worn, over-stuffed armchairs.

"Grrrrrrr!" Donny roared, and charged again. He narrowly missed Chuck, who dodged away and ran toward the den, the monster in close pursuit.

"Chuck! Donny! Stop it! Donny has to go to bed!"

"He got me! He got me!" Chuck screamed as Donny leaped onto his back.

"Look, I'm not being paid to baby-sit two babies!" Jenny cried, exasperated.

"I'm not a baby!" Donny insisted, hurt.

Chuck pulled Donny off him and climbed slowly to his feet. "She's right," he told Donny softly. "It's past your bedtime. We'll play again next time. I'll bring the mask if you want."

"There won't be a next time," Jenny said flatly.

"Awww, you're mean," Donny told her.

"You heard him," Chuck agreed, laughing.

"Bring him next time," Donny told her.

"Yeah. Bring me next time."

"Chuck — stop it. Come on, Donny. I don't want to have to give your mom and dad a bad report. Back up to bed."

"Only if he tucks me in," Donny said, pointing at Chuck.

Jenny shrugged and rolled her eyes. "Do it," she told Chuck. "And no clowning around up there. Tuck him in and come right back."

"Aye, aye, Captain," Chuck said, saluting. He pulled off the mask and tossed it to the floor. Then taking Donny's hand, he led him up the stairs.

Jenny went to the den and, with a weary sigh, sank into the big, white leather armchair. She yawned. All of the tension must be making her tired, she thought.

Chuck certainly was great with Donny. The two of them just hit it off immediately. That's because Chuck's a big kid himself. Playing that stupid practical joke with the mask. Why did he do that? Did he really think I'd find it funny? Or was he trying to scare me to death?

"You look so cute when you're scared," he had said.

What a sick thing to say.

She heard Chuck's footsteps in the living room. "I'm in here, in the den," she called to him. He appeared in the doorway and slid beside her into the big armchair, putting his arm around her shoulder.

"Stop," she protested.

He snuggled against her. "I just want to apologize," he said softly in her ear. "That was stupid of me. I'm really sorry." He pressed his face against her cheek.

He kissed her. She turned her lips to his. She gave in to the kiss. Then, with a little cry, she pulled away.

She decided she had to ask. She had to ask about the phone calls. She had to know. She would never be able to trust him, never be comfortable with him, never be able to relax with him, to really believe in him, to really believe they could be a couple unless she knew.

She stood up and walked to the desk. He looked very hurt. "What's wrong?" he asked, that little-boy look again.

"I have to ask you something," she said, leaning back against the desk, looking away from him, looking at the bookshelves instead.

"What? Why do you look so grim? I said I was sorry about the mask."

"It's not the mask. I have to ask you about something else. I hope you'll understand. I just have to ask."

He shrugged. "Okay. I'll understand. Ask me anything." He forced a smile, but he looked very nervous.

"Someone has called me. Here at the Hagens." She turned and stared into his eyes. "Was it you?"

His face turned bright red. He opened his mouth but no sound came out. "Yes," he finally managed to whisper. "Yes. I'm sorry, Jenny. It was me."

Chapter 12

Her eyes burned into his.

He looked down at the dark floor. His face grew even redder. He looks like a ripe tomato, Jenny thought.

Her thoughts bounced around in her head as she tried to decide what to do now. He had admitted it. He had confessed. He was sick. He may be dangerous. She had to get him out of there, away from her, away from Donny.

She could still feel his mouth on hers, still taste him on her lips.

How could I have kissed him? How could I have actually liked someone who made those disgusting calls to me?

How awful. How tragic. How scary.

Chuck must be out of control. Sometimes he can hold himself in and be a funny, likable, good-natured guy. Other times, his other side comes out, his sick side, his evil side.

What should she do now?

"I — I was going to tell you," he said. His

voice cracked. He didn't say any more. He shook his head and stared at the floor. "I — I didn't mean — "

A loud crash interrupted him. "Where'd that come from?" he asked quickly, looking up, obviously glad for the interruption.

"Not upstairs," Jenny said, heading to the doorway. It was more of a prayer than a statement.

He jumped to his feet and followed her across the living room. "No. It was outside. In the back, I think."

"I'm going to check upstairs," Jenny said, taking the stairs two at a time. Donny was sleeping peacefully, a stuffed tiger held tightly to his chest. They look just like Calvin and Hobbes, she thought. She hurried through the other upstairs rooms, not bothering to turn on the lights, hoping against hope that she wouldn't see or hear anything — or anyone.

She didn't.

Chuck was right. The crash must have been outside. She hurried downstairs and called to him. He was in the kitchen, looking out the window in the kitchen door. "See anything?" she asked.

"No. Not a thing. Guess we should forget about it."

"No. It was a loud crash. I can't ignore it. I'm in charge here. It had to be caused by something. By someone. By I-don't-know-what."

"Calm down, Jenny." He started to put his hands on her shoulders to comfort her, but she backed away. He immediately remembered why, and his face filled with embarrassment and shame.

"Okay. Let's call the police," he suggested, heading to the wall phone.

"No. Wait." She pulled his hand off the receiver. "What if it's nothing? A raccoon in the garbage or something? I don't want the police out. I don't want the Hagens to think I get hysterical and can't handle stupid little things."

He shrugged. "Okay. Then we'll ignore it."

She didn't reply. Instead she walked over to the sink and began searching frantically through the cabinet drawers. Finally she found what she was looking for, a silver-and-black flashlight. She tested it. "Good and bright," she said, shining it in Chuck's face.

He threw up his hands to shield his eyes. "What are you doing?"

"Going out to investigate," she said, pulling open the kitchen door. "You watch from here. If you see or hear anything wrong, call the police."

"But, Jenny — "

She was already out the door, following the narrow beam of light from the flashlight toward the garage.

The air smelled clean and fresh. She took a deep breath. Someone in a house nearby had a fire going. The dry fragrance of burning cedar invaded her nose, made the air smell warm and sweet. She turned back. Chuck was watching her from the kitchen.

Am I safer out here than inside with him? she

asked herself sadly. What do I think I'm going to find out here? I already know that the creep who made those horrible, threatening calls is already in the house, watching me from the kitchen.

Jenny shivered. Twigs cracked loudly under her feet. The ground felt as hard as rock. She shined the light around the yard, bouncing it along the tall, wooden fence at the back. Nothing there.

Round piles of leaves looked like craters in the dark. There was no wind now. The trees were still, silent onlookers.

What was *that* moving to her left?

Just a tall shrub. She took a deep breath and let it out slowly. The evergreen shrub was the same height as a person. But it stood straight and unmoving. Her imagination was playing tricks on her again.

She shined the white light onto other shrubs that dotted the yard. No sign of anything wrong. No sign of anything. Or anyone.

The crash had been loud, and it had been nearby.

"Maybe it *was* just a raccoon in a trash can," she told herself. But where was the trash can?

She followed a flagstone walk down a slightly sloping incline toward the garage.

Hold on a minute!

The garage light. Hadn't there been a bright yellow spotlight on the side of the garage when she arrived? It was dark now. No light at all.

Maybe she remembered incorrectly. Maybe the spotlight hadn't been on. But if it hadn't, how did she remember one being there?

She felt a sudden chill. It was cold out, cold enough to see her breath, hot and wet in front of her face, misting in the wavering light of the flashlight. She should have put on her jacket.

Maybe the spotlight had burned out. That was possible.

She heard a scraping sound. Shoes scraping against the hard ground? She raised the flashlight to the side of the garage.

She heard the scraping again.

Someone coughed. A man.

The scraping sound again, coming from the garage.

Jenny clicked off the flashlight.

Now what?

Call out to him? Try to sneak up on him? Run back to the house?

She clicked the flashlight back on, illuminating the garage door. The door was open. She could see snow tires hanging on the wall. A few lawn chairs. A small two-wheeler that must be Donny's.

She heard more scraping, boots against concrete, the concrete garage floor.

The man coughed again.

"Who's there?"

She didn't recognize her own voice. She hadn't meant to call out. Her heart was pounding now. She struggled to keep the light steady.

"Who's there?" she repeated, louder.

A man stepped into the circle of light.

"Sorry. Hope I didn't frighten you." He smiled at her.

It was Willers, the next-door neighbor. He was wearing the same plaid lumberjack shirt. He took a few steps toward her, then stopped. "I'm really sorry. You look frightened. Please don't be. It's only me." His voice was as rough as sandpaper. The way he kept insisting that Jenny shouldn't be frightened scared her even more.

"What are you doing back here, Mr. Willers?" she managed to say.

"I thought I saw a prowler. Back here in the Hagens' yard. I wanted to make sure that — "

The prowler story again. Willers didn't make it sound too believable.

"But what was that crash?" Jenny interrupted impatiently, keeping the light on Willers' dark, stubbled face.

"Crash? Oh. I tripped over Hagen's firewood pile. Sent the logs crashing." He pointed to the logs by the garage wall. They were scattered in disarray. "I'll pick them up for him in the morning."

"But — you have no flashlight. You came out without a light? Without anything?"

Willers smiled, a crooked smile, a smile that seemed to admit he had been caught lying. "I wanted to sneak up on the guy," he said. "You know, take him by surprise."

Suddenly the smile faded. "Are you all alone

in there?" he asked, his dark eyes searching for something in hers.

The question caught Jenny off guard. The way he said it, the rumble of his rough voice, sounded just like the whisperer on the phone.

But Chuck had already confessed. Chuck was the whisperer on the phone.

"No," Jenny told him. "I'm not alone. A friend is over. A friend came over to keep me company."

"I see," Willers said, scratching his black stubbly beard. "I wondered about the car parked out front."

What a snoop, Jenny thought. Does he spend all of his time watching the Hagens' house?

They stood staring at each other for a while. Jenny couldn't think of anything else to say. She shivered, almost dropping the flashlight.

"You'd better get inside," Willers said. "You'll catch your death."

Why did he say it that way? Was that some kind of threat?

"There's no prowler out here," he said. "Maybe I scared him away. Go on. Go back in. Sorry I scared you."

"Okay," Jenny said. "Night." She watched him walk away until he disappeared into the trees at the right of the yard.

By the time she got back to the kitchen, she was trembling all over. "You poor thing," Chuck said, taking her hands in his and rubbing them to warm them. "You were so brave. Come here. Let me warm you up."

She pulled away from him again. "No, Chuck. Let go."

"Jenny, that man out there — "

"Just the neighbor. He accidentally knocked over the woodpile. That was the crash. Now I think you'd better go."

"But, I want to — "

"No. I think you should just go. I don't think we have anything to talk about."

"Yes, we do," he said, suddenly sounding more forceful, as if he had just made up his mind about something. He pulled out a tall kitchen stool and climbed onto it. "I'm not leaving until you listen to me."

"I told you, Chuck. There's nothing more to say."

"But I want to explain, Jenny. About calling you. I know it wasn't right. I mean, I know there's no excuse for it. But I want to explain. Then I'll go. I promise."

She leaned back against the counter and closed her eyes. "Okay. Explain."

"Saturday night I got the Hagens' phone number from your mother."

"I know."

"I was just going to call and say hi. You know, just talk, nothing important. I thought maybe you were bored here all by yourself and we could talk. We could get to know each other better."

"Chuck, really — "

"Jenny, please — don't interrupt. This is really hard for me."

It's true, he really did look as if he were suffering. He had his hands so tightly clamped onto the back of the stool that his knuckles were white. His eyes kept darting back and forth. His chin was trembling as he talked.

"Sorry. Go on," Jenny said.

"Okay. I was really nervous about calling you. I mean, I'd never called you before. And you probably won't believe this, but I'm really very shy. I mean, all my joking and clowning around, I guess that's kind of a cover-up. I just do that because I'm nervous a lot of the time around people. I get scared, scared that they'll think I'm weird, or they won't like me, or something."

He was fidgeting on the kitchen stool. He wiped his sweaty hands off on his jeans legs. "So it isn't easy for me to call a girl, especially a girl I like a lot, like you. But I called you anyway. It took me over an hour to work up the courage to call — do you believe that?"

"I'm sorry," Jenny said.

"And when you picked up the phone, I guess I just panicked. I completely forgot what I was going to say. I started breathing real heavy. I felt weird, paralyzed, almost like I was going to faint or something. I wanted to talk to you, but I couldn't make a sound.

"It was so stupid. I heard you saying, 'Hello, hello,' and I was just too panicked to talk. So I hung up. After I calmed down, I felt ridiculous. And I realized you probably thought it was some kind of a nut or a joker calling."

"All I could hear was breathing," Jenny said. "I thought it was a creep who calls girls up and breathes at them."

"I'm really sorry. I was going to tell you on Sunday at the mall what had happened, but it was too embarrassing. I just wanted to forget about it. I had such a good time with you, I didn't want to spoil it by telling you what a dopey nerd I am in real life."

He wiped his hands again on his jeans legs. He was staring down at the linoleum floor, but he looked really relieved, as if he had gotten a great weight off his chest.

"Go on," Jenny said.

He looked up, confused. "What?"

"Go on. Tell me about the rest of the calls."

"What? What calls? That was it."

"What do you mean, Chuck? I want to hear your explanation for the rest."

"Jenny, there is no rest. I only made one call. It was such a disaster, do you think I'd call back?"

"But I got other calls. Someone whispering threats. Threatening to come here. Asking if I was all alone."

"Huh?"

"Saturday night. And tonight."

"Jenny, that's horrible! And you thought I made them?"

"No. I mean — I didn't know. When you said you were the one, I — "

"I only called once. You've got to believe me." He looked at her. "You *do* believe me — don't you?"

She ran to him in reply. She was in his arms. She was returning his kiss. He felt so warm, so good, so safe.

Did she believe him?

She wanted to. She really wanted to. . . .

But she wasn't sure.

Chapter 13

Twenty minutes later, they were still kissing on the white leather chair in the den when they heard a car door slam.

"The Hagens! They must be home early!" Jenny cried, shoving Chuck off the chair. He looked confused for a second, then realized why Jenny was so panicky.

"I'm out of here!" he cried. "Which way?"

"Go out the back! No — the front! Quick! The front! Get out of here!" Jenny screamed. Was that the back door opening? If so, the Hagens would be in the hallway in seconds. Could Chuck get out in time?

He flew across the living room, pulled open the front door, and vanished without looking back. "The door! You left the door open!" Jenny called, even though he was already out, already running through the darkness of the leaf-cluttered lawn toward his car.

Jenny slammed the front door just as she heard the kitchen door open. She glanced anxiously at the living room, trying to make sure no trace of Chuck had been left behind.

A few seconds later, Mr. Hagen came hurrying into the room, followed closely by Mrs. Hagen, who looked very upset and annoyed.

"You've got to stop doing this, Mike," she said, the tension in her voice revealing that this argument had been steaming for some time. "We had no reason to leave the Fischers' so early. Jenny is perfectly capable of — "

"Is Donny okay?" Mr. Hagen asked Jenny, ignoring his wife. His cheeks and ears were aflame. His small, steel-colored eyes burned into Jenny's, as if searching for trouble she might be trying to conceal.

"Fine," Jenny said, her heart still pounding over Chuck's narrow escape. "Just fine."

Mr. Hagen spun around, grabbed the bannister in his big hand, and bounded up the stairs, taking them two at a time despite his limp. Mrs. Hagen shrugged and rolled her eyes. She suddenly looked very tired and old.

Jenny didn't know what to say to her. She felt very awkward. And she felt bad that Mr. Hagen still didn't trust her.

But then, why should he trust me? she asked herself. I've been in the den making out with Chuck all this time instead of staying alert and doing my job.

"Donny was good tonight," she told Mrs. Hagen, trying to sound calm and normal, as if she didn't notice the Hagens were having a fight.

"He's a good boy," Mrs. Hagen said, wearily

pulling off her coat and draping it over the bannister.

Mr. Hagen reappeared at the top of the stairs, still looking troubled. "Donny's fine," he told his wife.

"Of course, he is," Mrs. Hagen said, frowning. "I'm sick of you and your hunches and bad premonitions, Mike. Donny's in good hands here. You have no cause for such alarm."

Again he ignored her and turned to Jenny. "I thought I saw a car out front, parked across the street," he said, leaning heavily on the bannister as he descended. "Do you know anything about it?"

"No. No, I don't," Jenny lied.

He limped over to the living room window, pushed aside the heavy drapes, and peered out. "That's funny." His voice was muffled by the drapes, making him sound far away. "I could have sworn it was parked right across the street. Not there now. . . ."

He stood looking out for a long while. When he returned, he looked at Jenny suspiciously. She wondered if he could read the guilt on her face. "You didn't hear any car doors or anything?"

"No. Not a sound. I was in the den most of the time." She wasn't a very good liar. Was he staring at her like that because he knew she was lying?

"You forgot to get Jenny's coat when you were upstairs," Mrs. Hagen said, obvious about trying to change the subject.

"That's okay. I'll go get it," Jenny said, eager to get going.

"No. No. I'll go," Mr. Hagen insisted. He was already halfway up the stairs.

"He had a bad day," Mrs. Hagen confided to Jenny as soon as he was out of earshot. "He's been under a lot of pressure, as I told you. Did everything go okay?"

"Well . . . actually," Jenny started reluctantly, "something kind of strange happened. This neighbor of yours — "

"Sshhh — he's coming back," Mrs. Hagen whispered. "Please — don't trouble him with it tonight." She gave Jenny a pleading look.

He handed Jenny her coat and headed back into the living room. "I'm going up to bed," Mrs. Hagen said, yawning. She patted Jenny on the shoulder and smiled. "G'night. See you Saturday."

"Wait a minute! What's this?" Mr. Hagen cried from the living room, sounding alarmed.

Oh no, Jenny thought. Did Chuck leave his jacket? No. He wasn't wearing a jacket. What could it be?

She hurried into the living room. Mr. Hagen was holding the rubber monster mask up by the long, red plastic hair, its protruding eyeballs flopping around in front of him. Chuck must have left it on the couch.

Mr. Hagen looked at her suspiciously. "Where'd this come from?"

"Oh. That silly mask," Jenny said, thinking

fast, forcing a smile to her face. "I brought it for Donny. I thought maybe he'd think it was funny."

The suspicious look didn't leave Mr. Hagen's face. He held the mask up and examined it closely. "Funny. I didn't see it when you came in."

"I had it in my backpack," Jenny said. "I'll take it home." She took it out of Mr. Hagen's hands. "Donny didn't really like it."

"He wasn't scared of it, was he?" he asked, a thin smile breaking over his face.

"No. I don't think so. He just said it was gross," Jenny told him. She hurried to get her backpack and stuff the mask inside. She didn't want it lying around the next morning. Maybe if he didn't see it, Donny wouldn't mention to his parents that a boy named Chuck had brought it.

"Mike, why are you cross-examining Jenny like that?" Mrs. Hagen asked from the doorway.

He looked up, surprised that she was still downstairs. "Was I? Gee, I'm sorry, Jenny. I didn't mean to. I guess I'm a little wound up tonight."

"That's okay," Jenny said brightly. "I'm ready to go now."

Driving her home, Mr. Hagen did seem more troubled than usual. He talked nonstop, his thoughts rambling from one subject to another, first talking about Donny and his schoolwork, then about a tree house he planned to build for Donny, then about a dog he'd had when he was Donny's age and how it had disappeared.

When they stopped for a stoplight a few blocks from her home, he finally grew silent. He turned to her with a serious look on his face. "There's probably no need to tell you this," he said softly, "but I like to make things clear. I have one important rule for our baby-sitters. And that's no visitors. I know a lot of times baby-sitters like to invite their friends over to keep them company. I guess some parents allow it, or at least, put up with it. But I don't. I just don't think it's a good idea. I want all of your attention on Donny. I hope you understand."

The light had changed, but he didn't move. Why was he saying this now? Did he figure out about Chuck's car parked across the street? About the mask? Could he read her mind?

"Yes. Sure, I do," Jenny said. "I understand." She could feel her face getting hot from the guilt she felt. She was glad he couldn't see her blushing in the darkness.

He pressed on the gas and the car rolled forward. "We had another child," he said, staring straight ahead through the windshield, his face suddenly blank, completely expressionless.

Jenny shifted in the seat and stared at him, waiting for him to say more. But he didn't. The words hung in the air. He seemed lost in thought. He stared straight ahead in silence the rest of the way to Jenny's house.

"Good night, Mr. Hagen," she said, climbing out of the car.

He didn't seem to hear her.

She slammed the door and watched him drive away, still staring straight ahead.

"Rotate! ROTATE!"

Miss Marks's powerful voice echoed off the tile of the gym walls. "Rotate, girls! Your serve, Jenny!"

"God, I hate volleyball," Jenny muttered to Laura as she switched to serve position on the floor, the other girls on her team all moving over one place.

"Here's a tip that might help you," Laura told her, leaning forward to catch her breath, her hands resting above her knees.

"What's that?" Jenny asked.

"Try to get it over the net this time!"

A few girls laughed. Jenny scowled at her friend, brought back her arm, raised the ball, and punched it with all her might.

Once again, it sailed into the net.

"One more try," Miss Marks called, looking on disapprovingly from the side of the net. "Get under it, Jenny. Get under it."

"I wish *you'd* get under it," Jenny muttered under her breath.

"What?" Miss Marks called.

"I said I'll try," Jenny told her. She raised the ball and brought her fist up fast and hard. This time the ball sailed under the net.

"Serve goes to the Blues. Rotate. ROTATE!" Miss Marks shouted.

Jenny kicked at the floor, feeling like a fool

and a failure. She looked up and caught Laura laughing at her.

"Well, you're certainly hostile today," she said. "What's your problem?"

The ball came flying over the net. Jenny tipped it straight up in the air. Sarah Robbins leaped and batted it over to the other side.

"Oh, I don't know," Laura said, slapping the ball easily over the net. "I guess I'm in a bad mood because I broke up with Bob Tanner last night."

"WHAT??"

"Rotate! ROTATE!"

"Laura, are you serious? Ulllp!"

The ball bounced off Jenny's chest. Her breath shot out like a balloon popping. She uttered a strangled protest and dropped to the gym floor. The lights seemed to flicker and flash. She tried to get up, but she was too dizzy.

Miss Marks's whistle blew. "TIME!" Jenny looked up to see the copper-haired gym instructor leaning over her. "You're okay, Jenny. You just had the wind knocked out."

If I had the wind knocked out, how can I be okay? Jenny thought. But she didn't say anything. She wasn't sure she could talk. She was still struggling to breathe normally.

"Laura, take Jenny to the locker room," Miss Marks instructed, patting Jenny on the back of her T-shirt, then jumping back up and returning to the game.

"ROTATE! ROTATE!"

Miss Marks's voice reverberated over the ringing in Jenny's ears as Laura led her slowly away. "It's okay. I can walk," Jenny said, pulling away from Laura.

"Listen, Jen. I'm sorry. That was my fault," Laura said, sweeping her hair off her shoulder. "Whew. Is it hot in here, or what?"

"It was my fault," Jenny said, her voice still thin and shaky. "I should've been watching."

"Can you breathe?"

"Yeah. I'm fine. Really," Jenny said, dropping down onto the wooden bench in front of her gym locker. "I feel a little light, that's all. You know, kind of feathery. But I'll be okay."

"Want me to sit with you for a while?"

"No. Really, Laura. You can go back to the game. I'm just going to catch my breath. Then I'll take a shower."

"Okay. See you later, Jen."

"Hey, Laura — sorry about you and Bob."

"Way it goes," Laura said, shrugging her tiny shoulders, and vanishing out the locker room door.

Jenny felt very dizzy. She leaned forward, elbows on her thighs, resting her head in her hands. After a while, the dizziness passed. Her head felt better, but her stomach felt as if it had a huge rock inside it. She opened her locker door and reached for her bag to get a tissue.

Inside the bag, her hand came upon a folded-up sheet of yellow notebook paper. She pulled it out. She didn't remember putting it in there.

She unfolded the sheet of paper. It appeared

to be some kind of a note. As she read it, she began to get dizzy again:

HI, BABES.

ALL ALONE IN THAT BIG OLD HOUSE?
DON'T WORRY. COMPANY'S COMING.

The bag fell out of her lap, spilling her hairbrush and mirror and several other items onto the concrete floor. She didn't notice. Her head was spinning. Her stomach ached.

She read the note again.

Again.

The big, block letters, printed so neatly, so carefully, seemed to jump off the yellow page at her.

COMPANY'S COMING.

DON'T WORRY. COMPANY'S COMING.

Who wrote it? Who folded it up and shoved it into her bag?

The phone caller and the note writer had to be the same person. But who? Who could have gotten to her bag?

Her heart skipped a beat as she mouthed the name of the only person who had been close enough to her bag last night to slip the note in.

Chuck. . . .

Chapter 14

The bus lurched and bumped across town. Since Jenny and a man in overalls, stretched out sound asleep on the long backseat, were the only passengers on this blustery Saturday evening, the bus driver was setting a crosstown record. He wasn't stopping at bus stops or even for traffic lights!

The town seemed really empty, as if the cold and the gloom had forced everyone into hibernation even though the winter was just beginning. Staring out of the smeared bus window at the silent streets and empty sidewalks, Jenny felt as dark and gloomy as the passing scenery.

Her stop came much too quickly. For a brief moment, she was tempted to stay on the bus, to keep riding round and round from one side of town to the other until the night was over. Only the thought of seeing Donny cheered her, made her forget her trepidation at going back to the Hagens' house, where so much fear awaited.

She stepped down off the bus, ducking her head to protect her eyes from the wind, which seemed to gust in all directions at once. The bare trees tossed and rattled their branches as she zipped up her down jacket as far as it would go and began to hurry toward the Hagens' house.

Friday's rainfall had frozen, leaving icy patches scattered over the lawns and sidewalk. Jenny slipped and almost toppled over backwards, but her speed propelled her forward and she regained her balance without slowing down.

She had gone nearly a block when she began to suspect she was being followed.

Walking even faster, she tried to listen over the roar of the wind. Was it just the clatter of tree branches overhead? Was she imagining it?

No. She heard ice cracking beneath someone's boots. Footsteps moving quickly over the frozen walk. Heavy breathing.

She turned her head quickly, saw moving shadows. Shadows sliding closer, closer. . . .

It was Willers, the creepy neighbor.

She began to run, slipping again, sucking in the frozen, wet air, running past dark, shifting woods now, no houses in sight, the entire world lit by a lone street lamp, casting more shadow than light, shadows that swirled and teased and tried to bewilder her as she fled.

Run, Jenny.

Run.

She wasn't fast enough.

She couldn't outrun him.

She *had* to outrun him.

"Wait up!" he called. But she just kept running.

A few seconds later, she was leaping onto the Hagens' front stoop, grateful for the yellow porch light, so bright, so warming, so safe. She looked back to see if Willers was behind her, but he had disappeared into the darkness.

Where had he gone? Why was he chasing her? Was he trying to terrorize her?

She realized she was shivering from the cold.

She raised her hand to knock — and the door swung open.

"Jenny, I *thought* I heard someone out here." Mr. Hagen said.

She dashed into the narrow front hallway, so grateful to be inside.

"Jenny — what's wrong?" he asked. "You look terrible."

"I'm sorry. Someone followed me from the bus stop."

"What? What are you talking about? Who?" He helped her pull off her down jacket.

"Mr. Willers. Your neighbor."

"Willers? I don't know anyone named Willers."

"He said he was your next-door neighbor."

Mr. Hagen held the jacket in front of him and stared at her, looking really troubled. "Neighbor? What neighbor? Jenny, we have no neighbors. That house next door has been vacant for six months!"

Chapter 15

"Can we play hide-and-seek?"

"Not now, Donny," Jenny said, giving his slender shoulders a gentle squeeze.

"This man said he was a neighbor? Said his name was Willers?" Mr. Hagen asked, his face aflame. He stood blocking the entrance to the living room, Jenny's jacket in his hand.

"I'm pretty sure I heard correctly," Jenny said.

"Maybe we shouldn't go out tonight," Mr. Hagen called upstairs to his wife.

She appeared at the top of the stairs, snapping on her earrings, a surprised look on her face. "What? Mike, you know the Spaldings are counting on us. Elaine will never speak to me again if we don't show up."

"But what about the attacks on those babysitters?" Mr. Hagen called, his face consumed with worry. "Donny could be in danger. Maybe this Willers — "

"Mike, we *have* to go," Mrs. Hagen called

down. "I'm sure if Jenny keeps the doors locked and all the lights on — "

"Okay, okay," he replied impatiently. "We won't stay out too late," he told Jenny. "If you hear anything at all, the tiniest squeak or creak, call the police. They can be here in less than five minutes."

"Okay," Jenny said. She had every intention of calling the police at the first suspicious sign. She reached into her jeans pocket and felt the piece of paper on which she had written Lieutenant Ferris's special number.

"What about hide-and-seek?" Donny whined, pulling Jenny toward the living room. "You promised!"

"I did not!" Jenny said, laughing. "I did not promise."

"No hide-and-seek tonight," Mr. Hagen said sternly. "Do something quieter. Why don't you watch that tape you made me rent for you?"

"Yeah! Yeah!" Donny cried enthusiastically, tugging Jenny harder. "Come on. Let's watch it."

"What is it?" Jenny asked, relieved that she wouldn't have to go running all over the house tonight playing hide-and-seek. "What did you rent?"

"*Poltergeist*," Donny said. "Have you seen it? It's really cool. She gets sucked into the TV set and she can't get out."

"Oh, great," Jenny said, rolling her eyes. Just what I needed tonight, she thought.

Donny settled down on the floor in front of the TV, and Jenny started the movie for him. The

Hagens left, after three more warnings by Mr. Hagen to call the police if she heard anything at all. He looked so overcome with worry, she was a little sorry she had told him about Willers. "Poor Mr. Hagen," Jenny told herself as the movie rolled across the TV screen. "*I'm* the one who should be scared. But he looked positively terrified!"

The movie seemed to be a series of loud, disconnected scenes. She couldn't concentrate on it at all. Donny kept insisting that he'd rather play hide-and-seek, and she kept refusing. Luckily he was falling asleep before the movie was half over. She got him up to bed before nine-thirty.

Now what? she asked herself, returning to the white leather chair in the den. I've got to do something to get my mind off Willers, and Chuck, and the calls, and the folded-up note, and . . . Chuck.

Was it just two nights ago that they had sat in this chair together . . . so together. . . .

She stared at the black telephone across the den on the desk. Was it going to ring tonight? Was her whispering caller going to renew his threats? Or did he plan to carry them out tonight?

She shuddered.

Then she heard the footsteps.

Someone was running fast in the back hallway. Donny?

No. The footsteps were too heavy, too fast.

Who was in the house?

She jumped up, reached in her pocket for the phone number. Would she have time to call?

No.

The footsteps were closer. Someone was running across the living room.

"MR. HAGEN!"

"Hi, Jenny." He limped toward her at full speed. His face red, filled with worry. "Everything okay?"

"Yes. You startled me. I didn't know who — "

"I hurried back. I just had a hunch. A hunch that something was wrong." He was breathing heavily, wheezing between his words. His shirt had come untucked from his trousers. He looked positively crazed with fear.

"Donny's fine. He went to bed early." Jenny squeaked out the words. She was still trying to calm down after the fright he had given her.

"He's okay? You're sure? He isn't sick or anything?"

"No. He's fine. Really."

"I just had a hunch. A bad feeling that something was terribly wrong."

She watched him clamber up the stairs until he disappeared on the landing. Then she slumped down on the bottom step, rested her head in her hands, trying to collect herself.

How many more times was Mr. Hagen going to frighten her like that? Would he ever trust her? Would he ever learn to relax? He had been so overcome with fear for Donny he hadn't even apologized for scaring her to death!

And what did he expect to find? What was he so afraid of?

Jenny pulled herself to her feet and leaned all

her weight against the bannister, waiting for Mr. Hagen to return from Donny's room. She yawned. Fear always seemed to make her feel tired.

"JENNY! JENNY!" Mr. Hagen's cries shattered her thoughts, startled her awake.

"Yes?"

He glared down at her from the top of the stairs. His normally small eyes were wide with terror. His face was twisted in shock.

"Donny's gone!" he screamed. "GONE!"

Chapter 16

"Where is he? Where IS he?" Mr. Hagen was screaming from the top of the stairs.

His words had no meaning for Jenny. Her mind had gone blank. She could hear his shouts, hear the sounds he was making, but the sounds had no meaning, as if the words were too horrifying to comprehend.

"This can't be happening to me," she told herself.

"Donny! Where are you?" Mr. Hagen shouted at the top of his lungs. "Where is he? WHERE IS HE??"

Jenny saw flashes of light, like flashcubes being popped right in front of her face. She blinked, trying to get away from the flashes, trying to see clearly.

"Donny! Donny! Where are you?" Mr. Hagen's voice was calling.

More flashing lights. Jenny struggled to clear her head, to force herself back to reality, to force the words to make sense again, to make this all go away.

Without realizing it, she had climbed the stairs. She was running into Donny's room.

If only the white flashes would stop.

If only she would wake up to find this was just a nightmare.

If only Mr. Hagen would stop shouting, maybe she could clear her head, figure it out, take responsibility.

"This can't be happening!" Mr. Hagen screamed at her. "Not again!"

What?

What did he say?

She stared at him, stared into his frightened eyes, stared into his red face, swollen in horror and panic, trying to see into his mind, trying to make sense of what he said.

"Where is he? Where is Donny?" He paced the small bedroom frantically, his limp more pronounced, his face so scarlet Jenny thought he might explode, repeating his question again and again, no longer able to shout, his voice a dry whisper.

"Donny — where are you?"

"Here I am," Donny said brightly, crawling out from under his bed.

He climbed to his feet and straightened his pajamas. "Gotcha!" he told Jenny, and started to laugh, pounding his little fists gleefully on top of his rumpled bedspread.

Jenny and Mr. Hagen were so startled, so overwhelmed by the sight of Donny, in perfect shape, unharmed, laughing, enjoying his ghastly joke, they stood staring at him openmouthed, almost afraid to move, afraid that if they made a sound or came closer, he'd disappear again.

And then Mr. Hagen let out a roar, a wild animal's roar, a roar of unleashed emotion. He lunged at Donny, picked him up by the waist, and pulled him close to his chest. "You're okay. You're okay. You're okay!" he cried again and again, hugging the surprised boy tightly to his chest.

"I was playing hide-and-seek," Donny offered, suddenly seeing the need to explain. "Jenny wouldn't play, so I played by myself."

"What on earth is going on up here? What's all the shouting about?" Mrs. Hagen burst into the room, her coat swirling behind her. She stared at her red-faced husband, squeezing Donny so tightly, still repeating, "You're okay, you're okay" into the boy's ear.

"Why are you doing that to Donny, Mike? You're squeezing him too hard!"

"We had a little scare," Jenny told her, finally finding her voice again, the flashing lights beginning to fade, her pulse beginning to return to normal.

"A scare? What kind of a scare?" she asked Jenny, walking across the room and pulling Donny away from Mr. Hagen.

"I was playing hide-and-seek," Donny reported with more than a little pride. "I fooled them. I fooled them both."

"Get back in bed, Donny," Mrs. Hagen said

sternly. "It's way past your bedtime." She turned angrily to her husband. "What are you doing here? Why did you leave the party? I thought you were downstairs shooting pool with Jack and Ernie. I didn't even know you had left."

"I just ran out for a minute. I had a hunch, a hunch something was wrong with Donny. I had to run home to find out. Then — "

"Look at you," Mrs. Hagen said, her anger softening as she realized how overwrought her husband was. "You're a wreck. You've got to stop this needless worrying, Mike. I mean it. You had no business running home like this. I'm very worried about you. Very worried."

Mr. Hagen looked past her to Jenny. "Please — let's not have a fight in front of — "

"I — I'll go downstairs," Jenny said uncertainly. "Now that we know Donny is okay, I — "

"No. Let's get your coat while we're upstairs," Mr. Hagen said. "I'll drive you home."

"No, you won't," Mrs. Hagen said, taking his arm. "I'm going to give you some pills to calm you down, Mike. I want you to stay home and try to get yourself together. I'll drive Jenny home."

"I'm together. Really," he insisted.

"Can I go, too?" Donny interrupted.

"No. Of course not," Mrs. Hagen said sternly. "You'd better be asleep in five minutes, Donny, or you're going to be in a lot of trouble." She shooed Jenny and Mr. Hagen from the room. "Go on. Out of here!"

Mr. Hagen retrieved Jenny's coat from his bedroom closet. Then, over his wife's objections, he grabbed the car keys and ushered Jenny out the door.

They rode in silence the entire way.

Normally Jenny would have found that very uncomfortable. Tonight she was grateful.

When he pulled up her driveway, he turned to her with a guilty half-smile. "I really should apologize," he said.

"No. It isn't necessary."

"I really should," he said. But then he stopped. His eyes were wet. Was he crying?

"I really should," he repeated. His voice sounded choked and small.

"Donny put us both through a real scare," Jenny said, and slid out of the car. She leaned back into the car, expecting Mr. Hagen to say something else. But he didn't, so she closed the door and hurried inside.

"You're home early," her mother said. She was in her bathrobe, bare feet up on the couch, reading one of her mystery novels.

"I know. The Hagens came home early," Jenny said. "Just as well." She yawned. "I'm really tired. Good night." No point in worrying her mother with all that was going on.

"Night," her mother replied, not looking up from the book.

Jenny climbed the narrow stairs to her room. Wish I could have a quiet Saturday night, she thought. Sitting home, reading a good book sounded pretty good.

She tossed her jacket onto her desk chair. Just a few more weeks. I'm going to work a few more weeks. Then I'll have more than enough money for Christmas. I'll tell the Hagens I have to quit, that it's interfering with my schoolwork. Maybe I'll baby-sit occasionally for Donny. But no more of this twice a week grind. No more frightening neighbors. No more frightening notes or creepy phone calls.

Just as she thought this, the phone on her desk rang.

She jumped and let out a startled cry.

Who would be calling this late on a Saturday night?

Laura? No. Laura would be out on a date with whoever had replaced Bob Tanner.

A second ring.

Was the creep following her? Did he have her home phone number?

A third ring.

"Jenny, aren't you going to answer that?" her mother called from downstairs.

She picked up the receiver. "Hello?"

"Hi."

"Chuck?"

"Yeah."

For a second, she was relieved. But her suspicions about Chuck quickly brought back her feeling of dread.

"Oh. Hi. I'm surprised. I mean — "

"I wanted to talk to you."

"Oh?"

"Jenny, you've been avoiding me."

"No, I — "

"Yes, you have. Come on. You walked away from me twice in the hall at school yesterday. And once I saw you deliberately go the other way when you saw me coming."

"I've just been busy, Chuck, and really — "

"Is it about Thursday night? Did I get you into trouble? Did Hagen see my car? I'm really sorry, Jenny."

"No. He saw the car, but he didn't know anything."

"Then what's the problem? I kind of got the idea that you liked me. And I like you. A lot. You know this is hard for me to do, call like this. So I wish you'd be honest with me. It's about that call I made, isn't it? When I scared you. I told you how sorry I was. I'll apologize a thousand times, if you want."

He sounded so sweet. And so sincere. He wasn't joking or trying to be funny. He really cared about her, Jenny thought. Once again, she began to feel guilty for suspecting him.

"I haven't been avoiding you. I've just had a lot on my mind. I got a scary note, Chuck. I found it in my bag. Someone had to be pretty close to me to put it there."

"And you thought it was me?" He sounded really hurt.

"I didn't know what to think. I still don't. I'm very mixed up."

"Why don't I come over and we'll talk?"

"No. It's too late. I'm exhausted. Donny

played a mean joke tonight and had us all in a panic."

"How about Thursday night?" he asked eagerly. Too eagerly? "We could study together. Please. I'll leave really early."

"Well. . . ." She didn't know what to say. She wanted to trust him. She wanted to be with him. But she just couldn't get rid of her suspicions. "Okay. I'll call Laura. Maybe she'd like to come, too. We can all study together." Safety in numbers, she thought.

"Well, okay. I guess." He sounded very disappointed. He laughed to cover it up. "You really think we need a chaperone?"

She forced a laugh, too. "Laura's my best friend. I like to spend time with her, too, you know."

"Okay. Good. Well, I'd better get off. Good night, Jenny."

"Night, Chuck."

"Thursday night will be special," he said. Then he hung up.

What did he mean by that?

Did his voice sound really strange when he said that?

Or was Jenny just imagining it?

Chapter 17

"Wipe that fiendish look off your face — this instant!" Jenny scolded.

Donny moved his hand down over his face as if using it to wipe off his expression. In its place, was a dopey, twisted grin.

"Wipe that expression off, too," Jenny said, unable to keep a straight face. "No hide-and-seek tonight. No more tricks on your baby-sitter. Understand?"

"Maybe," he said slyly, climbing into bed.

She ran her hand through his soft hair and pulled up his covers. "Now, go right to sleep."

"Is that boy coming over?" he asked, yawning.

"That's none of your business," Jenny said lightly. She felt a sudden pang of guilt. Had Donny told his parents about Chuck's visit?

I don't care, she thought as she descended the stairs. I don't want to be alone here. I'm glad Chuck and Laura are coming.

A few minutes later, she heard a knock on the door. She started to pull it open, thought better of it, and cautiously called out, "Who's there?"

"The Three Stooges," Chuck replied through the door.

Three?

She gratefully pulled open the door to find Chuck, Laura, and Eugene. "Hi, Eugene," she cried, unable to hide her surprise.

"How's it goin'?" he said, following the others into the entranceway. "Wow. Some house!"

"Looks more like a museum than a house," Laura said, pulling off her coat and tossing it onto the stairs.

Jenny gave Laura a look, as if to say, "What's Eugene doing here?" Laura just shrugged. "Why not?" she mouthed.

"Is this place a horror show, or what?" Chuck laughed, picking up a strange sculpture of an unrecognizable animal and examining it. "It's so creepy-looking. Can't you just picture vampires sleeping in coffins in the basement?"

Jenny gave Chuck a dirty look. "Stop that. Is that how you cheer me up?"

"Oops — sorry." He pretended to stab himself in the chest and then fell backwards onto the sofa in front of the fireplace.

"Hey, didn't anyone bring any books? I thought we were going to study," Jenny said.

"I knew we forgot something!" Eugene said, slapping his forehead.

"Eugene and I have to talk," Laura said, pulling Eugene's arm. "Is that the den over there?"

"Talk?" Jenny said. So Laura planned to use this opportunity to make out with Eugene.

"Yeah. That's the den. Great seeing you, Laura," she said sarcastically.

Laura just giggled.

"You guys all have to leave in a couple of hours," Jenny told them. "If Mr. Hagen comes home early and finds you here, I'll be out of here — for good!"

Chuck took Jenny's hand. "Don't worry. I'll make sure we all get out in time." He pulled her over to the couch. Laura and Eugene disappeared into the den and closed the door.

"Wonder what they're talking about," Chuck joked, looking toward the den. Then he suddenly turned serious. "Why'd you want me to bring them?"

"I didn't know about Eugene. I just thought Laura was coming. I already told you, I thought it would be more fun to study — "

"I had a feeling maybe you didn't want to be alone with me."

Jenny realized that she had underestimated how smart Chuck was, and how sensitive. "No, I — "

"I really want you to trust me, Jenny." He was still holding her hand. He squeezed it gently.

I'd really like to trust you, Chuck, she thought. I'd really like to trust you more than anything — but I don't know if I can.

He kissed her, softly at first, then harder, pulling her closer to him.

He couldn't be the one who's threatening me, she thought, kissing him back, trying to lose herself in the kiss, trying not to think about anything but him. It has to be Willers. It has to be.

But what about the note in her bag? Willers couldn't have put it there.

Chuck wrapped her in his arms and kissed her again. But she couldn't stop thinking. She couldn't stop doubting him, wondering about him, wondering. . . .

"Hey, Chuck — you left your headlights on." Eugene's head popped out from the den door.

"What?"

"I can see from the den window. Your headlights. They're on."

"Thanks, Eugene." Chuck disentangled himself from Jenny and climbed to his feet. "Sorry. I'll be right back." He headed quickly to the front door. "Save my place!"

Why did I let them come? Why did I do this? Jenny thought, watching Chuck disappear out the front door. Do I *want* to lose my job? Do I *want* Mr. Hagen to fire me so I don't have to be scared anymore?

Then she heard a sound. A footstep? A door opening?

It came from the direction of the kitchen.

Had Mr. Hagen come home early again?

Or was it a different visitor?

Company's coming.

Was this the night?

Was the kitchen door locked? She hadn't checked. Was someone in the house? She listened. Another sound.

Without realizing it, she was on her feet. Then she was in the back hallway. She walked quickly past the laundry room, past the small pantry, then slowed as she approached the kitchen.

"Who is it?" she called.

Silence.

"Hello? Anyone there?"

Chuck — please — hurry back. What's taking you so long?

The kitchen was silent, except for the loud hum of the refrigerator and the steady *plink plink plink* of water dripping from the kitchen faucet.

Was someone hiding in that silence?

Was someone waiting in that silence?

She crept a little closer, keeping near to the wall in the narrow hallway.

She tried to convince herself that she was being silly, that she was acting like a frightened child.

But she realized that her fear was justified. The phone calls had been real. The threats had been real. Willers prowling about in the garage, following her from the bus had been real.

She had real reasons to be afraid, real reasons to be cautious, to hesitate there in the hallway. This wasn't her imagination acting up again.

A sudden flash of memory. She was a little girl, seven or eight. Her parents had just divorced. She was adjusting to the sudden emptiness, the strange feeling of life with one parent where a short while before, there had been two.

She was standing in the hallway outside the kitchen door, in the old house before she and her mother moved to the house they had now. The memory was so clear, so bright, still so fresh in her mind.

A drop of blood. She spotted a bright red drop of blood on the hallway floor just outside the kitchen. Her mother was in the kitchen. She listened. She heard a chopping sound, a horrible sound, a sound she didn't recognize.

She stared at the drop of blood, glowing so red on the dark linoleum. She listened to the chop, chop, chop coming from the kitchen, so insistent, so steady, so mechanical.

She could still remember the terror from those long years ago.

What was making that chopping sound?

Why was there blood on the hallway floor?

Where was her mother? What had happened to her mother?

Propelled by her fear, she had burst into the kitchen, prepared to scream, to cry out her terror.

Her mother was standing at the sink, chopping carrots with a large knife.

Chop chop chop.

She had a Band-Aid on her thumb.

"Ma — the blood!" Jenny had screamed. She had to scream. She had to let it out. Even though her eyes told her everything was okay, she still had all that terror to let out.

"I cut my thumb," her mother said, holding the thumb up for a second for Jenny to see, then returning to the knife and the pile of carrots. Chop, chop, chop.

Clink clink clink.

Water dripped into the Hagens' kitchen sink.

The memory faded slowly. Then, propelled by the same fear she had felt as a little girl, Jenny burst into the kitchen.

No one there.

Except for the cat. The cat had knocked over the sugar cannister on the counter and was busily lapping herself into a sugar coma!

That explained the noise. Jenny ran to the kitchen door. It was locked. She leaned against the counter to catch her breath. "Got me again, kitty," she told the cat. "You bad cat." The cat ignored her and kept lapping up the sugar.

Feeling relieved, Jenny walked back to the living room. Chuck was waiting for her on the sofa. "Where'd you go?"

"Oh, I had to check on something in the kitchen," she told him.

"Come here and warm me up. It's freezing out there." He patted the sofa cushion beside him.

She was glad he was there. Her doubts about him were melting away. He genuinely liked her, he really cared about her, she thought. She had been foolish for suspecting him.

She dropped down beside him. He pulled her close.

She felt so safe now, so warm, so good.

The time seemed to fly by. She lost all track of time. She lost all track of everything.

She was still locked in Chuck's arms, still kissing him, when she looked up and saw Mr. Hagen glaring down at them from behind the sofa.

Chapter 18

He was standing so still, glaring at them with such a frozen face, his eyes unmoving, unblinking, clenched fists held straight down at his sides, that at first, Jenny thought he wasn't real. At first, she thought it was a statue, some sort of mannequin made to look like Mr. Hagen.

But as he opened his mouth to roar out his alarmed protest, she realized that he was real. And that she was caught.

Mr. Hagen lunged forward as if to grab Jenny and Chuck, his face reddening with rage. But before he could make a sound, before he got more than a step or two, Mrs. Hagen walked into the room. Her mouth dropped open in surprise. "Jenny? Who — ?"

Mr. Hagen stopped short. He was breathing heavily.

"Hey — what's going on?" Eugene called. He and Laura walked out quickly from the den.

"Uh-oh," Laura said, realizing at once what

was happening. Her lipstick was smeared all over her chin.

Mrs. Hagen ran immediately to her husband and put a hand on his shoulder, more to comfort him than restrain him. "It's okay, dear. It's okay," she said softly. "Jenny's friends will go home now. Then we'll have a quiet talk with Jenny about this."

She didn't remove her hand until Mr. Hagen seemed to calm down a little. He took a step back. He was still glaring at Jenny. He hadn't said a word.

"I'm sorry. I'm really sorry," Jenny said, jumping to her feet. "My friends stopped by to keep me company and — "

"We were just going," Chuck said, motioning to Laura and Eugene. He looked really frightened of Mr. Hagen. They all did. Mr. Hagen looked truly scary, as if it was taking all of his power to keep himself under control.

"I could drive Jenny home," Chuck said to Mrs. Hagen.

"Yes — " Jenny agreed quickly. "Save you a trip," she told Mr. Hagen. He didn't seem to hear her.

"No. You three go on ahead," Mrs. Hagen said, still holding on to her husband's broad shoulder. "I think we'll want to have a little talk with Jenny first."

"I'm really sorry," Chuck whispered to Jenny. "I'll wait for you at your house. Okay?"

She nodded, keeping her eyes on Mr. Hagen,

who seemed to be getting over his shock and rage.

"Let's go up and check on Donny," Mrs. Hagen suggested brightly to her husband. "Nothing terrible has happened here."

He nodded. "I guess you're right." The first words he had said. He let his wife lead him to the stairs.

She knows how to calm him down, Jenny thought. She's probably had to do this before. It's going to be okay. I'm going to be fired, but that's okay, too. I didn't really want this babysitting job anymore.

Her three friends, giving her looks of regret, hurried out the door. Jenny stood alone in the living room for a while, telling herself that nothing terrible had happened, that it was mostly embarrassing, that's all. No crime had been committed.

She decided to get her coat from the upstairs closet so that she'd be ready for Mr. Hagen to take her home. She climbed the stairs and entered the Hagens' large bedroom. It was lit by a single lamp on a table beside their four-poster bed. The closet was against the far wall on the other side of the bed.

I'm in for a long lecture from Mr. Hagen, Jenny told herself. But then at least I'll be out of here for good. She realized she'd miss Donny. But she wouldn't miss anything else. Wow, did Mr. Hagen look mad! He was going to have to do something to control his temper!

She slid open the closet door and searched for her down jacket among all the clothes. The closet smelled of Mrs. Hagen's perfume, strong and flowery. The hangers were all full. Jenny spotted her jacket on a high shelf above the hangers.

Reaching up on tiptoe to pull it down, she knocked a cardboard shoe box off the shelf. The box hit the closet floor and bounced open, the lid flying onto Jenny's sneakers.

Bending down to put the box back together, she was surprised to see that it was stuffed with newspaper clippings. She started to replace the lid, but then some headlines caught her eye:

BABY-SITTER ATTACK REPORTED ON EAST SIDE.

BABY-SITTER BLAMED IN BABY'S DROWNING.

Jenny felt a cold chill run down her back. Her hands shaking, her heart beginning to pound, she riffled through the clippings.

POLICE ISSUE WARNINGS AFTER THIRD BABY-SITTER ATTACK.

BABY-SITTER ADMITS TO KIDNAPPING CHILD.

BABY-SITTER RESPONSIBLE FOR CHILD'S DEATH.

All of the neatly clipped articles were about baby-sitters, Jenny realized. Dozens and dozens of clippings. All about baby-sitters and the recent attacks on baby-sitters.

It was too dark by the closet to read the clippings, and her hands were shaking too badly, but Jenny noticed that certain words had been circled in red. She picked up the box and pulled out a few clippings to see more clearly.

The names.

The baby-sitters' names had been circled in red marker.

"No!" Jenny gasped.

She dropped the box to the floor, the clippings scattering across the rug.

Mr. Hagen — why has he collected these? He must be CRAZY! she told herself. I've got to get out of here!

She picked up her jacket and started to turn away from the closet. "Oh!" She cried aloud when she realized Mr. Hagen was standing right behind her.

Did he see the box of clippings? Did he see that she had discovered the box?

"Ready to go home?" he asked, pulling on his black leather gloves.

She couldn't tell. He looked very calm now. She stood up quickly and closed the closet door. Maybe he hadn't noticed that the box was down on the floor. It was pretty dark down there, after all.

"Ready?" he repeated.

"No. Uh . . . It's so far for you to drive, Mr. Hagen, and you look so tired," she said, thinking frantically. "Why don't I take the bus tonight?"

He shook his head no.

She didn't want to ride with him. Not now. Not ever again. Not after seeing his collection of baby-sitter stories.

The question repeated in her mind as she

stared back at him in the dim light: Did he know she had seen the clippings? Had he seen the open box on the closet floor?

She couldn't tell.

"I won't hear of it, Jenny," he said, taking her coat out of her hands and helping her into it. His steel-gray eyes burned into hers, revealing nothing. "I won't hear of it. You're coming with me."

"Really, Mr. Hagen. I don't mind — "

He frowned, turned, and headed to the stairs. "Let's go," he said quietly.

Chapter 19

"Good night, Jenny. See you Thursday," Mrs. Hagen called from Donny's room. "Mike — don't lecture her all the way home!"

Jenny wanted to stop and call to her for help. "Please don't make me ride with him!" she wanted to say. "I think he's crazy. I saw the clippings! Please — don't make me ride home with him!"

But she stopped herself. "Good night, Mrs. Hagen," she called softly.

She scolded herself for letting her imagination run away with her. What did the clippings mean anyway? Sure, Mr. Hagen was nervous and excitable. But he had always seemed very sweet underneath his nervousness. And he certainly did love his child.

There were a lot of reasons why he might have kept those clippings, she told herself. It didn't necessarily mean he was a sicko.

She was feeling a little better by the time she climbed into the front seat of the car. Mr. Hagen smiled at her as he closed her door.

I'm just completely exhausted, she thought. I've got to calm down now. It's all over. All of the creepiness is over.

"Quite a night, huh?" Mr. Hagen said, shaking his head as he climbed behind the wheel. "Quite a night."

He backed down the drive and headed up Edgetown Lane. Jenny rested her head against the seatback and wearily closed her eyes. A loud click made her open them. Mr. Hagen had touched a control button and locked all the doors.

Funny, Jenny thought. He's never done that before.

She settled back again, determined not to imagine any new terrors. There was nothing wrong with locking the car doors, after all. In fact, it was considerate of him.

She closed her eyes again. He was silent, not questioning her about her friends, not lecturing her. What was he waiting for?

When she opened her eyes a few moments later, she didn't recognize where they were. "Is this Millertown Road?" she asked, peering out into the darkness.

"No," he answered softly.

She waited for him to tell her what road it was, but he drove on in silence. Outside the frosty window, there were no houses or stores. She made out an occasional barn and silo, and farm houses as dark and silent as the fields that surrounded them.

"Where are we? We seem to be heading out

of town!" she said, sitting straight up, no longer tired.

He didn't say anything. He kept his eyes straight ahead on the flat, uncurving road.

"Mr. Hagen — why are we going this way?" Her voice revealed her growing fear.

"I'm going very fast," he said finally. "I wouldn't try anything if I were you."

"What?" She wasn't sure she heard him correctly. He couldn't have said that — could he??

She leaned forward to look at the speedometer. He was doing 85.

"Mr. Hagen — please — "

"I'm sorry you saw my clippings," he said, his eyes straight ahead, his voice even, emotionless, almost machinelike. "But it really doesn't matter."

"I — I didn't see anything," she lied. It didn't sound at all convincing. "Please — where are you taking me?"

I've got to get out of here, she thought. But how?

"Please, Mr. Hagen," she said, forcing her voice down, forcing herself not to cry, not to scream. "Please take me home now."

He drove on in silence, his large hands at the top of the wheel.

He's crazy, she thought.

He's crazy and he's out of control.

Where is he taking me? What does he plan to do?

I'm going to get away. I'm going to be okay.

She repeated those words again and again,

staring out the window at the shifting night shadows. They were way out of town now, and heading farther out, roaring toward the empty flatlands where the fields ended, where no trees grew, where no one lived, where no one went unless they were on their way somewhere else.

"Company's coming," Mr. Hagen whispered, staring straight ahead, talking to himself, smiling a strangely satisfied smile. "Don't worry. Company's coming."

"It was YOU!" Jenny screamed.

"SHUT UP!" he yelled with sudden fury. He raised his left hand from the wheel and slapped her face, a stinging blow.

The loud sound of it surprised her more than the slap itself. Pain shot up her head and down her neck. She was too hurt, too shocked, too frightened to scream.

"I tried to warn you," he whispered, the hoarse whisper she had heard on the phone. "But now you'll get what's coming to you."

"But I didn't *do* anything!" Jenny cried. Her head throbbed like a giant toothache. She turned away and stared out the side window, as if not seeing him might make him disappear, might make this entire nightmare disappear.

"I had a baby," Mr. Hagen said, still in that hoarse whisper, talking to himself now. "I had a baby. A little girl. She was only two. But the baby-sitter wasn't quick enough. The baby-sitter wasn't smart enough. The baby-sitter wasn't GOOD ENOUGH!"

Jenny didn't turn around, didn't reply, didn't

react in any way. She remembered the girl in the photograph, the girl who looked just like Donny.

"My little girl died," Mr. Hagen said. "Now it's your turn."

Her head hit the dashboard as he slammed on the brakes.

The car squealed for several hundred yards, sliding over smooth ground, then finally stopped.

When Jenny looked up, he was already pulling open the door, already grabbing her, jerking her out of the car.

"Let go," she said, just mouthing the words, an almost silent plea. He was too strong. There was no way she could fight him.

He slapped her again, this time catching her jaw, snapping her head back.

Then he grabbed her by the shoulders and shoved her in front of the car, into the bright cylinders of light from the headlights. "Move!" he ordered, pushing her shoulders.

She stumbled and started to fall, but he pulled her up. Her eyes adjusted slowly to the bright light. She was walking on solid rock now.

Two more steps, three more. She realized where he had taken her. It was the quarry. The old rock quarry, about ten miles out of town. The quarry had been deserted for years.

There wasn't a sound. There didn't seem to be air to breathe.

The world was silent, except for their shoes moving over the hard rock surface as he pushed her toward the quarry.

The headlights shot out in two straight beams. Then the light suddenly vanished.

"No!" Jenny cried aloud.

She realized why the light suddenly stopped. It stopped at the edge of the quarry, the edge of the deep, empty pit.

"Move!" Mr. Hagen repeated, giving her a hard shove that took her right to the edge, to where the light stopped.

She looked down. It was a sheer drop, hundreds of feet down to jagged rocks below.

"This is what you deserve, Jenny," he screamed.

"I didn't kill any baby!" Jenny cried.

The look on Mr. Hagen's face was almost as terrifying as the thought of the quarry. It went beyond cold. It went beyond hatred. It went beyond inhuman.

He looked like one of those hideous undead monsters that stagger through the horror movies, eyes ablaze with fury, everything else about them zombielike and dead.

"I had a baby. This is what you deserve."

He didn't move his lips when he talked. He didn't blink.

"I didn't do anything!" Jenny's voice came out in a desperate cry.

"It's time to die."

"No! Mr. Hagen — please!"

She knew he couldn't hear her. His face was no longer alive. Even his eyes had narrowed and nearly closed. It was as if he were retreating, pulling into himself, so that he wouldn't see what he was about to do to her.

"No — please!"

"Good-bye, Jenny."

"No! Think about Donny! Think about — "

"Do you want to jump now. Or should I push you?"

What? Was he giving her a choice? Was this her opportunity to stall?

"Choose fast, Jenny. Jump or be pushed?"

"Mr. Hagen, listen to me — "

"Okay. That's your choice. You choose to be pushed."

He raised his arms and moved forward, his eyes still dead, his face expressionless.

Jenny backed up. She was on the very edge now. Her left heel rested on air. She nearly toppled backwards, down, down into the deep pit, onto the rocks so far below.

Struggling to regain her balance, to get back on firm footing, she tried to inch forward, but he wouldn't let her. He came toward her slowly, preparing to push her back. A smile spread across his face. He was enjoying her fear.

"Stop right there, Hagen!"

A man's voice from behind the car.

Mr. Hagen spun around, startled. Jenny stared into the headlights. She couldn't see. The lights were blinding. She looked away, bright yellow circles following wherever she looked.

"Who's there?" Mr. Hagen called, peering into the darkness.

A man stepped in front of the headlights.

Jenny blinked, trying to clear her eyes, trying to see who it was.

She saw the plaid wool lumberjack shirt.

Willers!

What did he want? Did he want to kill her, too?

Willers raised the pistol in his hand. He moved a few steps closer.

"What are you doing here?" Mr. Hagen shouted angrily.

"Saving you from ruining your life," Willers shouted back, brandishing the pistol.

Mr. Hagen threw back his head and laughed, a crazy, exaggerated laugh.

Jenny tried to move away from the edge of the quarry. But he was still blocking her way. She felt dizzy. Her head was spinning. She didn't know how much longer she could stand with nothing but air behind her.

"My life is already ruined," Mr. Hagen said bitterly.

"I can't do anything about that, Hagen," Willers said, taking another cautious step forward. "But I can stop you from committing a murder."

"No, you can't," Mr. Hagen told him.

He lunged toward Jenny and gave her a hard push.

Chapter 20

Jenny dodged to the left and collapsed to the ground.

Mr. Hagen sailed over her and plunged over the quarry side.

His scream cut through the air like a fading police siren. Then she heard a sickening crash, like a full carton of eggs hitting the sidewalk.

Then silence.

It happened so quickly it didn't seem real to her.

She looked up, expecting him to still be there, standing over her, his small, gray eyes burning into hers with such insane hatred.

But she saw only headlights.

Then two legs in front of the headlights, legs walking quickly toward her.

Then Willers's dark stubbled face was down low near hers.

"Are you okay? Can you get up?"

The words didn't make any sense at first. The siren was still blaring in her ears. The short siren of Mr. Hagen's scream followed by the cracking sound, the sound of his body hitting the rocks below. What language was this man speaking? What was she doing out here on the edge of the old quarry in the middle of the night?

And then suddenly, as Willers stared down at her, as he offered his hand to help her up, the words made sense. "Yes. I'm okay," she said, a little surprised that she could form words herself.

What did she expect?

Did she expect to be dead right now?

Yes. That was it. She expected to be dead.

But someone else was.

Mr. Hagen was dead. Down at the bottom of the quarry.

She climbed to her feet. "I'm not hurt," she told Willers.

Even in this strange, harsh light from the car headlights, he looked very shaken. "I — I tried to stop him," he said, his voice trembling. He took Jenny's arm. She thought he was trying to help support her, but she quickly realized he wanted to lean on her.

"I tried to stop him. I tried to save him."

"There was nothing you could do," Jenny said softly, ignoring the smell of stale cigar smoke that clung to Willers's shirt.

Jenny shivered. The air was cold and wet, and she was perspiring from the horror of her close call. Holding onto her arm, Willers began to lead her to his car, which was parked in the darkness behind Mr. Hagen's car. Along the way, he stopped and turned off Mr. Hagen's headlights, plunging them into total darkness. Jenny looked up to the sky. There was no moon.

She made her way slowly, her eyes adjusting to the dark. She listened to the crunch of her sneakers over the hard ground. She had never realized how good that sound could be, so solid, so real, so alive.

"I should introduce myself," Willers said, stopping in front of his battered old Honda Civic. "You probably guessed that my name isn't Willers and I'm not the next-door neighbor."

"Yeah," Jenny said, shivering. She reached for the door handle. She wanted to get inside the car where it was warmer.

"My name is Ferris. Lieutenant Ferris."

"You're the policeman?"

"That's right. I'm with the town police. I was assigned to this case."

"C-can we g-get into the car?" Jenny stammered. "I'm not feeling too well."

"Oh. Sorry." He pulled open the door for her and she collapsed into the tiny bucket seat. The car started reluctantly. Ferris let it warm up for a while, then pulled out onto the road.

"Where are you taking me? The police station?" Jenny asked, shaking all over, unable to get warm.

"No. I'm going to take you home," Ferris said. "I think you've had enough excitement for one night."

"How did you know to — how did you know he — ?"

"I've had Hagen's house staked out for a

month. When the complaints started — "

"Complaints?"

"Well, I should say attacks. The attacks on baby-sitters. I was assigned the case."

"Baby-sitters. Mr. Hagen had clippings about them all," Jenny said. Her head was spinning with images, frightening images, pictures of everything that had happened that night.

Ferris looked at her, surprised. "Clippings?"

"Up in his closet."

Ferris shook his head. "He was one of the main suspects right from the beginning. Two years ago, his daughter died mysteriously. No one ever knew the cause. He went berserk. He blamed the baby-sitter who was taking care of her. It wasn't the girl's fault, but Hagen just went nuts. He attacked the girl, beat her up pretty badly. It went to court. He got off lightly because he had been in a disturbed emotional state.

"Then he moved to the other side of town and took a new job. When someone started beating up baby-sitters a few months ago, he was our prime suspect."

"When you chased after me at the bus stop — " Jenny started, trying to get it clear, trying to clear her mind from the whirling, confused images.

"I tried to warn you," Ferris said, eyes on the road. "But then when you ran, I changed my mind. I wanted to see what Hagen had planned."

"You used me?"

He was silent for a while. "Yeah. I guess you could say that."

"But how could you do that to me?" she cried, suddenly angry.

"Give me a break," he muttered, a low growl. Her question seemed to hurt him. "This didn't turn out the way I'd hoped. Believe me."

Jenny realized she shouldn't be angry at Ferris. He was just doing his job. Besides, he had saved her life.

Her life.

She was alive.

And Mr. Hagen was lying crushed and crumpled at the bottom of the quarry.

"His poor family," she said, her voice a choked whisper.

"Poor everybody," Ferris said bitterly.

He stopped the car, shifted into park, and pulled on the handbrake.

"Why are you stopping?" Jenny asked suspiciously.

He gave her a weary smile. "You're home."

She looked out. They were in her driveway.

Ferris walked her to the door, then followed her inside as Jenny's mother greeted her with a long, emotional hug. "You're okay? Where were you? Chuck said he left the Hagens' over an hour ago."

"I've been worried out of my head," Chuck said, appearing suddenly from the kitchen and putting his arm around Jenny.

"This is Lieutenant Ferris," Jenny said. "It's all a long story, a long, frightening story. But it's over. Could I have some tea? I can't stop shaking."

As Mrs. Jeffers hurried to make tea, Ferris told them quickly what had happened. After asking Jenny at least a dozen times if she really was okay, her relieved mother hugged her again and, looking dazed, dropped down onto a kitchen chair. "Such a sad story," she muttered, shaking her head.

"It's a very sad story," Ferris said softly. "And it's going to get sadder. Now I have to go tell Mrs. Hagen what happened." He shook his head, then turned to Jenny. "I'll pick you up tomorrow and bring you to the police station to make a statement, okay? In the meantime, get some rest."

After Ferris left, the three of them settled down in the warm kitchen, sitting at the bright yellow Formica counter, drinking soothing hot tea with honey. Conversation was awkward. They were each thinking of what a close call Jenny had had that night.

"It's good to be here," Jenny said finally, sipping the fragrant tea.

"Yeah," Chuck agreed. "This is a nice kitchen."

"I meant it's good to be alive," Jenny said, smiling at him.

"Oh. Right," Chuck said, embarrassed.

"I have the feeling things are going to be good from now on," Jenny said, still looking at Chuck. "I don't think I'll live in such a fantasy world anymore, letting my imagination run away with me all the time. The real world is interesting enough!"

"A reality trip," Chuck said, smiling back at her.

"I guess there's something to be learned, even in such a terrible tragedy," Mrs. Jeffers said. "But the important thing is that you're safe. You're here. You're all right. Oh. I almost forgot." She put her mug down hard on the counter. "Mrs. Milton — you know, down the block with the twins? She called tonight, Jenny. She wants to know if you can baby-sit next week."

Jenny stared at her mother in disbelief. "Mother, I — well, I — No. I don't think so. I think maybe I'll give it a miss."

"That's right," Chuck said, taking Jenny's hand. "She has a steady baby-sitting job on Friday nights, Mrs. Jeffers."

"What?" Jenny's mother looked very confused.

"From now on, she's baby-sitting me!" Chuck said.

Chuck was the only one who laughed.

"Thank you, Chuck," Jenny said. "That was the perfect dreadful joke to end a perfectly dreadful evening." She pulled him up from the counter and, holding his hands tightly and leaning wearily against him, she walked him to the door to say good night.

THE BABY-SITTER II

Chapter 1

"I — I killed him," Jenny said, shifting uncomfortably on the couch.

"I can still hear his scream. So loud at first and then fading to . . . nothing. No matter how I try to look at what happened, I just can't get it out of my mind that I killed him."

She twisted a strand of her dark hair as she talked. Her eyes, so round and black, stared at the cracks in the wall beside her. She licked her lips, a nervous habit she just couldn't stop.

"I'm sorry," she said, taking another strand of hair and twisting it between her slender fingers. "You asked me to begin at the beginning, and I skipped to the end. It's just . . . so hard."

She took a deep breath and began again. "It was last fall, just a few weeks after school began. I go to Harrison. I'm a junior this year. I guess you already knew that." She let go of her hair and let her arm drop down, clasping her hands tightly in her lap.

"Well, I took this baby-sitting job. Twice a week with this adorable little boy named Donny. Donny Hagen. Donny had the most amazing white-blond hair you ever saw. He was so cute, and the two of us just hit it off right away.

"The Hagens lived in this creepy old house on the other side of town. It used to take me over half an hour to get there on the bus." Jenny paused. "I guess that isn't a very important detail. But sometimes I think about all those long bus rides, that nearly empty bus bumping across town in the dark, taking me to — to that frightening old house.

"Well, anyway, after I'd been baby-sitting for Donny for a short while, I started getting these really scary phone calls. I'd pick up the phone and hear this ugly whisper. And always the same words. *'Hi, Babes. Are you all alone? Don't worry, company's coming.'* "

Jenny shuddered. As she said the words, she heard the whispering voice once again in her ear. And felt the fear all over again.

"There had been all these attacks on baby-sitters all over town," she continued. "I kept hearing about them on the news. And here I was, all alone in this frightening old house on the other side of town. I had this new boyfriend. I guess you'd call him a boyfriend. We really hadn't gone out all that much. He was new at Harrison. His name was — is — Chuck. Chuck Quinn."

Jenny's features tightened into a frown. "I'm not

seeing Chuck anymore. He's — he's a real joker. You know, a class clown type. He's very funny, actually. But after . . . after what happened . . . I don't know. I guess I didn't feel much like laughing and joking all the time. So I told Chuck I didn't want to see him anymore. He was really upset. He got very angry. He has an angry, moody side, too, and — Oh. Sorry. I'm getting away from my story."

Her hands felt cold and clammy. She wiped them on her jeans. "I started to let Chuck come to the Hagens' house when I was baby-sitting there. I — I just felt safer when he was there. I mean, because of the scary phone calls. But then I started getting the calls at my own home. Always the same. *'Hi, Babes. Company's coming.'* It was so frightening.

"I started thinking maybe it was Chuck who was making the calls. I guess I was just freaked or something. But I didn't know Chuck that well. And he was a joker, always clowning around and playing practical jokes.

"I was so scared. I wanted to quit my baby-sitting job. But Mom persuaded me to stay. We really needed the money, see. Mom is a legal secretary. She doesn't make a very big salary. The Hagens were paying me five dollars an hour, and with Christmas coming up . . .

"So I stayed. And then one night I found the newspaper clippings up in Mr. Hagen's closet. They were all clippings about children who had died because of baby-sitters' carelessness. And clippings about the attacks on baby-sitters that had been happening all over town. And the baby-sitters' names were all circled in red!

"It was Mr. Hagen! He was the one, the one attacking the baby-sitters. Donny had had a sister. And the sister had died. And Mr. Hagen blamed the baby-sitter. I guess it destroyed his mind or something, made him crack up. And now he was out to get back at all baby-sitters.

"He — he was the one making the calls. He was the one — This is all so terrible. As I'm telling it to you, I'm seeing it all again." Jenny was clasping her hands together so tightly, it hurt. Suddenly realizing it, she let go and forced her hands down to her sides.

She waited awhile, waited for her heart to stop pounding. She took the glass from the table beside her and sipped some water. Then she took a deep breath and in a low, steady voice, resumed her story.

"Mr. Hagen came up behind me in his bedroom. He saw me reading his newspaper clippings. He knew that I knew. He — he said he was driving me home. But he didn't.

"It was very late. There were no other cars on the road. He drove to the old rock quarry. You know the one? About ten miles north of town?

"He pulled me out of the car and he hit me. *'This is what you deserve,'* he kept saying. *'This is what you deserve.'*

"He backed me up right to the edge of the quarry.

174

It was so dark. I was standing right on the edge, nothing but air behind me. It was such a nightmare. The headlights from his car were shining in my eyes. I was blind. But I knew if I took one more step back, I'd go over to the bottom of the quarry.

"And then he pushed me. I mean, he rushed at me. He meant to push me. But somehow I — I dodged away from him. And he went flying over the edge.

"I didn't see him. I only heard him. That scream. That horrified scream. I heard the scream all the way down. Then I heard the cracking sound his body made when it hit the rocks below."

Jenny paused, trying to catch her breath. "I still hear that sound. *Crack*. Like an egg breaking."

She was playing with her hair again, nervously braiding a strand of dark brown hair, still staring at the wall, but not seeing it, not seeing anything.

"Of course, I realize it wasn't my fault," she continued. "I mean, he was crazy. He was trying to kill me. I know that. I mean, I can tell myself that over and over. But I still have this . . . knowledge, this awful knowledge that I killed him, that I'm responsible for Mr. Hagen's death. That Donny doesn't have a father because . . . because . . ."

Her mouth felt as dry as cotton. She stopped to take another sip of water. The water was warm and tasted of minerals. She made a face, but took a long drink.

"When Mr. Hagen fell over the quarry edge, it was all over. The nightmare, I mean. He was dead.

No more attacks on baby-sitters. No more phone calls or threats. Donny and his mother moved away. I don't know where.

"I was safe, but it wouldn't go away. I mean, I tried to force it all out of my mind. But then the dreams started. The nightmares. Just about every night.

"They're so real, so vivid. I see them in color. I'm sure of it. And I remember them when I wake up in the morning. Every detail.

"In most of them, I see Mr. Hagen. I see him crawling up to the top of the rock quarry. His face is all twisted, all distorted, and he's covered with blood. In the dreams, I'm standing there watching him as he pulls himself up to the top. Then he starts to stagger toward me, like Frankenstein, only covered with blood, his clothes all torn. Sometimes his skin is all torn, too, and chunks of it are falling off his body. Sometimes he has a skull instead of a head, a bleeding skull.

"And I — I just stand there. I want to run away from him — but I can't. I'm paralyzed or something. And he comes closer and closer until . . . I wake up screaming."

Breathing hard, Jenny stared up at the tiled ceiling.

"I think we'd better stop there," Dr. Schindler said softly. "This session is almost up. We'd better save your dreams for next time."

He reached across his cluttered desk and clicked

off the tape recorder. Narrowing his green eyes in concentration, he popped the cassette from the machine and began to label it with his pen.

Dr. Schindler doesn't really look like a shrink, Jenny thought, turning her gaze on him. For one thing, he is too handsome. And too tanned. With his wavy, coppery hair, those blond eyebrows and startling green eyes, she imagined him as an actor or maybe a model.

And he looks too young to be a shrink, Jenny thought. Shouldn't he have a beard or something? Or wear thick, rimless eyeglasses? Or smoke a pipe?

He didn't look the part, but he had the diplomas to prove that he was the real thing. They were carefully lined up in rows on the wall behind his enormous mahogany desk.

"Next time — " he started to say, flipping through his appointment book.

"But what about my problem right now?" Jenny interrupted. She turned and pulled herself to a sitting position on the couch, dropping her feet to the floor. "You know. About the baby-sitting job."

The question seemed to catch him off guard.

He's forgotten everything I said at the beginning of the hour, Jenny thought, groaning to herself. No *wonder* he has to tape everything!

"Well, Jenny . . ." His eyebrows lowered, and his face assumed a more serious expression. "How do *you* feel about it? What do *you* think you should do about the job?"

Jenny sighed.

Was he just going to ask questions? Wasn't he going to *help* her?

"I don't know," she said, biting her lower lip. "Normally, I guess I'd have a real summer job now. But I was so upset, and so tired from never being able to sleep much, I just didn't think I could manage a full-time job."

She looked to him to reply, but he just stared back at her with those sparkling green eyes, his face completely expressionless.

"I need money for school in the fall," Jenny continued uncertainly. "And the Wexners seem like really nice people. They only live a few blocks from my home. And their son, Eli, is ten, so he probably won't be that much trouble."

"How often do they want you to baby-sit for Eli?" Dr. Schindler asked, fingering his silver-and-jade desk clock.

"Two days a week and two nights," Jenny told him. "It isn't too bad. And I really need the money. But — "

He stared at her, waiting for her to finish her sentence.

" — I'm really frightened."

"Frightened of — ?" he asked, leaning forward.

Jenny thought for a while. "I don't know," she replied. "Just frightened."

"Frightened that Mr. Hagen will come back?"

"No, of course not," she said quickly, feeling her face flush. "I know that's stupid. I don't know.

178

Should I take the job? I really should — shouldn't I?"

She expected him to react, but his face remained expressionless. "I hate to sound like a psychiatrist," he said softly, "but what do you *want* to do?"

"I want for it all to have never happened," Jenny said with more emotion than she had planned.

"That would be good," Dr. Schindler said, finally smiling. "But we can't go back in time. We can only go forward." He glanced at his desk clock.

"I — I think I should take the job," Jenny said, suddenly surprising herself by making a decision. "Yes. I do. I think I should take it. There's no real reason not to. And I really need the money. And maybe — maybe it'll help me get over all the fear. You know, like getting back on a horse after you've fallen off."

"You've made a decision," Dr. Schindler said. He seemed pleased by it. Or was Jenny just guessing about his reaction?

"Yes. I guess I have," Jenny said, tossing her shoulder-length hair back, smoothing it with one hand. "My problem is that I have this wild imagination. My mom — I mean, everyone — they're always telling me that my imagination runs away with me and — "

Dr. Schindler startled her by standing up.

He's so tall, Jenny thought. He's too tall to be a shrink!

"I'm sorry," he said, his eyes on the clock. He straightened his navy-blue necktie. "Perhaps we can talk about your imagination next week. I'll also want to hear how you're doing with your new job."

"Yes. Okay," Jenny said, feeling foolish. Her time was up, and here she was dithering on about her wild imagination.

Well, he doesn't have to be *such* a clock-watcher, does he? she asked herself. Is keeping to his schedule all he cares about?

"Would you like me to prescribe some sleeping pills?" Dr. Schindler asked, walking her to the door.

"Will they stop the bad dreams?" Jenny asked hopefully.

"I'm afraid not," he said without smiling, one large hand gently on the shoulder of her T-shirt.

"Well, then, I — I don't think so," Jenny said.

"Okay. But feel free to call me anytime if you'd like a prescription," he said. "Please see Miss Gurney on the way out."

As Jenny pulled open the door, revealing Miss Gurney, the receptionist, seated at the desk in the tiny waiting room, Dr. Schindler quickly removed his hand from her shoulder.

Jenny started to say good-bye, but he had already returned to his desk. She crossed the small room with its four brown leather chairs and stepped up to Miss Gurney's low desk in front of a wall of gray filing cabinets.

Miss Gurney was a plump, middle-aged woman, with gray-streaked black hair tied tightly behind her head in a bun. She was dressed in a gray skirt and white high-necked blouse, very conservative-looking except for her eyeglasses, which had bright red plastic frames dotted with rhinestones. She finished writing a long entry in a logbook of some sort, then looked up at Jenny.

"What a pretty T-shirt," she said in a surprisingly husky voice, looking Jenny up and down through the bizarre eyeglasses. "What do you call the way the colors all run together?"

"It's . . . uh . . . tie-dyed," Jenny told her, looking down at her T-shirt to remind herself what she was wearing. Her mind was still swirling from all that she had just relived in Dr. Schindler's office.

"Very pretty," Miss Gurney muttered, searching her desk for something. She found the pad she was looking for and wrote something on it, scribbling quickly in jagged, bold letters.

"This is just a reminder of your next session," she said. She tore off the note and started to hand it to Jenny but then sneezed loudly.

"Gesundheit," Jenny said.

"Lots of germs around here," Miss Gurney said, reaching into her desk drawer for a tissue. She handed Jenny the note.

"See you next week," Jenny said.

Clutching the note in her hand, she stepped out of the office, down the hall, and out the street door. She had expected to see bright sunshine. It was four in the afternoon. But the sky was evening dark. Puddles on the sidewalk indicated that it had rained while Jenny was in the doctor's office.

I wish I had driven here, Jenny thought, looking

up at the dark sky. Too bad Mom needed the car. It's going to start raining again any second. "Oh, well," she said aloud.

She turned and, chilled by the cool, wet air, began walking quickly down Wooster Hill. Dr. Schindler's office was located in a low office building at the top of the hill, surrounded by other office buildings and a few old residence hotels. The bus stop was at the bottom of the hill, four blocks down.

It began to drizzle, a cold drizzle for June. Being careful not to step into the deeper puddles, Jenny hurried down the hill.

The sky turned even darker. It was as black as night now. A cold wind seemed to follow her down the hill. Her sneakers splashed against the wet concrete sidewalk.

"Where *is* everyone?" she asked herself, looking around at the deserted street. "Guess everyone else has the good sense to stay in out of this cold rain."

She was in the middle of the third block, shivering from the cold, her hair wet, her T-shirt soaked through, when she heard the footsteps behind her.

Suddenly frightened, she turned back to see who it was.

No one there.

Strange.

She started walking down the hill again, taking longer strides.

Come on, Jenny. Don't start thinking things. Don't let your imagination start running away with you.

The rain came down harder.

She heard the footsteps again. They were hurrying, too, keeping pace with her.

A familiar fear gripped her chest.

I'm being followed, she realized.

Chapter 2

Without looking back, Jenny started to run.

"Hey — " a voice called angrily.

Whoever it was started to run, too.

The steady rain continued to fall, whipped by sudden, cold gusts of wind. The sidewalk dipped steeply, following the hill down to the bottom. Jenny's sneakers slid and slipped as she ran, jumping over puddles now.

A car turned up the hill from Oakland Avenue, its headlights on despite the early hour. The double lights caught Jenny, as if in a spotlight, and she shielded her eyes from the shock of the brightness.

And a hand grabbed her shoulder roughly.

She opened her mouth to scream, but no sound came out.

"Jenny — what's the matter?"

She spun out of the grasp, turned to face him, breathing hard. "Chuck!"

"Hey — why'd you run? Didn't you hear me call-

184

ing you?" His expression was serious, concerned. He didn't have his usual, goofy Huck Finn grin. His curly blond hair was matted down on his head from the rain. Water ran down his freckled cheeks.

He was wearing a faded Bart Simpson T-shirt over jean cutoffs. His white Nikes were mud-stained and soaked.

"Chuck — what are you doing here?"

"Getting wet," he said. He never could resist making a joke.

"You — you really scared me," Jenny said angrily, her heart still pounding.

"I didn't mean to," he said. "Why'd you run like that?"

"I — uh . . . I thought you were someone else," she said, thinking hard to come up with an answer.

Why *had* she run like that?

It seemed pretty silly now.

And not silly. So many things frightened her now.

So many things reminded her of . . . other things.

"I *am* someone else," Chuck cracked. "That's why I was running. I was running from myself."

"Well, maybe you should keep on running," Jenny said coldly. She hadn't meant it to come out as harsh as it did.

Chuck gave her his hurt-little-boy expression. The dimple in his right cheek appeared, the dimple she used to be so crazy about.

Now she didn't feel anything.

He's so big, she realized. He's built like a wrestler. Did I ever notice how wide he is, how powerful he looks?

"Chuck, it's raining. I've got to get to the bus," she said impatiently.

"Your mom said I'd find you up here on Wooster Hill," he said, ignoring her impatience. And then he added meaningfully, "Your mom still likes me."

"Then why don't you go pester *her*?" Jenny snapped. She turned and crossed Oakland Avenue against the light. He hurried to keep up with her.

"Aw, come on, Jen — "

She kept walking, taking long strides. The bus stop was on the next corner. The street sparkled from the rain, all reds and purples.

Suddenly nothing looked real. The colors were all wrong. The sky was an eerie chartreuse. The street was a glowing purple. Everything seemed to be so wet, so shiny.

I'm walking in a dream, Jenny thought.

Chuck grabbed her arm again, gentler this time, bringing her back to reality.

She turned around, not quite sure why she felt as angry as she did. "Chuck — what do you want?" she cried, pronouncing each word slowly and distinctly, her voice hard and shrill.

"I just wanted to talk with you," he said, his eyes searching her face for some warmth. "I don't think we ever really talked after . . . " His voice trailed off.

"We talked and talked and talked," Jenny said

wearily. Half a block to go to the bus stop. The hill began to level off as it met Hunter Street. Beside her just beyond the sidewalk, rainwater poured down the curb, a steady downhill river. "I don't want to talk anymore, Chuck. I said everything I had to say. I don't want you following me anymore. I don't want you waiting for me, jumping out at me wherever I go."

The words seemed to pour out of her like the water rushing down the hill. She suddenly felt flooded with emotion, angry and sad at the same time.

"But, Jenny," Chuck said, refusing to let go of her arm. "I don't want to lose you."

Having said this, he let go of her and looked away.

He can't stand being this open, this vulnerable, Jenny thought. He makes jokes all the time, usually to cover up his true feelings. But here he is, letting me know how he really feels.

If only I had some feeling for him.

She stared at his face, so open, so fair and blue-eyed . . . so hurt.

She didn't want to hurt him. She felt a sudden pang, a sudden urge to say, "Okay, Chuck. Let's go talk. Let's go back to the way things were." But she knew that wasn't her true feeling. She knew she never could do that.

"I'm not the same person," she said flatly, wiping rainwater off her forehead with her hand.

"But, Jenny — " he pleaded.

"So much happened to me, Chuck. I'm just not the same person. It — it's not your fault. Really. It's all me. I know that. It's all my fault. But you've just got to accept it."

"I *can't* accept it!" he shouted.

His sudden anger startled her. She stepped back, into a deep, cold puddle. The water went over her sneaker, covered her white sock.

"I *won't* accept it!" he shouted.

Jenny tried to concentrate on him, tried to figure out what to say to him to make him realize once and for all that it was over between them. But the shimmering colors distracted her. The oddness of it all. The green sky that didn't look like afternoon or evening. The sparkling, slick streets. The glowing patches of blue grass beyond the sidewalk.

The two white circles of light that approached so quickly.

It was all out of focus now, all shimmering together.

And it took Jenny so long to realize that the two approaching lights, so white now, so bright, so close, were actually the twin headlights of the crosstown bus she'd been waiting for. It took her so long to make them seem real, she almost missed the bus.

But just before the driver gave up and reached to push the button to close the double doors, she leaped onto the step and pulled herself inside.

She could hear Chuck yelling angrily behind her, pleading with her to stay.

And as the doors closed with a soft *whoosh* and the bus strained away from the curb, its windshield wipers scraping across the rain-dotted glass, arcing to a steady, clicking rhythm, Jenny heard him threatening her and cursing.

Poor Chuck.

But she was being pulled away from him now, pulled away from his angry words, pulled as if in a dream, away, away, away.

I'm free, she thought, seeing Chuck grow smaller and smaller in the rear window of the bus. I'm free. . . .

"Hey — it's not free!"

The husky voice brought Jenny back to earth. "What?"

"The bus. It's not free," the driver barked. "You gonna pay?"

"Oh. Right. Sorry." Jenny searched her pockets for change.

I shouldn't have come here, Jenny told herself.

The sky was flat and starless. No moon. No clouds. The blackness was solid and deep.

I shouldn't have come here.

She stood on the hard ground, staring into the darkness, staring ahead to the bottomless pit that stood only a few feet in front of her, stretching out in both directions.

The rock quarry.

What brought her back here, back to the scene of all the horror?

What forces drove her to face it again? What did she hope to see *this* time?

Jenny, Jenny, said a voice inside her, you can't lose memories by chasing after them.

What a mysterious thing to say.

The darkness turned even darker, but she knew the treacherous hole was there. She knew she was standing near the edge, so near the edge she could almost *feel* the emptiness, almost *feel* the sheer drop of it.

I shouldn't have come here.

You can't lose memories by chasing after them.

What did it mean?

She had no time to figure it out.

Even in the darkness she could see the two hands shoot up on the top of the quarry edge. Even in the darkness she could see them grasp onto the rock.

Two hands from the pit. Two hands from down below.

Spattered with blood, they dug into the hard rock.

The man's head appeared next.

The hands pushed. The arms strained. The head seemed to rise up, like a pulpy, bloodstained moon. Like a dark-eyed, lopsided moon rising over a canyon.

"Mr. Hagen — no!"

He pulled himself up out of the hole and onto his knees. Part of the flesh of his face had been torn away, revealing curved bone under his cheeks. The rest of his flesh hung loosely about his fixed grin.

His eyes never left hers.

"Mr. Hagen — no!"

He laughed. The sound was nothing but wind, dry, dry wind. The sound of ashes.

He staggered toward her, his arms outstretched, bone protruding from the elbow of one arm.

"Mr. Hagen — it wasn't my fault!"

Even though her voice was coming from her own mouth, it sounded far away.

She tried to run. Her legs wouldn't move.

She couldn't even turn away from him. Couldn't even *look* away!

"Mr. Hagen — please!"

And she started to scream.

She opened her mouth, her eyes wide open, and screamed.

"Jenny — please! Jenny, Jenny!"

He was holding her. He had his broken arm around her. He brought his flesh-torn face close —

No!

"Jenny! Jenny — wake up!"

It was her mother who was holding on so tightly.

The dream, the horror of the dream, faded slowly.

"Mom — ?"

"Jenny. Jenny, wake up. You were dreaming again."

"What? I — "

"It was just a dream, Jenny. Another nightmare," Mrs. Jeffers whispered.

The room came into focus. The blue lamp on the

dresser. The curtains fluttering softly at her window. Her mother. Her mother looking so much older all of a sudden. Her mother looking so worried, so . . . frightened.

"I'm sorry, Mom," Jenny said, her voice tiny, still filled with sleep. "It was the same dream. I had it again."

"Jenny, Jenny," her mother whispered soothingly, her arms still tightly around Jenny's shoulders.

"It — it was so real," Jenny said.

"But it wasn't real," Mrs. Jeffers told her.

"It seemed as if I were really there. Standing there again."

"Jenny, Jenny," her mother repeated, "it wasn't real. Believe me, child — nothing like that will ever happen to you again."

Chapter 3

"Well, here goes."

Jenny stood at the foot of the gravel driveway, looking up the gently sloping lawn to the Wexners' house. It was a two-story, gray-shingled house, not very large, sort of a box without any style. A red-and-white boy's BMX bike stood leaning against the front stoop. The hedges that ran along the house from the stoop to the far side were neatly trimmed, and the grass looked as if it had been mowed with great care.

Her sneakers crunching up the gravel drive, Jenny felt a little bit less nervous. At least it's not a run-down old mansion like the Hagens' house, she told herself. The Hagens' house, she recalled with a shudder, looked like the setting for a horror movie. The Wexners' house, on the other hand, looked well cared for and inviting, Jenny thought.

From the drive, Jenny could see around to the backyard, which was also neatly mowed and dotted with tall evergreens. The sun was setting behind the trees, the sky a beautiful rosy gray.

Jenny climbed the three steps onto the stoop. She raised her hand to knock on the screen door, and a man appeared in the doorway.

"Oh, hi," he said, holding open the door. "I saw you coming up the drive. Did you walk here?"

"Yes," Jenny said, stepping into the house. "It's only two blocks from my house."

"Oh. Right. I think you told us that." He motioned for her to go into the living room, which was small but nicely furnished with a white leather couch and matching armchair around a glass-and-chrome coffee table. Three watercolor paintings of different-colored orchids were hung stairstep-fashion on the wall behind the white couch.

"I like the paintings," Jenny said.

"Oh, really?" Mr. Wexner seemed pleased. "Rena painted those. My wife. She's really quite talented. I keep after her to paint more, but she hasn't had the time."

He was a short, slightly built man, about thirty-four or thirty-five, Jenny guessed. His narrow, pleasant face was topped with thinning, light-brown hair that he wore combed straight back and as neatly trimmed as his front lawn. He was wearing a navy-blue, button-down sportshirt and neatly pressed chinos.

"Rena and I won't be out very late," he told Jenny, motioning for her to have a seat in the armchair. "We're just visiting friends."

"Where's Eli?" Jenny asked, looking out the front

window at a rabbit hopping near the stoop.

"Good question," Mr. Wexner said, smiling. "My guess is he's up in his room, building something or other. Eli, as you will quickly find out, is quite mechanical." He chuckled. "You will quickly find it out," he added, "because Eli will tell you what a mechanical genius he is. I'm afraid he's not too modest."

"Most ten-year-olds aren't," Jenny said, laughing.

"I wish Eli acted more like other ten-year-olds," Mr. Wexner said, his smile fading, his face filling with concern. "Oh, well. Back in a minute." He turned and hurried up the stairway across from the front door.

What did he mean by that? Jenny wondered.

She walked to the window and looked for the rabbit, but it had disappeared. A bookcase under the window contained three shelves of mysteries. She read the titles for a while, feeling nervous, wishing Mr. and Mrs. Wexner would leave so she could play with Eli or just relax.

"Hi, Jenny. Sorry to rush out without a chance to talk. I've written down the number where we can be reached on this pad." Mrs. Wexner, standing at the foot of the stairs, spoke rapidly in a soft whisper of a voice that barely carried across the living room.

She was a small, thin woman, shorter than Jenny, with blonde hair cut boyishly short, dramatic dark eyes, and three diamond studs in her left ear. She was wearing a pale blue, long-sleeved T-shirt over white tennis shorts, and sandals.

"Hi, Mrs. Wexner," Jenny said, stepping away from the bookcase.

"Please — call me Rena. Eli is upstairs in his room. Why don't you go up and say hi? He's expecting you."

"Okay — " Jenny started.

But Mrs. Wexner just kept right on talking. "Don't let him walk all over you, if you know what I mean. Sometimes you've got to be firm with Eli. But not *too* firm, if you know what I mean. He's very emotional. I mean — well, you'll see. He's so smart, you see. Sometimes we forget he's only ten, and — "

"Come on, Rena," Mr. Wexner called from the kitchen. "You'll scare Jenny away before she even starts!"

"Okay. Sorry," Mrs. Wexner said, her whispery voice making her sound like a little girl. "Sometimes I talk too much. But there are worse crimes, right?"

Jenny laughed. She didn't know how else to react. Mrs. Wexner seemed a bit surprised by her laughter. She picked up her bag, quickly fingered through it, then closed it, and hurried out toward the kitchen. "See you later, Jenny. Help yourself to anything," she called.

Jenny heard the kitchen screen door slam. A few seconds later, she heard a car start up. Jenny watched from the window as the Wexners' car, a blue Volvo station wagon, backed down the drive.

196

"Guess it's time to go meet Eli," she said aloud. As she climbed the stairs, she thought about Mrs. Wexner's words of warning. She seemed so nervous, Jenny thought. Why did she feel she had to warn me to be careful with Eli?

Is he some kind of monster or something?

Jenny's imagination immediately took over. She pictured a monster waiting for her at the top of the stairs, a short, hunched creature with bulging red eyes and an open, drooling mouth, giggling hideously to himself, waiting to pounce on her the second she came into view.

Stop it, Jenny, she scolded herself. He's probably just a little high-strung, she decided, reaching the top of the stairs. A narrow hall led to two bedrooms and a bathroom.

The door at the end of the hall proved to be Eli's room. Jenny stopped in the open doorway and peered into the room. Eli was seated at a long white counter that ran the length of the back wall. The counter was filled with all kinds of electronic equipment and tools. An M.C. Escher poster was the only artwork on the walls, a confusing abstract of tangled, interwoven shapes that seemed to double back on themselves endlessly.

Eli had his back to the door. He was typing rapidly on a computer keyboard, his face and body outlined in the amber glow of the monitor.

"Hi," Jenny called from the doorway.

He continued to type.

"Hello!" Jenny called, nearly shouting.

He typed a little longer, then spun around on his desk chair. "Hi," he said without smiling.

Jenny saw that he had a narrow, intense face like his father's topped with thick blond hair, which obviously hadn't been brushed that day. He had his mother's dark eyes, which were even more startling on him since his skin was so fair and the rest of his features were so pale.

He was wearing a "Turtle Power" T-shirt over green spandex bicycle shorts.

"I'm Jenny," Jenny said, venturing a few steps into the room.

"I know," Eli said, scratching one ear. "You're Jenny Jeffers. You live two blocks away on Sycamore. You go to Harrison High. You're going to baby-sit me two days and two nights a week."

"Hey — you're right," Jenny said. "I'm impressed."

He shrugged. "I don't need a baby-sitter," he told her, his face remaining expressionless, not unfriendly, not friendly.

"Maybe I do," Jenny joked.

"I built this computer," he said, ignoring her joke.

"You did? You built it? I really *am* impressed," Jenny exclaimed, moving closer to take a better look.

"From a kit," Eli said. "But I modified it. I put in a graphics card and extra memory."

"Wow," Jenny said, leaning over him to stare at the monitor screen.

"You know anything about computers?" Eli asked, sounding doubtful before Jenny even answered.

"A little. Enough to do my homework on."

He smiled for the first time. He doesn't look so grown-up and serious when he smiles, Jenny thought. Such a sweet smile.

"I really don't need a baby-sitter," he said, turning serious again. "You could go home right now, and I'd be perfectly fine."

Jenny couldn't help it. She felt a little hurt by his repeating this. "Would you *like* me to leave?" she asked.

He turned back to his computer. "I'm a mechanical genius, you see. At least that's what the testing people said. I took all these tests at this place downtown, and they said I was a mechanical genius. Know what my IQ is?"

"No. What?" Jenny asked, a little appalled by the boy's boasting.

"It's over 180. That's really high. And it'll probably go higher when I get older and know how to take tests better."

"Wow," Jenny repeated, not sure whether she should be encouraging him or lecturing him on why he should be more modest.

"What's *your* IQ?" he asked.

"I don't know," Jenny replied.

"No. Really," he said, reaching out and pulling her arm. His hand was so small, it startled Jenny. How did such little hands build this big computer?

"Tell me your IQ," he said, tugging her arm.

"I really don't know," Jenny insisted. "I don't think I've ever taken an IQ test."

"Why? Because you're too dumb?" He burst out laughing, a goofy, high-pitched laugh.

"That's not nice," Jenny said, unable to suppress a giggle. "I'm not dumb."

"Then why wouldn't they let you take an IQ test?" he asked, still holding onto her arm.

Is he being friendly? Jenny wondered.

Why is he holding onto me so tightly?

"I don't know. Let's change the subject," Jenny said impatiently. "Tell me about your computer. What do you do with it?"

"You wouldn't understand," he said, sighing.

"Why wouldn't I?"

"Because you're not a mechanical genius like me."

"That's not a nice thing to say, Eli."

Oh, brother, Jenny thought. Here I am with this kid for five minutes, and I'm already making with the lectures.

"I'll show you something else I built," he said, his large, dark eyes glowing in the amber monitor light. He held a finger up to his mouth. "*Ssshhh.*"

"Is it a secret?" Jenny asked, whispering.

"It's a secret from my parents," Eli said, pulling a cardboard carton out from its hiding spot beneath the counter.

"Maybe you shouldn't show it to me if it's a secret from them," Jenny suggested.

"It's okay. You're only the baby-sitter," he said.

I think he *meant* that to be cruel, Jenny realized.

I think maybe he's testing me, seeing how far he can go, how mean he can be. He's too smart not to know that he was insulting me. Or is he? He's only ten, after all.

Eli is definitely going to be a challenge, Jenny thought.

"See?" Eli asked, pulling a metal-and-wire contraption out of the carton.

"Wow," Jenny said, trying hard to figure out what it was.

He handed it to her. "It's a phone. Rena and Michael don't want me to have one."

"Rena and Michael?" Jenny asked, a little surprised.

"You know. My parents," he said impatiently. He took the homemade phone back and deposited it carefully in the carton. "They don't want me to have a phone. They're afraid I'll get spoiled."

"So you built your own?"

He nodded. "It really works. I tried it. There's a phone jack right under the counter there. See it?" He bent down to point it out to her.

"Who do you call with your secret phone?" Jenny asked.

He shrugged. "No one really. I mean . . . I don't have too many friends." His face remained expressionless as he said this.

Jenny felt uncomfortable with Eli's sudden openness. He was such a strange combination. One minute he was insulting her, telling her she was only the baby-sitter and he really didn't need her. The next moment he was holding onto her arm and confiding in her what had to be a painful secret.

"Do you *try* to make friends?" she asked.

"Friends are stupid," he said.

"What?"

"They're stupid. The kids at school. They're dweebs. Stupid dweebs."

Jenny didn't know how to respond to this. She didn't want to get into a heavy-duty discussion with the kid about the value of friendship. But she knew it wasn't right that he thought all the other kids were too stupid to be his friends.

"I'll show you my real friends," he said, pulling her by the arm.

"Your real friends? Eli — where are you taking me? Don't pull so hard!" He was surprisingly strong for such a skinny little kid.

"I just want to show you this," he said. "Close your eyes a minute."

Jenny obediently closed her eyes. When she opened them, Eli was holding a shoe box in front of her face. "What's in the shoe box?"

"Go ahead," he urged. "Reach your hand in."

"What?"

"It's okay, Jenny. I promise. Slide back the lid and put your hand in."

"No, I won't," Jenny insisted warily. "No way."

"Come on — I promise," he said. He looked upset, hurt that Jenny wasn't trusting him. "I promise. Please. Stick your hand in."

"Well. Okay. If you promise it's okay," Jenny said reluctantly.

He probably has a turtle in there, she thought. Or maybe a hamster or a guinea pig.

I don't want him to think I'm a dweeb, too.

She slid back the lid a few inches and plunged her hand into the box.

And then she opened her mouth wide and began to scream.

Chapter 4

"It was a tarantula," Jenny said, her voice trembling, just thinking about it. "Do you believe it? The kid put a tarantula in the box. He has three of them. They're his pets."

She stopped to scratch her arm. She suddenly felt itchy all over.

Dr. Schindler leaned forward at his desk, rolling a silver letter opener in his hand. "So what did you do?" he asked, his first words since Jenny had begun describing her first evening of baby-sitting for the Wexners.

"I — I screamed and dropped the box," Jenny said, picturing the big, hairy tarantula as she spoke. "The thing fell out of the box and started to run right toward me."

Dr. Schindler's face remained expressionless. He continued to twirl the letter opener.

"I dodged out of its way," Jenny continued. "I *hate* spiders. I've always hated spiders. But Eli, he thought it was hilarious. He was in hysterics. He laughed until tears rolled down his cheeks. I — I wanted to kill him."

"Not really," Dr. Schindler said quietly. He looked over at the tape recorder, checking to make sure the tape hadn't run out.

"Not really," Jenny agreed. "But it was such a mean trick. I mean, making me reach into that box. And then he thought it was so hilarious that he had frightened me, that his trick had worked.

"The look on Eli's face, it was . . . evil. That's the only way to describe it — evil. He just laughed and laughed."

"Then what happened?" Dr. Schindler asked, glancing at his clock.

"Eli put on a glove and picked up the tarantula, and carried it back to the glass case he keeps them in. He never even apologized. I told him that was a horrible trick to play on someone, and all he said was, 'Tarantula bites can't kill a person.' "

"He's ten, right?" the psychiatrist asked, writing a quick note on his desk pad.

"Yeah. But this wasn't like a ten-year-old's prank," Jenny insisted, suddenly feeling defensive. "He — he enjoyed it too much."

"What do you mean, Jenny?"

"I mean . . . he thought it was so funny that I got so frightened. I just had the feeling that he wanted to hurt me."

"Are you sure you're not reading too much into this?" Dr. Schindler asked.

"I don't think so," Jenny said. "I really don't."

"Well, what happened next? After he put the tarantula back in its cage?"

"I forced myself to calm down. But I was still very upset, and I told Eli how angry I was. I told him he should never play a mean trick like that again."

"Did he take you seriously?"

"I really don't know," Jenny replied, thoughtfully. "After I scolded him, he got real sullen. He turned away from me and went back to his computer. He wouldn't talk to me the rest of the night."

"Not at all?"

"Not at all," Jenny said, shaking her head. "I went downstairs and watched TV. I didn't see him the rest of the night. He even put himself to bed. I couldn't believe it."

"How do you know he put himself to bed?"

"I went upstairs to check on him about ten-thirty, and he was sound asleep, all tucked in his bed. It was so weird. I mean, I was angry at him. I don't think he had a right to be angry at *me*."

Dr. Schindler smiled for the first time in the session. "I don't think we should talk about *rights* when it comes to a ten-year-old."

Jenny frowned. "When his parents came home, I told them what had happened. They just looked at each other, like, 'Oh, brother, here we go again.'"

"What did they say to you?"

"Rena, Eli's mother, all she said was that I should try not to get Eli angry. She said once he gets angry, it's hard to win him back. They weren't apologetic or anything. And they didn't say anything about punishing Eli for what he did to me.

"They were only worried that maybe I got Eli mad at me. That's all they cared about. I got the feeling that Eli has had a *lot* of baby-sitters. He's so smart, but he seems to be real difficult."

"Do you think you can handle him?" Dr. Schindler asked.

Jenny shrugged. "I hope so. The Wexners are paying me five dollars an hour. I really would like to keep this job."

"Have you had any more nightmares?" Dr. Schindler asked. But then he looked at his clock. "Oh. Sorry. We'll have to talk about that next session." He clicked off the tape recorder and stood up.

Jenny stood up, too, feeling awkward. She never knew what to say after he turned off the tape recorder.

"Eli sounds like an interesting kid," Dr. Schindler said, raking his hand back through his coppery hair and then stretching. "Maybe he'll be sitting on my couch soon." He chuckled at his little joke.

Jenny said good-bye and hurried out to the waiting room. Miss Gurney was standing at a cabinet against the back wall, filing away tape cassettes. She turned quickly when Jenny entered the room and picked up an envelope from the desk. "Here's the doctor's bill to take to your mother," she said.

Jenny took the bill and tucked it into her canvas bag.

"I like your hair. Such a pretty color," the receptionist said in her hoarse, scratchy voice.

"Thanks," Jenny said, returning Miss Gurney's smile.

"Dr. Gurney is such a wonderful man," Miss Gurney said, returning to the tape cabinet. "I — I mean, Dr. Schindler," she corrected herself quickly. "I was a patient of his, too."

"That's nice," Jenny said awkwardly. She didn't know quite how to respond. "Uh . . . see you next time," she said, and quickly walked out of the office.

Her friends Claire and Rick were waiting for her at the mall, at the Pizza Oven. A large pepperoni pizza was on the table, several slices already devoured.

"Thanks for waiting, guys," Jenny said, rolling her eyes. She slid into the red vinyl booth beside Claire.

"Rick was starving," Claire explained, wiping tomato sauce off her chin with a paper napkin.

"Claire was starving," Rick explained, shoving the pizza tray toward Jenny. "It's still warm." He grinned at her, his wide grin.

Claire and Rick were Jenny's new friends, friends she had made after the horrifying events involving the Hagens. She had known Claire since elementary school, but they had never been close until now. Rick had been a longtime buddy of Claire's. Now they formed a very comfortable trio.

Rick was a big, good-looking jock with curly black hair and a goofy smile. Claire was as serious as Rick was unserious. She was very tall and thin, nearly a foot taller than Jenny, and had straight brown hair, which she usually wore behind her in a single braid, and serious brown eyes. She wasn't really pretty, but she would be one day. A lot of boys made fun of her because she was so tall.

Jenny liked Claire, she realized, because she was so serious.

Claire seldom made jokes. She almost never "got" jokes. She was serious and caring and sympathetic, which was more of what Jenny needed. These days, she often didn't feel like being teased or kidding around.

"Chuck was here," Claire said. "He said he was looking for you."

Jenny sighed. "He just doesn't give up."

"Chuck's a good guy," Rick said, just to annoy Jenny.

"Then *you* go out with him!" Jenny cracked.

"He's not my type," Rick said, reaching for another pizza slice.

"I'm glad you guys could meet me on your lunch break," Jenny said, changing the subject. Claire and Rick both had summer jobs at Rick's uncle's shoe store in the mall.

"It's nice to talk to someone who doesn't smell

like sneakers," Rick said and laughed at his own joke.

"How's it going?" Claire asked, sounding concerned.

"Oh, okay, I guess," Jenny said with a shrug. "I started that baby-sitting job Tuesday night."

"And?" Claire asked eagerly. She and Rick both knew how important the job was to Jenny.

"And the kid turns out to be this ten-year-old evil genius brat," Jenny said.

"Oh, wow," Claire said. "Is he really a terror?"

"Well, listen to this," Jenny said. "He raises tarantulas."

"Gross," Claire declared.

"You sure know how to pick 'em!" Rick said, and then looked very embarrassed, having realized what he said.

"Maybe you should quit this job and find another one," Claire suggested.

"Yeah. You could come help us lace sneakers all day," Rick said.

Jenny shook her head and swallowed a large chunk of cheese. "No. I'm going to try and stick it out. I think it would be good for me to try to stay with it. And the money's really good." She shrugged. "After all, what's a few tarantulas? Maybe they'll keep me on my toes."

Rick laughed and Claire forced a smile. They talked about the coming school year for a while, naming the teachers they hoped to get and the teachers they hoped to avoid. Then they talked about Rick's unsuccessful attempts to persuade his parents to buy him his own car.

"Uh-oh, we're going to be late," Claire said, staring at her watch as if it couldn't be telling the truth.

"Oh, no! If we're late, Uncle Bill will take away my shoehorn!" Rick declared with exaggerated horror. He slid out of the booth and jumped to his feet.

Jenny grabbed her bag and slid out so Claire could get out. "What are *you* going to do now?" Claire asked.

"Oh, I don't know. Wander around the mall, look at clothes, I guess," Jenny said, glancing toward the door. She half expected to see Chuck lurking there, waiting to spring on her, but he wasn't there. "If I stick with this job, I'll actually be able to afford some new clothes for school."

"Well, see you around," Rick said, giving her a little wave. He and Claire walked through the crowded restaurant and out the door, hurrying back to the shoe store, which was at the far end of the mall.

Jenny took a last slurp of her Coke, then wandered out into the brightly lit mall filled with midday shoppers, mostly housewives pushing strollers. Across from the restaurant, a new Buick revolved on a circular platform. BIG DRAWING ON SATURDAY, a Day-Glo-blue-and-orange sign proclaimed.

She looked through a couple of small clothing boutiques, then walked aimlessly through Sutton's, the large two-leveled department store in the center of the mall.

She pulled a few blouses off the rack and studied a very short, black suede skirt for a while. But her mind wasn't on shopping. She was thinking of her session with Dr. Schindler, of the things she had told him about her first encounter with Eli, of her feelings about how she had handled — or mishandled — the whole tarantula incident.

It was always hard to push the sessions with Dr. Schindler out of her mind. They seemed to follow her out of his office and stay with her, bits of conversation and thoughts swirling about, refusing to fade away, forcing her to sift through what she had said over and over again.

Whenever she saw the doctor, she felt unsettled for the rest of the day. It was as if their conversations stirred up all of her troubling thoughts, stirred up her imagination, which really didn't *need* stirring up, causing her to feel jumpy and out-of-sorts for many hours after the session ended.

Without realizing it, she had wandered into Blasters, the record store. It was a long, narrow store with hot red walls lined with big posters of music performers and a single aisle that led all the way to the back of the store, shelves of CDs on one side, cassettes on the other.

She bent down to look at some rap cassettes, then moved down the aisle to the pop-rock section. She was returning a cassette to its shelf when she noticed the boy watching her.

Glancing down the aisle at him, then quickly looking back at the cassettes, she saw that he was sort of tough-looking. He had short, spiky blond hair, so light it was almost platinum, and he was wearing black denim jeans and a red-and-black Aerosmith T-shirt.

He came closer, loping down the narrow aisle, taking big strides with his long legs.

Is he staring at me? Jenny wondered. She took a few steps toward the back of the store, then glanced back at him. He had a gold stud in one ear, she saw. And he had blue eyes.

Blue eyes that continued to look at her.

Yes, yes. He's staring at me. But why?

He continued to lope nearer, staring boldly.

Suddenly frightened, Jenny turned and began to walk quickly along the aisle toward the back.

What does he want? she wondered.

Why is he coming after me?

Is he coming after me? He looks so tough. Is he just trying to scare me?

There was no back exit to the store. Looking desperately around, Jenny realized that she was about to be trapped at the end of the aisle.

There was no one else around.

The lone sales clerk was at the register up near the front door, completely out of view.

The tough-looking blond boy came after her, his blue eyes now riveted to hers. Jenny saw that he had a scar along the bottom of his chin.

What does he want?

Why is he coming after me?

She was against the back wall now. Nowhere to run.

I'm trapped, she thought.

Completely trapped.

He wasn't stopping. He was coming for her.

Chapter 5

"You dropped this," he said.

Jenny's mouth fell open. "What?"

He handed her a small white envelope. It was the bill from Dr. Schindler's office. "It dropped out of your bag. When you bent down to look at cassettes."

Feeling like a complete fool, Jenny struggled to force her breathing back to normal and stop her pounding heartbeat, and reached out for the envelope. Once again, her wild imagination had led her down the wrong path.

"Thanks," she said. She knew her face was bright red. He must think I'm a real dweeb, she thought.

His sky-blue eyes did seem to be laughing at her. "I've never been in this store," he said.

"It's pretty good," Jenny said, still feeling embarrassed and uncomfortable. "But they have a bigger selection at Hit Power. It's across the street from the mall."

She wanted to get out of there, but he was blocking her way. He smelled of cinnamon for some reason. Jenny tried not to stare at the scar on his chin, but it was hard to avoid looking at it.

He's actually very good-looking, she thought. Although he does seem to be enjoying some private joke. His eyes seem to be laughing all the time.

"You live here?" he asked.

"You mean in the store?"

They both laughed. Nervous laughter. He looks like a little boy when he laughs, Jenny thought.

"I meant this town," he said, his blue eyes seeming to twinkle in the bright store light.

"Yeah," she said.

"I just moved here. A few weeks ago." He shifted his weight, then leaned against the display rack, still blocking the aisle. "Where do you go to school?"

"Harrison," Jenny told him.

"Hey, I'll be starting there in the fall."

I really like his smile, Jenny thought.

"It's not a bad school," she said, stuffing the envelope back into her canvas bag. "It's kinda big, though. I mean, if you're used to a smaller school."

"I'm used to a lot of schools," he said, growing serious, the laughter fading from his eyes. "My family travels around a lot. I'm sort of an army brat. Except my dad isn't in the army."

"That makes sense," Jenny cracked.

They both laughed again.

"Are you into Aerosmith?" she asked, making a face as she stared at his red-and-black T-shirt.

"No. I used to work in a T-shirt store," he said.

"This is one that nobody wanted, so I got it half-price."

Jenny laughed. "You're joking, right?"

He laughed, too. "No, I'm serious." He looked back down the long, narrow aisle, which was still empty except for the two of them, then turned back to her. "You hate heavy metal, huh?"

"Well . . . I used to like Def Leppard a little." Jenny took a step forward, trying to indicate to him that she wanted to leave. She realized she was feeling trapped.

"My name's Cal," he said.

"I'm Jenny. It was nice to meet you, Cal. I've got to get home now."

He stepped aside so that she could pass. Jenny started up the aisle, then realized he was following right behind.

"Hey, Jenny — "

She kept walking. She was nearly up to the front now. "I've really got to go," she called back to him.

He followed her out of the store. They stopped just outside the open doorway. A group of laughing teenagers hurried by, on their way to the movie sixplex just around the corner.

"Jenny — "

"Cal, really — "

"You wouldn't go out with me Friday night, would you?" he asked shyly, his hands jammed into his pockets. For once, he didn't look her in the eyes. Instead he stared past her at the kids heading to the movie theater.

"I don't know you. I — " Jenny stammered.

"This guy in my neighborhood, he goes to Harrison. Maybe you know him. Jim somebody."

"Jim Somebody?" Jenny joked. "Never heard of him."

"Jim . . . I don't remember," Cal said, scratching the back of his head. "Anyway, he invited me to a party Friday night. Maybe you could come with me, or something."

"I can't," Jenny said, shaking her head. "I have to baby-sit Friday night. I have this regular baby-sitting job, see."

"Hey, I meant *Saturday* night," Cal said, slapping his forehead. "Did I say Friday? No. I meant Saturday." He flashed her a warm smile. "You probably don't go out with guys you just meet at a mall, huh?"

"Well, I never have before," Jenny told him, shifting her bag to the other shoulder.

His grin grew wider. He still had his hands jammed into his pockets. "I'm not a bad guy. Really," he said. "Why not take a chance? Come to the party with me Saturday night. If you hate it after ten minutes, I'll take you right home. Promise."

Those eyes. Those incredible, pale blue eyes. Why did they always seem to be laughing at her?

Jenny stared into Cal's eyes, thinking hard, trying to decide.

Should she take a chance?

Should she go out with him?

* * *

"Got to run. We're a little late," Mr. Wexner said, picking up his sports jacket from the banister. Then he shouted up the stairs, " 'Bye, Eli. Have fun with Jenny!"

Mrs. Wexner came hurrying down the stairs, buttoning the sleeves of her blouse. "Hi, Jenny. How are you?" she asked, picking up her purse from the low table by the doorway. "Eli's watching TV upstairs," she said, before Jenny could answer. "He's been in a cranky mood all day. I'm sorry." She shook her head. "Just try to go along with him tonight. You know — go with the flow."

"I'm sure Jenny can handle Eli," her husband said. He chuckled, but his tone was tense and scolding. "Eli isn't really a monster, you know," he added, rolling his eyes. "You're going to frighten Jenny away."

"Oh, right," Mrs. Wexner snapped. "Like I frightened away all the other baby-sitters. I suppose it was my fault."

Mr. Wexner avoided Jenny's gaze. He looked very embarrassed.

"Why do you always have to defend Eli?" Mrs. Wexner continued angrily. "Why don't you defend *me* once in a while? That kid drove me crazy all day, and you want to ignore it and pretend he's a perfect angel!"

"Rena — *please!*" her husband pleaded. "Can we continue this discussion later? *Much* later?"

He gave Jenny a quick wave, his face filled with

embarrassment and annoyance. "See you later," he said wearily.

"Good luck," Mrs. Wexner added. And the two of them headed toward the back door.

Sounds like I'm in for a thrilling evening, Jenny thought. She dropped her bag by the living room couch and, taking a deep breath, headed up the stairs to Eli's room.

She found him sitting on his bed in the dark, watching some kind of horror film on a TV set a few inches away from the foot of his bed. "Hi, Eli. I'm back."

He didn't look up.

"What are you watching?"

"TV."

At least he answered me, she thought.

"Can I watch it with you?" she asked, moving toward the edge of his bed.

"If you want. Watch this." He pointed to the screen. "This guy's gonna get killed." He said it gleefully, an eager smile on his face.

Sure enough, the guy on the screen walked into a cabin and had his head cut off.

Yuck, Jenny thought, turning away to avoid seeing the blood splattering all over the cabin walls.

She watched Eli's reaction, his pale face reflecting the red from the TV screen. He started to giggle, then laugh out loud.

He thinks it's hilarious, Jenny realized with sudden revulsion.

"Eli — do you think you should be watching this

movie?" she asked. On the screen, a deranged-looking man was running through the woods carrying an ax.

"Who's gonna stop me?" Eli asked, challenge in his voice.

"I just mean — "

"I can watch whatever I want," he said angrily, his eyes not leaving the screen. "It's *my* room."

I don't want to turn this into a battle, Jenny thought, watching the man with the ax start chopping away at a teenage girl who looked a lot like Jenny.

Eli started laughing again, a high-pitched, gleeful laugh.

Is that what Eli would like to do to me? Jenny thought. Chop me to bits with an ax?

He's enjoying this awful flick way too much.

"I didn't have a good day," he said suddenly, turning away from the screen to look at her. The red and blue from the TV danced across his face, making him look like some kind of multicolored creature.

"I'm sorry," Jenny said sympathetically. "What was the problem?"

He thought about it for a moment. "My parents don't like my pets."

I can understand why! Jenny thought. But she didn't say it.

"I'm sorry," she said again. "Maybe you and I could have some fun tonight. Why don't you turn off the TV, and we'll — "

"No way." He turned his attention back to the screen.

"Come on, Eli. Let's play a game or something," she pleaded.

He ignored her, staring straight ahead at the screen.

"Eli — "

He continued to ignore her.

"Okay then. I'm going downstairs. I don't want to watch this horrible movie."

"It isn't horrible," he insisted. "It's good."

"See you later. I'm going downstairs."

He didn't reply.

She turned and walked out of the dark bedroom. As she reached the hallway, she heard him shrieking with laughter again, most likely at another hideous murder.

She went down to the living room, pulled the copy of *Sassy* she had brought out of her bag, and sat down in the big leather armchair to read.

As she flipped through the pages, she found herself thinking of Cal. Why on earth had she agreed to go to the party with him Saturday night?

I've never done that before, Jenny thought, feeling very uneasy. I don't know a thing about him. He seems sort of tough, not my type at all.

Why did I say yes?

Then she abruptly changed sides in the argument with herself. Why not take a chance? she asked herself. What have you got to lose?

She was still thinking about Cal when the phone

on the table beside her rang. Startled, it took her a few seconds to realize what the sound was.

Her heart was still pounding when she picked up the receiver. "Hello?"

The voice on the other end was just a whisper. *"Hi, Babes. I'm back."*

Chapter 6

There was a loud click, and the line went dead in her hand. Jenny clutched the receiver tightly, so tightly her hand hurt, hearing the whispered words again and again.

Hi, Babes. I'm back.

My nightmare is coming true.

That was her first thought.

The terrifying dream that she had had night after night. The dream in which Mr. Hagen came back for his revenge.

But it's impossible, she told herself, still clutching the phone receiver.

He's dead.

Mr. Hagen is dead.

I saw him fall over the quarry edge, down to the rocks below. I heard the *splat* his body made when it hit. I heard the *crack*.

I'll hear it as long as I live.

It *can't* be Mr. Hagen. People don't come back from the dead.

Do they?

The receiver started to buzz loudly in her hand. She returned it to the phone with a trembling hand.

"*Hi, Babes. I'm back.*"

It wasn't a voice at all. It was just air, just wind.

Like a voice from beyond the grave. Like a voice a dead man would have, a dead man back from the grave.

It wasn't Mr. Hagen, Jenny told herself, gripping the arms of the chair. The magazine slid from her lap, but she didn't bother to pick it up.

But if it *wasn't* Mr. Hagen, how did he know the same words? The same exact words Mr. Hagen had used all those times he called to terrify Jenny?

"*Hi, Babes.*" That's just what Mr. Hagen had said, whispered just the way he had whispered.

"This can't be happening to me again!" Jenny cried aloud.

Suddenly she was back in her dream, the dream that caused her to wake up screaming every morning.

There she was, back at the rock quarry, surrounded by blackness, blacker than the blackest night. There she was, staring at the gaping hole beyond the rock ledge, unable to move, unable to turn away, unable to leave.

Staring, staring at the black emptiness as the hand appeared on the quarry edge. First one hand, then the other. Mr. Hagen was pulling himself up.

His head appeared, the skin torn off one side of his face, pale skeleton showing through from underneath. One eye was missing, the gaping, empty socket bulging with pulsating veins.

Now Mr. Hagen pulled himself to his feet. One arm lay limp at his side. He shuffled toward her, pulling one leg stiffly as he moved, seeming to stare at her with the empty eye socket.

"Hi, Babes. I'm back."

"No! No!" Jenny jumped out of the chair, shaking her head hard, as if trying to shake away the dream.

It was *only* a dream after all. Only a nightmare.

And nightmares don't come true.

I'll go upstairs and see what Eli is doing, she decided.

She started walking toward the stairway, but stopped.

A sound.

It was coming from the kitchen.

She froze, listening hard.

It was the sound of the back door opening.

"Hi, Babes. I'm back." The whispered words repeated in her mind.

She forced them away, forced herself to listen to the sounds from the kitchen.

Yes. Yes. She hadn't imagined it.

She heard the kitchen door open.

And now, someone was walking through the kitchen.

Someone was about to find her, standing there, frozen in fear.

Chapter 7

"Mr. Wexner!" Jenny gasped.

"Sorry," he said, giving her an apologetic smile. "Hope I didn't startle you."

"No. I — I just didn't know who it was," Jenny said, wishing her heart would stop pounding so hard, wishing her voice didn't sound so high and frightened.

"Rena and I were so busy arguing when we left, I forgot the tickets," he said. He grabbed them up from the low table by the door. "What a night."

He started to leave, then poked his head back into the room from the doorway. "Everything okay here? Eli okay?"

"Yes. Fine," Jenny told him. "He's watching a horror movie. Do you usually let him watch really scary movies?"

Mr. Wexner sighed. "We really don't have much control over what he watches," he said.

"It's a pretty gory movie. I just wondered — " Jenny said.

"Well, maybe he'll get the blood and gore out of his system that way," Mr. Wexner said. "I've got to run." He disappeared to the kitchen. Jenny heard the back door slam behind him.

Get the blood and gore out of his system?

That's a strange thing to say, Jenny thought. She wondered if Mr. Wexner had any idea how much Eli enjoyed the blood-spattered murder scenes in the movie. How hard he laughed every time someone got killed.

Mr. Wexner's unexpected return had made Jenny forget about the frightening phone call for a minute.

It was obviously someone playing a very mean practical joke, Jenny decided. But who?

Puzzling about it, she climbed the stairs and peered into Eli's room. The TV had been turned off, to Jenny's surprise. The lights were on, and Eli was standing in the corner, staring into the glass cage that held his tarantulas.

"The movie over?" Jenny asked, walking up to him.

"No, but I didn't want to see the end," Eli said, his nose pressed against one side of the glass cage. Inside, three ugly, hairy tarantulas were scrambling over each other. "I don't like it when they kill the bad guy," Eli said, "so I turned it off."

He's definitely twisted, Jenny thought, her eyes on the scrabbling legs of the tarantulas.

"I've seen it four or five times already," Eli said. "I just fed my tarantulas. You missed it."

"What a shame," Jenny said sarcastically.

"They get all excited when I feed them. Just like real pets."

"Do they have names?" Jenny asked.

"That's babyish," he answered quickly, his eyes on the tarantulas.

Jenny glanced at the cat clock on the wall above the bed. Its tail was clicking back and forth, its eyes sliding right, then left in rhythm with the tail. "I like your clock," she said.

"It's babyish, too."

"Well, it may be babyish, but it's way past your bedtime," Jenny told him.

"Babyish," he said.

"Come on, Eli," she pleaded. "Don't give me a hard time — please."

"Babyish," he muttered, ignoring her plea. "I saw a movie on TV with a bunch of giant tarantulas. They were bigger than this house. They could eat you up in one bite."

"Yuck," she said, making a face.

It was the right reaction. He laughed.

"If I keep feeding mine, maybe they'll grow up to be giants, too."

What a sick mind, Jenny thought. "And who would you want your giant tarantulas to eat?" she asked.

"Everybody," he answered, without having to think about it.

Sweet, she thought. That's real sweet. "Come on, Eli. Bedtime. Go brush your teeth."

He yawned. "I'm not tired."

"Eli — no arguments," she said sternly, beginning to lose her patience.

"I'm not tired. Really," he whined, sounding like a little boy suddenly. "If I get into bed, can I read for a while?"

"Well . . ."

"Please please please please?"

Jenny laughed. "Okay. I guess. For a little while. What are you reading?"

He walked over to his counter, picked up a book, and returned with it. "This. It's really neat."

Jenny took it from him and stared at the title. "A Stephen King book? You're reading a Stephen King book?"

He shrugged. "So?"

"This one is supposed to be really gruesome," Jenny said. "Why don't you read something for kids your age?"

"Bor-ing," he said in a singsong voice, taking the Stephen King novel back from her.

It must be hard being ten and being so smart, Jenny realized. He can't really be a kid and read children's books and do other things normal ten-year-olds enjoy. But he can't really act like a grown-up, either.

"Will you tuck me in?" he asked sweetly.

Jenny quickly agreed, unable to stifle a laugh. Here he was, reading this gruesome horror novel, asking to be tucked into bed in a tiny voice.

Of course it took another half hour to actually

get him into bed. First he needed a drink of apple juice. Then he decided he was hungry and needed a bowl of cereal. Then he suddenly wanted to chat.

By the time Jenny got him tucked in, it was nearly eleven o'clock. The Wexners returned home a little before twelve, surprised to find Jenny sitting in the living room staring out the window into the darkness.

"Jenny, are you okay?" Mrs. Wexner asked.

"Yes. Fine," Jenny replied, jumping up from the chair. No point in telling them about the phone call, she decided.

"You look very tired," Mrs. Wexner said, her eyes studying Jenny's face. "I hope Eli didn't give you a hard time tonight."

"No. He was fine," Jenny told her, gathering up her backpack. "He watched a movie. Then he played with his spiders."

Mrs. Wexner made a face. "Those disgusting tarantulas. I'm so sorry I let him talk us into getting them for him. He said it was for a science fair at school. But then he got so attached to them, he wouldn't let us get rid of them."

"They're not the *cutest* pets in the world," Jenny said, laughing.

"I'm glad he wasn't . . . difficult," Mrs. Wexner said.

Wow, Jenny thought. Eli must be a real terror sometimes. His mother seems totally amazed that I'm not ready to quit already.

Just how bad *is* the kid?

"Want me to drive you home?" Mr. Wexner asked, appearing in the doorway.

"No. No, thanks," Jenny replied. "It's such a short walk. There's no need."

"Are you sure?" Mrs. Wexner asked, her face filled with concern. "It's so late."

"I'll be home in less than five minutes," Jenny assured her. "Really. I'll be fine."

A few minutes later, adjusting her backpack on her shoulders, she stepped out into the night. It was surprisingly warm and still. A half moon hovered above the trees in a smooth cloudless sky.

Her sneakers crunched loudly down the gravel drive. There were no other sounds. The other houses on the block were all dark.

People go to bed early around here, she thought, turning at the foot of the driveway, following the street toward her house. She had a sudden chill. For no reason at all.

Or *was* there a reason?

What was that sound?

Footsteps on the grass?

The sound was so close. Right behind her.

Someone was there.

She spun around and saw him.

He grabbed her before she had a chance to scream.

"Jenny — I've been waiting for you."

Chapter 8

Jenny's mouth dropped open in a silent gasp of surprise. She struggled to find her voice.

"*Jenny—I've been waiting for you.*"

He gripped her shoulders tightly.

"Chuck—what are you *doing* here? Let *go* of me!" she cried.

She tried to pull away from him, but he refused to let go.

His eyes were wild. His blond hair was in disarray. The front of his sleeveless T-shirt was stained with sweat.

He's so big and strong, she thought. He could crush me if he wanted to. "Let go!" she insisted.

"Not until you agree to talk to me," he said, holding on tightly to her shoulders.

"You're *hurting* me!" she cried.

He let go, but didn't step back. His chest heaved. His breath felt hot on her face.

"Chuck — what are you doing? What do you want?"

"I just want to talk, that's all," he said, breathlessly, staring into her eyes as if searching for something inside them, something that was no longer there.

"You — you really frightened me," Jenny said, taking a step back along the low curb.

It suddenly grew darker. She turned and saw that the Wexners had just turned off their porch light.

"Why won't you talk to me?" Chuck insisted, his voice a loud whisper.

"There isn't anything to talk about," Jenny said, calming a little, still watching his face warily.

"Don't say that!" he shouted angrily. "Stop saying that!"

"But, Chuck — "

"Why won't you give me a chance?"

"I've explained to you."

"You haven't explained anything." He took a step toward her. Was he trying to frighten her?

"You're supposed to be Mr. Jokes," she said. "Always cracking everyone up. What's happened to your sense of humor, Chuck? Why are you acting like this is such a tragedy?"

"Do *you* think it's funny?" he asked accusingly, his eyes growing wild again. "It's just a joke to you?" His face filled with anger.

"No — that's not what I said," Jenny cried.

"You were the best thing that ever happened to me," he said, his eyes burning into hers. "And then, you dumped me. No explanation."

234

"No explanation?" she cried. "Chuck, I went through a nightmare. I was being stalked by a crazy man. I was responsible for that man being killed. My life was like a horror movie. Afterward, I needed a change. A complete change. I'm still haunted by . . . by everything that happened. I still can't get rid of that nightmare. What *more* of an explanation do I have to give you?"

He didn't reply. Just stared at her, his features tight with anger.

"I'm sorry," she said, her voice cracking. "Sorry if I hurt you. But . . . but I can't stand to be reminded of what happened. And you — you — "

"I remind you of what happened? Jenny, I was there for you. I was there for you when you needed me. And now — you repay me by — by — " He was so angry, he couldn't speak.

Taking another step back, Jenny had a sudden, frightening thought. "Chuck — did you call me tonight?" she asked.

Was he the one?

Was he the one who called and said, "Hi, Babes. I'm back"?

It *could* have been Chuck, she realized. It *could* have been him. Who else knew Mr. Hagen's exact words?

"Did you call me?"

"Yes," he admitted, his anger not cooling.

"You *did*?!" she cried. "You called me at the Wexners'?"

"Huh?"

235

"You were the one?"

"Whoa," he said, raising a hand as if to hold her back. "I called you at your house. Your mother told me where you were."

"And you didn't call me at the Wexners'?"

"Don't change the subject!" he screamed.

She tried to read his expression, tried to read his eyes, to determine if he was the one who had tried to terrify her. But she could see only anger there.

"Chuck — I want to go home now." Her words, spoken so softly, seemed to hover in the still night air.

"No! You can't! You've got to stay. We've got to talk."

She couldn't fight the tears back any longer. They ran down her cheeks, hot and sticky. "Chuck — please. What more can I say? It's over. Just face it. I'm so sorry. But it's over."

"No!" he screamed, in a rage.

He grabbed her shoulders hard.

"Chuck — let go — "

She jerked away, tried to free herself. But he was so strong, and his rage seemed to make him even stronger.

"No!"

"Chuck — what are you going to do?" Her voice revealed her fear.

He was out of control, she realized. Completely out of control.

"No! No! Let *go!!*"

With a loud groan, he heaved her down onto the pavement.

"Ow!" she cried out as the back of her head hit the curb. "What are you doing? What are you going to do to me?"

He stood above her, breathing noisily.

Is he going to kill me? Jenny wondered.

This isn't happening, she thought, the back of her head throbbing with pain, her thoughts swirling in her mind. This isn't Chuck. Chuck was always so lovable, so . . . funny.

What have I done to him?

What is he going to do to me?

"Chuck — "

He was standing above her, gulping air.

She tried to sit up. She felt dizzy at first, but it passed quickly.

"Chuck, I have to know — was it you who called me tonight?"

He didn't reply.

She climbed unsteadily to her feet. "Chuck — "

"You'll be sorry," he whispered, still breathing hard. He was looking past her now, off into the dark trees across the street.

"Chuck, I've got to know — "

"You'll be sorry, Jenny."

Then, without looking at her, he turned and ran.

Tears drying on her face, her head throbbing, she stood and watched him run. He turned the corner, running at full speed. His car was parked under the trees. She saw the light go on as he opened the car door, saw him climb into the car, shielded her eyes as the headlights flashed on, and the car squealed away, following its own white rectangle of light.

She waited until his car was out of sight, until she could no longer hear the roar of its engine, and then she began walking toward her home, taking long but unsteady strides.

He hates me so much, she realized.

I hurt him so much.

I hurt him. He hates me.

The words repeated and repeated, followed her home, followed her up the stairs to her room, followed her into the shower.

I hurt him. He hates me.

The words followed her into her bed, wouldn't let her get to sleep. Wouldn't let her think about anything else.

I hurt him. He hates me.

She had almost drifted off when the phone beside her bed rang.

She reached out her hand and grabbed the receiver.

Should she pick it up?

Despite the heat of the night, she suddenly felt cold all over.

Cold dread.

It rang a second time.

If I don't pick it up, it'll wake Mom, she thought.

But I don't want to pick it up.

I don't want to hear that whispered voice again, that whispered voice from the grave. . . .

She picked up the receiver and raised it to her ear. "Hello?"

There it was. The whispered voice on the other end.

"Jenny? It's me."

Chapter 9

"What — what do you want?" Jenny cried, sitting up in her bed, the covers slipping to the floor.

"*Jenny — it's me.*" The whispered voice, followed by a high-pitched giggle.

Her room seemed to tilt, first to one side, then the other. "Chuck — why are you doing this?" She was so frightened, she didn't recognize her own voice, so hoarse, so tight.

Another whispered giggle. Followed by crackling static on the line. Then: "*Jenny — it's me. Eli.*"

"What?"

She hadn't heard correctly — had she?

Was her mind playing tricks on her? Had she scrambled her brains when she bumped her head against the pavement?

"It's Eli," came the little boy's whispered voice. "I'm calling on the phone I made." Another hushed giggle.

"Eli — it's you?"

She could hear him breathing on the other end.

240

"Eli?"

"Isn't this *neat*?" he asked in his normal voice, forgetting to whisper.

"Eli — why are you calling me?"

"Mom and Dad don't know," he said. "It's so awesome! My phone really works!"

"Awesome," Jenny repeated, her heartbeat starting to return to normal. She reached down and pulled the covers up off the floor. "Listen, Eli — it's very late."

"I know."

"And I'm coming to baby-sit for you all day tomorrow. So how about hanging up, and we'll both get some sleep?" Jenny didn't mean to sound as annoyed as she did, but he really had frightened her. And after her run-in with Chuck, she didn't need another scare that night.

"I can call you whenever I want," Eli said, ignoring her request. "Isn't that awesome?"

If he says "awesome" one more time, I'll be forced to murder him, Jenny thought.

"I'm going to hang up now, Eli," she said, yawning. "Good night." She replaced the receiver and glanced at the clock on her bed table. Nearly two-thirty. What on earth was Eli doing up at two-thirty?

Phoning her, of course!

She was still trying to rearrange the covers when the phone rang again.

Another stab of terror.

This time . . . this time . . . who would it be?

She picked up the receiver before the second ring. "Hello?"

"Hi. You didn't let me say good night."

"Eli — get off the phone! Go to sleep!"

He sounded very hurt. "I just wanted to say good night."

"Well, good night."

"Good night, Jenny." He giggled and hung up.

What an evil giggle, she thought.

It took her nearly half an hour to finally fall into a light, dreamless sleep.

"Great party," Jenny said, rolling her eyes sarcastically.

"Glad you're into it," Cal said, grinning.

Someone had turned off the lights in the living room, and couples were sprawled all over the floor. There were couples making out in the den, too. And in the dining room, some guys who had somehow gotten hold of a keg of beer were puzzling over it, trying to figure out how to get the tap to work. Rap music boomed from speakers set up all over the house.

Cal was wearing black, straight-legged jeans and an oversized, short-sleeved Hawaiian shirt. Jenny wore a green T-shirt over an orange sleeveless T-shirt over white tennis shorts. It was hard to tell what anyone else at the party was wearing. It was too dark!

Cal clasped Jenny's hand as they looked in vain for a quiet place to sit down. "How about the front yard?" Jenny said, leaning against Cal and screaming over the music.

Cal tripped over a couple entangled on the living room carpet and would have fallen if Jenny hadn't held onto him. They both laughed.

"Where's the guy you said invited you to this?" Jenny asked.

"What? I can't hear you."

"Where's our host?"

"I don't know." Cal shrugged. "Maybe he's here. I don't really remember what he looks like."

"Come on," Jenny said, tugging his arm. "This isn't exactly my kind of party." She pulled him toward the front hallway.

"But it's just getting started," he protested.

She dropped his arm. "You're not serious. You really want to stay?"

He shook his head. "No. Let's go."

They stumbled out the front door and hurried out of the house. Two guys with long, greased-down hair, both wearing denim jackets over plain white T-shirts, came swaggering up the walk. "This where the party is?" one of them asked Cal while the other looked Jenny up and down.

"No. It's next door," Cal said with a straight face, pointing.

"Thanks, man." The two of them turned and headed across the lawn to the house Cal had pointed to.

"Poor neighbors," Jenny whispered. "What a mean joke."

"Let's get out of here," Cal said, grinning as he pulled Jenny to his car, a scratched-up Dodge Dart that had seen better days.

He was still smiling as he started up the car, hurriedly backed down the drive, and then squealed away. But as soon as they were a few blocks from the party, Jenny noticed that his mood had changed.

His smile had faded, replaced by a grim thoughtfulness. He drove in silence, his eyes straight ahead on the road.

"Hey," Jenny called, sliding a bit closer to him. "Where are we going?"

He didn't answer, didn't seem to hear her.

"Hey, Cal — yoo-hoo!" she called, confused. "What's wrong?"

He shrugged, his expression unchanging. He ran his finger slowly along the scar on his chin.

What's going on here? Jenny wondered. One minute he's laughing and playing practical jokes. The next minute he's as quiet and somber as a tomb!

"Cal?"

"Sorry," he said, his spiked hair shining, his eyes suddenly flashing bright blue as they drove under a streetlight. "It's just that I — I'm so . . . embarrassed."

Jenny wasn't sure she heard him correctly.

"What did you say?"

"I'm embarrassed, that's all." He said it with a flash of anger.

"I don't get it."

"I wanted to show you a good time," he said,

staring straight ahead, avoiding her glance. "You know, impress you. But instead I took you to that stupid party with a bunch of creeps acting like animals."

Jenny couldn't help but laugh. "I've been to wild parties before, you know."

Her laughter seemed to make him more upset.

"I just wanted to make a good impression, that's all," he said. "Instead, there we were, stumbling around in the dark with a bunch of dorks who couldn't figure out how to work a beer keg."

Jenny started to make a joke, but stopped when she saw how upset Cal was. "Just forget about it," she said, touching his hand.

"I can't," he insisted, frowning and looking away.

"It's no big deal," she said. "Come on, Cal. I spent the entire day with a ten-year-old who thought everything I suggested we do was too boring and too babyish. No matter *what* we do tonight, it's got to be an improvement on that!"

"Oh, that makes me feel a *lot* better," he said, sounding like a child himself.

"Pull over," Jenny said suddenly.

His expression changed to one of surprise. "What?"

"Pull over," Jenny urged. "Right now."

"You're getting out?" he asked. "We're in the middle of nowhere. At least let me drive you home — "

"Will you just pull over?!" Jenny insisted.

He obediently swung the car to the curb,

stopped, and pushed the gearshift to park. Then he turned to her. "Listen, I'm real sorry — "

Before he could finish his sentence, she flung herself across the seat onto him, threw her arms around his shoulders, and pressed her lips against his in a long, hard kiss.

"Okay," she said when the kiss had come to an end, "you can go on driving now."

"Jenny — "

"I've been wanting to do that all night," Jenny said, feeling really happy for the first time in many months. "I guess you made a good impression on me after all, Cal."

She started to settle back into her seat, but he grabbed her, pulled her back to him, and kissed her again. This time, he wouldn't let the kiss end.

He's so . . . needy, Jenny thought, kissing him back, her eyes shut tight. Maybe that's what we have in common. Maybe that's why I feel so attracted to him, even though I hardly know a thing about him.

We're *both* so needy.

She pulled away from him. "Cal — we'd better stop."

He looked disappointed. She settled back in her seat, straightening her T-shirt. Her heart was pounding. She wanted to kiss him again. And again. And again.

So needy. . . .

"It's still early," she said. "Why don't we do something?"

246

He smiled at her, his blue eyes sparkling from the light of a streetlight above them. He reached for the gearshift on the steering column and slid it back into drive.

"I know! Let's go skating!" Jenny said.

"Roller skating?"

"Yeah. There's a rink just past Halsey Manor — you know, on the North Road."

"But we don't have skates," he protested.

"They rent them, silly," she said.

For a brief second, his eyes went cold, his expression hardened.

Jenny caught the change of expression and immediately understood. He doesn't like to be called "silly," she realized.

He certainly is sensitive, she thought.

She started to apologize, but his expression had softened, his smile returned. "Do you skate?" she asked, staring at him as he drove, dark trees and hedges rolling past the car windows in a shadowy blur.

"I'm willing to give it a try," he said.

"You mean you've never skated in your life?" she exclaimed.

He shrugged. "I've had a tough life."

She stared into his eyes, trying to determine how seriously he meant that. But she couldn't tell.

Headlights from an oncoming car suddenly illuminated them both, as if a spotlight had been turned on them. In the sudden brightness, Jenny was struck by how tough Cal looked, how hard. The silver stud in his ear glistened, and his short, spiked hair glowed white and then faded back into shadows as the oncoming car passed by.

What am I *doing* here with this boy, this tough-looking stranger? Jenny asked herself.

Enjoying yourself. Having a good time. For once. She answered her own question.

"Come on, Cal — turn here. The skating rink is right over this hill. It'll be fun."

"Fun," he repeated uncertainly, but he obediently turned and headed toward the rink.

The rink was crowded, and noisy, and . . . fun. An endless stream of rock and dance music flowed from the enormous speakers on the rafters. Jenny had trouble at first. She hadn't skated in quite a while, and one of her rented skates had a wheel that kept sticking.

To his own surprise, Cal turned out to be a natural skater. He whirled around the rink with ease. He was so good, Jenny accused him of having skated before. He laughed in reply, and explained that he was just a natural athlete.

Again, she couldn't tell if he was serious or not. It was so hard to tell when he was putting her on. But she didn't care. She really liked him.

She didn't want the evening to end. But at a little past midnight, he pulled up her driveway, and then walked her up to the front porch.

They kissed under the porchlight, shyly this time. Too briefly, Jenny thought.

"See you soon," Cal said casually.

Then Jenny saw a hedge rustle at the side of the house.

Too fast, too hard to be the wind.

Someone's hiding there, she realized.

She grabbed Cal's arm. "Cal — look," she whispered, pointing.

The hedge moved again. She heard the crackle of dry leaves.

"Hey — who's there?" Cal shouted angrily.

The hedge shook in response, and they both heard shoes sliding over the dry, crackling leaves on the ground.

Then someone running hard.

"Hey — " Cal shouted. He took off in the direction of the footsteps, running at full speed.

"Stop!" Jenny cried. "Cal — come back!"

It could be . . . it could be . . . Mr. Hagen.

The thought flashed into her mind.

It could be Mr. Hagen, back from the dead, waiting for her in the darkness.

Stupid thought. But she couldn't help but think it.

"Cal — come back!"

He stopped. He turned and came jogging back to her.

Was it Chuck? she wondered.

"Someone was definitely hiding over there," he said, breathing hard. "Probably a burglar."

"Probably," she said.

A burglar. Of course. That was the normal thing to suspect.

But it hadn't even occurred to Jenny that it might be a burglar.

"You were very brave," she said.

"I was very stupid," he said, shaking his head.

"You're not stupid. Don't say that." She kissed him quickly on the cheek, surprising him, turned, and hurried into the house.

She made sure all the doors were locked, then ran up the stairs, turned off the hall light, and stood on the second-floor landing, listening to Cal's car roar off. She undressed quickly, forcing herself not to think about the person lurking behind the hedge. Instead, she thought about Cal, about what a good skater he was, about how sensitive he seemed, remembering how sullen and embarrassed he had become because of the party.

After changing into her oversized, black-and-white-striped nightshirt, she didn't feel at all tired. She pulled an old copy of *Seventeen* off her shelf, turned on the light over her headboard, and settled into bed to read for a while.

She was just beginning to feel drowsy when the phone rang.

She glanced at the clock on her night table — 1:17.

She grabbed up the receiver before it could ring a second time. "Listen, Eli — I told you not to call this late!"

"It isn't Eli," said a hoarse, whispered voice.

Jenny's breath caught in her throat.

"Jenny, I'm back."

"No! Stop it!" she managed to yell.

"Are you all alone, Babes?"

The same words Mr. Hagen had used.

"Leave me alone! This isn't funny!" Jenny cried. She was gripping the phone so tightly, her hand ached.

"Company's coming," whispered the voice.

Again, the words of Mr. Hagen's that had terrified her months before.

Why did the whispered voice sound so far away?

"Who *is* this? What do you *want?*"

Her questions were greeted by a crackle of static on the line. And then silence.

Chapter 10

Small puddles of water glistened across the pavement like hundreds of glowing eyes. The endless stretch of asphalt seemed to shimmer and gleam.

To Jenny's eyes, the rain had transformed the parking lot, washed away its solid reality, turned it into a dark, sparkling jewel spread out around her feet.

Nothing is real, she thought.

Not the darkened stores of the mall, not my car in this vast, empty parking lot, not this old-fashioned-style street lamp I'm standing under.

The rain has enchanted everything, like fairy dust. She let her eyes blur until everything seemed to come together as one glistening, dark light. Then she brought it all back into focus, scraped her wet sneakers against the pavement, and looked for Cal.

Where was he? He was supposed to meet her here at the far end of the Walker Mall parking lot. Behind the Doughnut Hole, he had said. Off in the back corner of the endless lot, back where they kept the large green bins for people to drop in old used clothing for some church charity.

The rain had stopped nearly fifteen minutes ago. Jenny had arrived early, had parked and watched the stores go dark, one by one, as if in a chain reaction. Then she had watched the last of the cars drive off into the glowing, wet darkness.

All alone on this unending parking lot. She had climbed out of the car, grateful for the fresh smell of the air, the cool dampness of it. It felt so good on her skin. The air was so wet that droplets formed in her hair.

Where's Cal?

She began to pace from her car to the clothing bins, under the yellow cone of light from the tall, curved street lamp.

It was late. Very late.

Why had she agreed to meet him so late at night? Why had she agreed on this strange, unearthly meeting place, this empty, cratered planet of a parking lot?

Because she wanted to see him.

Because he had asked her to meet him here.

I'm all alone, Jenny thought. I can do anything. I can dance. I can sing.

This whole, glowing, fresh world is mine!

She began to hum to herself as she paced from the car to the big green bins, then back again. It grew darker suddenly. The pavement lost its sparkle. Jenny looked up to see that a thick curtain of clouds had covered the moon.

There were no stars.

The sky was black and solid, tar-black.

She began to feel impatient.

It wasn't right of Cal to keep her waiting in this corner of the dark, empty lot.

It wasn't right.

She felt a drop of water on her forehead, cold and startling. Then a drop on her shoulder. It was beginning to rain again, a cold sprinkle.

Cal, where are you? Hurry, please.

You know I'm waiting out here for you.

She stopped when she heard the scraping sound. Where was it coming from?

Just the wind?

The wind didn't *scrape*, did it?

"Cal — is that you? Cal? Are you here?"

The parking lot was so dark. Most of the other street lamps were out for some reason. Knocked out by the rain, maybe.

Someone groaned. Very nearby.

"Cal?"

She felt a sudden, cold tremor of fear avalanche down her spine.

Something moved. Something scraped. Someone groaned. Again.

"Cal? Please!"

Her heart seemed to stop. She had to force herself to breathe.

Then, standing under the yellow light, the cold rain beginning to fall, standing halfway between the car and the clothing bins, she saw the hand, and then the arm.

"Ohh."

There was a hand sticking out of the clothing bin.

"No!"

Is it . . . Cal?

Has something horrible happened to Cal? Is that his hand, his arm?

Without thinking, without hesitating, she ran to the bin, pushed on the lid, grabbed the hand — so cold, such a cold hand — and pulled.

As she tugged, the cold hand came to life. It gripped her hand in an icy hold.

"Hey!" she cried.

She pulled, and the figure climbed out of the bin, emerged as if floating out. Still gripping her hand, he stepped under the light.

"No!" she screamed, struggling to free herself from his grasp.

"Please — *no!*"

He grinned at her, his face olive-green under the street lamp.

Mr. Hagen grinned at her. One eye was missing, revealing a dry, empty socket. His skull showed through where pieces of his cheek and forehead flesh had decayed and fallen off.

The stench. The stench was so strong. The stench swirled around him, swirled around both of them, holding her, drawing her toward him, not letting her run.

"Jenny — " he whispered, holding her so tightly in his icy grip.

When he opened his mouth to utter her name, she could see the gaps in his mouth, the rotting, black teeth.

"Jenny — " he repeated, his voice nothing but dry, rancid air.

A black bug crawled over his swollen tongue. He repeatedly licked his dry lips, but his tongue was dry and caked with dirt.

"No!" Jenny screamed. "Let me go! I'm *begging* you! You're dead! You're dead! Let me go!"

"Jenny — I'm back!"

Chapter 11

"Then I woke up, screaming my head off," Jenny said, twisting and untwisting a dark strand of hair. "Mom was already in my room, sitting on the edge of the bed, trying to wake me up, trying to get me out of that horrible dream."

Dr. Schindler cleared his throat, but didn't say anything. He fiddled with his desk clock, waiting for Jenny to continue.

"It was kind of the same dream I've had before," she said, "except it was in a different place. And it seemed more real somehow."

"More real?" the psychiatrist asked, his green eyes suddenly coming to life.

"Yes. All the rain. I could feel the rain, feel the dampness of the air. And the colors. And the smell." Jenny made a disgusted face, remembering. "I swear, Dr. Schindler, I could still smell the stench of Mr. Hagen, that smell of decay, of rotting meat, even after I woke up."

"A very vivid dream," Dr. Schindler muttered,

checking his tape player, then returning his glance to her. "You say it took place in a different location this time?"

"Yes. All the other times I dreamed it, I was at the rock quarry," Jenny said, nervously twisting the strand of hair. "Not at a mall parking lot. I don't know *why* I was at that parking lot."

The room was silent for a while. Jenny could hear the soft hum of the tape recorder and the bubble of water in the coffee maker across the room from her. She stared at Dr. Schindler's carefully lined-up diplomas on the wall, waiting for him to say something, wondering if he was waiting for her.

"Can you think of something *else* that's different about this dream?" he asked finally. It was obvious to her that he had something in mind. Why didn't he just *say* it? Why did he only ask questions and force *her* to do all the work?

"Something else different?" Jenny thought hard, staring at the diplomas until they blurred into one big diploma. "Well . . . I guess it's the first time Cal was in the dream."

"He wasn't really *in* the dream, was he?" the doctor asked quietly, leaning forward on the mahogany desk.

"Well, no. But he was the reason I was in the parking lot."

"He was the reason?"

"Yes," Jenny answered sharply. What was Dr. Schindler leading her to?

"Why do you think he was in your dream in this manner?" he asked her.

Jenny thought about it. "I don't know."

"Do you think maybe you're unsure about Cal?" Dr. Schindler asked. "Are you maybe unsure of his motives? Are you possibly a little suspicious of Cal?"

"I don't know. I don't *think* so," Jenny answered quickly, feeling confused.

"These frightening phone calls you were telling me about," the doctor continued. "Do you think that somewhere in your mind you might suspect Cal of making them?"

"Cal? No!" Jenny exclaimed. "How could I? I mean, how could *he*? How could Cal know what Mr. Hagen whispered to me when he made those frightening calls?"

"I'm just trying to get you to think about the dream," Dr. Schindler said, settling back in his big leather desk chair. "Tell me more about the phone calls."

"There isn't much more to tell," Jenny said, her mind whirling with too many thoughts at once. "I get them late at night. The same hoarse whisper. The same words. It — it's just so scary!"

Jenny sat up, hoping to clear her head. "Dr. Schindler — am I going crazy? These calls — "

"Sometimes after such a violent trauma," said the doctor, "our imagination doesn't settle down for a while."

"What?" Jenny jumped angrily to her feet.

259

"You — you think I *imagined* those phone calls?"

"Please let me finish," Dr. Schindler said calmly, motioning for her to resume her place on the couch. "I'm not trying to upset you, Jenny. But we have to think about these things very carefully and consider all kinds of possibilities."

Jenny was too angry and upset to sit down. She stood in front of the couch with her arms crossed tightly in front of her. "And you think the phone call I got the other night was all in my imagination?"

"I think the phone calls might be like your dreams," the doctor said, clasping the edge of his desk with both hands. "Your dreams are so vivid, so lifelike, you can even smell them. Who's to say that the same impulses that drive these dreams aren't also driving you to — ?"

"I don't understand what you're saying!" Jenny screamed.

He looked at his desk clock, raking his hand quickly through his coppery hair. "Our time is up for today. It's just as well, I believe. We need to be calm if we are to discuss this properly."

"How can I be calm?" Jenny cried.

She felt hurt. Betrayed, even.

Dr. Schindler obviously thought she was crazy!

How *could* she be imagining those terrifying phone calls?

They were real. They *had* to be real.

Or was she really cracking up?

"Would you like to schedule an extra session for

tomorrow?" Dr. Schindler asked, standing up, staring at her intently.

"An extra session?"

"If it would help make you feel better," he said, stretching.

"No. I can't," she said, her head spinning. "I have to baby-sit for Eli all day. I was there all morning, and I have to work tomorrow, too. The Wexners need me more often than they thought they would."

"How did it go with Eli this morning?" the doctor asked, walking her to the door.

"Not well. Eli was mad at me for some reason. I couldn't get him to tell me why. He said he hated me, then wouldn't say another word."

"You've had an upsetting day," Dr. Schindler said sympathetically. "Can I prescribe something to calm you? Some sleeping pills?" He opened the door to the waiting room with one hand and put his other hand on Jenny's shoulder. Miss Gurney looked up from her desk outside the door. "It really wouldn't hurt to take a sleeping pill tonight," he told Jenny softly.

"Okay," Jenny relented. "Maybe it's a good idea."

He walked her over to Miss Gurney's desk, his hand on her shoulder, and quickly scribbled a prescription in the illegible handwriting that all doctors share. He tore it off the pad and handed it to her with a warm smile, the first time Jenny had seen him smile all afternoon.

"A little sleep should help," he said, turning back

toward his office. "Please call me any time if you need to." He closed the door behind him.

Jenny collected her bag from the coat closet.

"You look tired today," Miss Gurney said, studying Jenny's face.

"I didn't sleep too well last night," Jenny replied. She said good-bye to the receptionist and headed out to the street.

It was a hot, humid afternoon, the sun still high in the sky. A wall of dark gray clouds appeared to be moving closer from the south. It was probably going to rain again.

Walking quickly down the hill to the bus stop, Jenny reached into her bag to see if she had remembered to bring bus fare.

To her surprise, she felt something prickly in her bag. Prickly and squishy.

Had something spilled?

What could it be?

She wrapped her hand around it and pulled it out of her bag.

Several people nearby on the sidewalk turned, startled, as Jenny screamed and dropped her bag.

She screamed again, staring at the dead tarantula in her hand.

Chapter 12

Jenny ran into the house, slamming the door behind her, tossed down her bag, and headed for the phone. She punched in the Wexners' number, her heart still pounding.

She couldn't overlook this horrid joke of Eli's. She had to tell Mrs. Wexner about it. For one thing, it was a really cruel joke for Eli to play on her, knowing that she was afraid of spiders. But more importantly, had he actually *killed* one of his pets just to play a joke?

His parents had to know about this, Jenny decided.

The phone rang once, twice. After the eighth ring, she slammed the receiver down in frustration. "YAAAAAAAII!" she screamed at the top of her lungs, knowing she was the only one home.

It didn't make her feel any better.

What a spectacle she had made of herself on the sidewalk near Dr. Schindler's office. There she was, shrieking like a crazy person, all of her belongings strewn about her feet, a dead tarantula in her hand.

Everyone on the sidewalk thought I was totally nuts, Jenny thought, shaking her head.

Maybe I *am* totally nuts.

Dr. Schindler thinks so, too. She thought of how he suggested that she might be imagining the whispered phone calls from Mr. Hagen and felt the anger well up inside her all over again.

Could he be right?

She had always had a wild imagination. Her fantasies and daydreams had often seemed as real to her as things that actually happened. And her dreams had always been vivid and lifelike.

But could she be so confused about what is real and what isn't that she fantasized those frightening phone calls and then believed them to be real?

Thinking about this was giving her a headache. She walked into the kitchen and took a Coke from the refrigerator. After several long gulps from the can, she glanced up at the clock over the stove. Four-thirty.

"Oh, no!" she cried aloud.

She was supposed to meet Claire and Rick at four-thirty at the tennis courts behind the high school. They were getting off work early so they could play a few games of tennis with her.

Jenny ran upstairs, grabbed her tennis racquet, looked at herself in the mirror, gave her tousled hair a quick brush, then hurried out of the house, planning to jog the three blocks to the school.

"Hey — Jenny!" a voice called at the foot of the drive.

She cried out, startled. "Cal — what are you doing here?"

"Just wanted to say hi," he said, running up to her and giving her a shy smile, his blue eyes burning into hers.

"I'm late," she said awkwardly. "I'm supposed to be playing tennis with my friends."

"Oh, I see." His face filled with disappointment.

"Hey — do you play?" she asked. "We could use a fourth, actually. Then we could play real doubles."

"I could give it a try," he said, smiling.

"That's what you said when I asked if you'd ever skated before," Jenny said, laughing. "And you turned out to be great at it."

"Beginner's luck," he said with a shrug. He was wearing a denim workshirt and faded jean cutoffs. Jenny thought he looked really great.

She ran back into the house and got a tennis racquet for him. They started together toward the school.

"Which end do you hold? This skinny part here?" Cal asked, flipping the racquet in his hands.

"Very funny," Jenny said, making a face.

"You're in a swell mood today," he said as they jogged across Henry Street. Jenny waved to Mrs. Russell, out pulling up weeds as usual.

"Oh, you noticed," Jenny replied. "I'm not exactly having a great day."

"Until I arrived?" he asked innocently.

"Let's see what kind of tennis player you are," she said, making a halfhearted attempt at a joke.

When they arrived at the courts, the afternoon sun beginning to lower behind the three-story brick high school, Claire and Rick were already playing. Rick was clowning around as usual, trying to return the ball from behind his back. Claire looked a lot like a flamingo, Jenny thought, her long legs exposed under white tennis shorts.

As Jenny and Cal pulled open the gate and entered the court, Claire and Rick stopped their game. Jenny apologized for being late.

"I'm sure you have a good excuse," Rick said, flashing her his goofy smile, sweat pouring down his broad forehead.

"Yeah. Somebody put a dead tarantula in my bag," Jenny said bitterly.

"Aw, come on. You can do better than that," Rick joked.

Jenny didn't laugh. She gave him a dirty look instead. Then she introduced Cal to them.

"I'm going to Harrison in the fall," Cal said, pointing to the high school with his racquet.

"Lucky duck," Rick said sarcastically.

"Can we play?" Claire urged, looking at her watch. "It's getting late."

They divided up, Claire and Rick on one side, Jenny and Cal on the other. They warmed up a bit and then began to play. It became quickly obvious to Jenny that, as with the skating, Cal was not quite the beginner he claimed to be. In fact, he was a skilled player.

What a phony, Jenny thought, watching him serve. Why does he always have to act as if he's never tried something before?

"Out! That was out!" Rick called, sounding angry for some reason.

"It was in, I think," Cal said quietly.

"No way! It was out!" Rick insisted heatedly.

Cal sighed, shrugged, and served again. Rick hit it back hard, nearly taking Cal's head off.

"Hey — " Cal cried, ducking back, surprised.

"Come on — show us something," Rick challenged him, gripping the racquet in his beefy hands.

"Rick — chill out. What's your problem?" Claire asked.

Rick ignored her. He continued to challenge Cal.

I've never seen Rick like this, Jenny thought. He's usually so relaxed, so easy-natured.

"That was out!" Rick called, red-faced.

It was clearly in, Jenny thought. What is Rick trying to prove?

As the game continued, the two boys seemed to forget the girls were there. This isn't a game, thought Jenny. It's a personal battle of some kind.

Shouting and cursing, the boys batted the ball back and forth. Both of them seemed to grow angrier and angrier.

"Double fault!" Rick cried.

"What?" Cal screamed and angrily tossed his racquet at the net. He came running toward Rick, fury in his eyes. Rick moved forward, dropping his racquet, prepared for a fight.

But Cal stopped at the net. He was breathing hard, glaring at Rick.

Rick stopped, too, and bent to pick up his racquet.

"That's it," Claire declared. "I quit."

Rick turned around, looking startled to find her still there. "Hey — sorry," he called to her, raising his T-shirt to mop his sweaty forehead.

"What's with you today, Rick? What's all the yelling and carrying on?" Claire asked him, clearly disgusted.

"It works for McEnroe," Rick declared, his good humor beginning to return.

"I've got to get home anyway," Jenny said, feeling confused about what had just happened.

"Nice meeting you guys," Cal said, bending over to pick up the racquet he had thrown.

Claire walked over to Jenny and bent down to whisper in her ear. "I think Rick put on his little show for *you*."

"Huh? What do you mean?" Jenny asked, bewildered.

"I think Rick was showing off for *you*. Why else would he be acting so weird?"

"I don't know. Maybe his tennis shorts are too tight," Jenny cracked.

As usual, Claire didn't laugh at Jenny's joke. Her face, flushed from the exertion of the game, remained thoughtful.

Jenny suddenly noticed that Rick was staring at her, as if seeing her for the first time. His face was bright red. His black hair was matted down from all the sweat.

"See you," Jenny said, giving him a little wave.

"Yeah," he called. "Come to the shoe store sometime. I'll show you how to work a shoehorn."

Jenny laughed even though it was a stupid joke. She waited for Cal to catch up with her. They crossed the street and headed toward her house. "Some game," Jenny said.

Cal apologized. "He kept egging me on, challenging me," he explained. "I guess I just got carried away."

"He's usually not like that," Jenny said, taking his arm.

"Neither am I," Cal replied. "Hey — I forgot to tell you," he said, stopping and turning to her. "I got a job. At Mulligan's. You know — the ice-cream store in the mall. For the rest of the summer."

"That's great!" Jenny exclaimed. "Can you get me a discount on a double-scoop cone?"

"Sure," Cal said, smiling. "You'll have to come meet me there sometime. I can probably get you sprinkles on it, even. If you're good."

"Oh, I'm very good," Jenny said playfully.

They were at the bus stop. "This is where I get

off," Cal said. "I've got to get home. Here comes the bus." He reached into his pocket for change.

"See you soon," Jenny said. "Save me some mint chocolate chip. That's my favorite."

She watched him climb onto the bus, still thinking about the angry competition of the tennis match. Cal seems so nice, she thought, watching the bus pull away. But he sure lost his temper at Rick.

She wondered if she was seeing the real Cal when they were together, or whether he put on an act for her.

She hoped she was seeing the real Cal.

Then carrying both racquets, still replaying the events of the day in her troubled mind, she walked slowly home.

"I don't believe it!" Mrs. Wexner cried, holding her hands up to her face to show her surprise.

Sitting at the kitchen counter the next morning, Jenny had just told her about the dead tarantula.

"That's impossible," Mrs. Wexner insisted, gulping down the last drop of coffee in her cup, nearly dropping the cup as she tried to replace it on its saucer. "Why would Eli do that, Jenny?"

"As a joke, I think," Jenny replied. "A practical joke."

"But Eli cares about those awful tarantulas as much as — as anything he owns," Mrs. Wexner said. "I just can't imagine him killing one of them in order to play a stupid joke on you."

She glanced nervously at her watch, stood up,

and carried the cup and saucer to the sink. Her toast lay on its plate, uneaten. "I'm late, but we've got to get to the bottom of this."

She motioned for Jenny to follow her, and the two of them hurried up the stairs to Eli's room. They found him tapping away at his computer keyboard even though he hadn't had breakfast yet.

"Eli — " his mother called cautiously.

He typed a while longer, then turned around. He looked at his mother, then at Jenny. His face didn't reveal much emotion at all, just mild annoyance at having been interrupted.

"Eli, did you play a joke on Jenny?" his mother demanded accusingly.

"Huh?" His narrow face filled with innocent surprise.

"Did you put a dead tarantula in Jenny's bag?" Mrs. Wexner asked, getting right to the point.

"My tarantulas aren't dead!" Eli exclaimed, looking over at the cage. The idea seemed to upset him immediately.

Mrs. Wexner gave Jenny a puzzled glance.

Jenny stared at Eli, trying to see through this innocent act he was putting on.

"Eli, no one's angry at you," Mrs. Wexner said softly. "We just want to know if you played a joke on Jenny."

He shook his head no.

Mrs. Wexner is afraid of her own son, Jenny thought.

"You didn't give her a tarantula?"

"They're *my* tarantulas!" he insisted. "I'm not giving them to anybody."

"But, Eli, I found a tarantula in my bag yesterday," Jenny said, speaking softly as his mother had done. "You're the only person I know who has tarantulas. So — "

"Take a look," Eli said, jumping up and walking over to the glass cage.

Jenny and Mrs. Wexner quickly joined him there.

"Look," Eli said, pointing. "One, two, three. They're all here."

Jenny counted them, too. Sure enough, all three tarantulas were inside, two of them crawling around, one of them motionless, pressed up against one of the corners.

"I'm sorry, Eli," Jenny said quickly, feeling very confused and embarrassed.

"You shouldn't say I did bad things when I didn't," Eli said angrily, crossing his thin arms over his chest.

"Jenny said she was sorry," Mrs. Wexner said, coming quickly to Jenny's defense. But she gave Jenny a suspicious look.

"I'm really sorry," Jenny said, leaning down and putting her hands on Eli's slender shoulders.

He immediately pulled away from her. "Go away," he said sullenly. He turned and started to walk away. And then suddenly, he uttered a loud wail and burst into tears.

Jenny froze in surprise. She'd never seen him cry before.

His mother rushed to comfort him, throwing her arms around him and pulling him into a tight hug.

But Eli continued to wail, a high-pitched wail like a baby might make, his eyes shut tight, large tears rolling down his cheeks.

"Eli, I'm sorry. I'm sorry!" Jenny called. But he was crying too loudly to hear her.

With a loud burst of anger, he pulled out of his mother's hug and flung himself face down on the bed, crying into the bed sheet, slapping his fists in a fury against the mattress.

"We'd better leave him alone for a while," Mrs. Wexner whispered. Horrified, feeling terribly shaken and guilty, Jenny followed her back downstairs.

Why on earth is Eli carrying on like this? Jenny asked herself, her mind racing from thought to thought. Is he *that* hurt that I accused him unjustly? Or is he making a big scene to cover up his guilt?

I *didn't* imagine the tarantula, Jenny thought. I *didn't* imagine it!

"I'm afraid you've gotten off to a bad start with Eli this morning," Mrs. Wexner said, shaking her head as she glanced at her watch. "But he'll come around. Just let him cry it out. Then be really nice to him."

"I feel so bad — " Jenny started.

"Oh, I'm really late. Got to run." Mrs. Wexner grabbed up her car keys from the low table by the door.

"I guess someone else played the joke on me," Jenny said uncertainly.

Who? Who would do that? Who else would get a dead tarantula to stuff in her bag? Who could get into her bag without her knowing it?

Mrs. Wexner didn't seem to have heard what Jenny said. "Good luck with Eli. Just be careful with him. Once he stops crying, be extra nice to him," she instructed, and disappeared out the back door, heading to the garage.

She didn't care at all, Jenny thought bitterly, hearing the car grind for a few seconds and then start up. She doesn't care about anything but keeping Eli calm.

The little monster had to be the one who put the tarantula in the bag. He *had* to. And then he replaced the dead one with a new one.

But I'll never prove that.

And what's the point?

One more story to tell Dr. Schindler. One more thing for him to suggest maybe I made up.

She slumped onto the bench in front of the kitchen counter and chewed off a bit of Mrs. Wexner's cold toast. It tasted like cardboard. She could barely swallow it.

Dr. Schindler isn't helping me at all, she decided. I feel more uncertain about things, about myself, now than ever. I don't feel any more confident. I don't feel as if I'm getting anywhere.

And what if I really did imagine those phone

calls? What if I really am cracking up?

She shook her head as if trying to shake away the glum thoughts. Then she walked to the stairwell and listened.

Silence. The crying seemed to have stopped.

She listened for a while longer. Then, satisfied that he wasn't crying, shouted up, "Eli! What do you want for breakfast?"

No reply.

"Eli?"

"Go away!" he screamed, still sounding angry and out of control.

She started up the stairs. "Eli — you've got to have breakfast."

"Go away! Go away! Go away! I don't want to see you! I *don't*!" he shrieked.

She was halfway up the stairs when she heard a loud crash. Eli screamed. Then she heard another crash that sounded like something heavy falling.

"Eli — what was that?"

Silence.

She flew up the rest of the stairs, two at a time.

"Eli — are you okay?"

Silence.

Into his room, a scene of disarray.

The bedclothes had been stripped off the mattress and tossed in a tangle on the floor. The desk chair lay on its side in the middle of the room. Books and papers and art supplies were scattered everywhere.

And sprawled on his back on the carpet lay Eli, his eyes frozen in a glassy stare, his head tilted at an odd angle, his mouth hanging slack and unmoving, one arm bent underneath him, a puddle of dark blood under his head.

Chapter 13

"Eli?"

This isn't happening, she thought.

The room began to spin. She grabbed the side of the door for support.

The puddle of blood seemed to grow brighter until it glowed. She looked away. Then looked back. It had returned to its wine-dark color.

"Eli?"

She ran to him, knelt down on her knees, lifted his head in her hands. He stared up at her with glazed, unseeing eyes.

"What have you done? How did this happen?"

"Beats me," he said, and started to giggle.

"What?" Jenny screamed, dropping his head in shock.

He laughed and sat up.

"Eli — " Jenny's heart was in her throat. She felt as if she were going to be sick.

He picked up the puddle of blood. It was fake. Some sort of plastic. He tossed it at her, laughing hysterically, slapping his hand on the carpet.

"Why did you do this?" Jenny shrieked, anger rising up from her chest, feeling herself losing control. "How could you scare me like that?"

"Easy," he said. He stopped laughing, but couldn't keep a wide, pleased grin off his face.

"Didn't you know how much that would scare me?"

"Yes."

That grin — Jenny wanted to wipe it off his face. She wanted to hit him. She wanted to make him cry, make him *bleed*.

She *hated* him!

No.

Get control, Jenny. Calm down. Just calm down. He's a little boy. He's only ten years old. And he's very confused.

Calm. Calm. Calm.

No matter how many times she repeated the word to herself, it just wouldn't work.

"Hey — you said you wanted me to play a joke on you," Eli said, tugging her sleeve.

"I did not, Eli. That's not what I said at all."

His grin faded, replaced by a look of disappointment. "You said I played a joke on you before, but you were wrong. So I decided to play a joke on you now."

"But that was a *horrible* joke. You scared me to death!"

He laughed, still holding her T-shirt sleeve. "That means it was a *good* joke."

"Don't ever do that again," Jenny scolded. "To anyone."

He picked up the plastic sheet of blood and rolled it around in his hands. "I'm hungry," he said. "I want breakfast."

He isn't sorry at all, she realized. In fact, he's the happiest I've ever seen him.

"Come on downstairs," she said, finally feeling strong enough to climb to her feet. "Let's see what we can make you for breakfast."

He led the way out of the room, skipping gleefully to the hallway. Jenny stopped at the doorway and glanced back at the tarantula cage. All three of them were scrabbling all over each other in what appeared to be a concerted attempt to get out.

The phone rang at four-thirty, interrupting their Monopoly game. "Don't answer it," Eli said, shuffling through his property cards.

"I have to," Jenny told him, climbing up from the living room floor. "It might be your mom and dad. You know, they're not coming home till very late tonight."

"You're staying with me?" he asked, a worried expression on his face.

"Of course. I wouldn't leave you here alone," Jenny said, hurrying toward the phone, which had already rung three times.

Eli had acted insecure all day, clinging to her, practically attaching himself to her, never letting her out of his sight. He's such a strange kid, Jenny

279

thought. Sometimes he can be so cold and aloof, so grown-up in a way. And today he's been acting like a little baby.

She picked up the phone receiver and heard loud breathing on the other end. A cold shudder of dread rolled down her back.

"Hello?"

"Hello, Jenny?"

She didn't recognize the voice immediately.

"Jenny, it's me."

She felt her throat catch. Her fear, she realized, was always right below the surface, ready to take over, ready to grab hold of her at the slightest provocation.

"It's me — Chuck," the voice said.

She felt her anger push away the fear. "Chuck — what do *you* want?" she asked coldly. Eli looked up at her from across the room, startled by the harshness of her voice.

"Jenny, I — "

"You hurt me, Chuck," she interrupted, the painful memory flooding over her, feeding her anger.

"I — listen, I know. I just need to talk to you." His voice trembled with emotion.

She realized she didn't care.

"Chuck — have you been following me around?" she demanded.

He didn't reply.

"Well? Have you? Have you been spying on me?" Still no reply.

"You really hurt me, Chuck."

"I know. I just — "

"Stop calling me." She was shouting now, probably upsetting Eli, but she didn't care. She couldn't help herself. "I mean it. Stop spying on me, and stop calling me."

"Now, wait just a minute, Jenny — "

"Don't ever call me again." She slammed down the receiver.

Keeping her back to Eli, she stood in front of the phone, trying to calm down, taking deep breaths, waiting for her heartbeat to return to normal.

I shouldn't have yelled like that, she thought. I don't want to alarm Eli. He's been so strange and insecure all day.

She turned around to face him, prepared for his questions, prepared to try to deal with his confusion and anxiety.

To Jenny's surprise, he had a smile on his face. "You landed on Park Place," he said. "You have to pay me."

The rest of the day went smoothly. Jenny put a frozen pizza in the oven for dinner. Eli ate two slices hungrily, even though he complained that it was too tomatoey. Then he ran up to his room to work on his computer.

Jenny sat on the sofa by the living room window, staring out at the front yard as the sky faded from pink to gray, and then to black.

The darkness seemed to renew her fears, bring them out from their hiding place, make them dance across her mind. Staring out the window, she heard the frightening whispers again.

"I'm back."

"Company's coming."

Who could it be?

Who was trying to terrorize her? Who knew those words, those exact words that held such terror for her?

Chuck knew them. Chuck knew the whole story.

A few other friends knew the story, too.

And, of course, Mr. Hagen knew them.

Crazy Mr. Hagen. *Dead* Mr. Hagen.

"Jenny, I'm back."

She stood up, determined to find something to do, to drive these thoughts away, to force the fear back to its hiding place, when she heard the knock on the front door.

A hard, forceful knock that caused her to cry out in alarm.

The knock repeated, louder.

She stepped into the front hallway.

"Who's there?" she asked, unable to keep her voice from trembling.

Chapter 14

Jenny pulled open the front door.

"Hi, Jenny."

She stared at Rick and Claire as if she didn't recognize them. "Hey — what are you two doing here?"

Rick stepped past her into the hallway. "Some greeting," he muttered.

Claire held out a package of M&M's and dumped some in Jenny's hand. "Your mom told us you were here," she said, following Rick into the house.

"Hey — not bad," Rick said, admiring the living room.

"How's it going?" Claire asked, around a mouthful of candy.

"Not bad," Jenny said uncertainly. "We had a bad incident this morning, but — "

"Where's the little spaz?" Rick asked, looking around the living room.

"Don't call him that, whatever you do," Jenny warned. She suddenly realized that she had become as frightened of Eli as his parents were.

"I love little spazs," Rick said, grinning his goofy grin. "I was a little spaz myself once."

"*Now* what are you?" Jenny couldn't help but crack.

Rick looked hurt. He plopped down heavily on the couch.

"Hope you don't mind us coming here," Claire said, bending down to scratch a scrape on her knee just under the hem of her tan shorts. "We thought you might like some company."

"Well, I'm not sure it's such a good idea," Jenny said, feeling more than a little apprehensive.

Her eyes went up to the top of the stairs where Eli suddenly appeared. "Who are they?" Eli demanded, sounding suspicious.

"There he is!" Rick said, laughing for some reason. "Hi, guy. I'm Rick."

Eli ignored him. "What are they doing here?" he asked Jenny.

"These are my friends," Jenny said. "Come down and meet them."

"I don't want to," Eli said, shaking his head.

"Well, then stay upstairs and meet them," Jenny told him. "This is Claire and this is Rick."

"But what are they *doing* here?" Eli repeated, whining.

"They came to visit me. You're being very rude, Eli," Jenny said.

"You like to play basketball?" Rick asked, grinning up toward Eli.

"Want some candy?" Claire held up the envelope of M&M's.

Eli continued to ignore them. "I don't want them here," he told Jenny.

"Eli — that's not nice. These are my friends," Jenny said impatiently.

"I don't care. I don't want them here."

"We're only going to stay a short time," Claire said, looking at Jenny.

"Tough little dude," Rick muttered, pushing the sofa cushion as if testing it out.

"It's my house," Eli said.

"Aren't my friends welcome in your house?" Jenny asked, sounding more shrill than she had intended.

Eli didn't reply.

"Sure you don't want some M&M's?" Claire offered again.

"Maybe," Eli said, softening just a bit.

"I'll bring 'em up to you," Claire said, smiling at him and starting up the stairs. "Can I see your room? Jenny told me you've got a lot of great stuff in your room."

Eli shrugged. "Yeah. I guess."

Claire was definitely winning him over, Jenny saw.

"You into Ninja Turtles?" Rick called up to Eli.

Eli ignored him and, as Claire joined him on the upstairs landing, held out his hand for her to pour candy into. Then he and Claire disappeared into Eli's room.

"I think the spaz is hard of hearing or something," Rick griped.

"I think he was ignoring you," Jenny said, laughing. She sat down on the other end of the couch and tucked her legs beneath her.

"Kids love me," Rick said, brushing back his dark, curly hair. "They're usually all over me."

"He's not a regular kid," Jenny said.

"If I ever talked to company like that, my parents would really come down on me," Rick said.

"I don't think Eli gets punished too much," Jenny replied, whispering in case Eli was listening. "I don't think he'd react too well to being punished. He's very high-strung. He has an IQ of 800 or something."

"Weird," Rick said. Then suddenly he reached over and took Jenny's hand. "Hey — your hand is cold."

"Is it? I hadn't noticed," Jenny said uneasily.

He rubbed her hand as if trying to warm it. Then he slid over to Jenny on the couch and put his arm around her shoulders, pulling her close.

Jenny was so surprised, she didn't react at first.

Rick had never acted the least bit interested in her — except as a friend. What was this about?

His big arm felt heavy on her narrow shoulders. He leaned forward, moving his face toward hers, about to kiss her.

"Rick — whoa!" She tried to pull away, but he had her pinned down. "Hey — stop."

He immediately pulled his arm away. She jumped to her feet.

"What's going on?" she asked, more puzzled than upset.

He shrugged. "Just kidding around," he said. But his face was bright red, and his hurt expression revealed that he was more serious than he was letting on.

"Rick, you and Claire and I have been friends — " Jenny started.

"Forget it," he snapped, his face still crimson. "Just forget it." He seemed really angry.

Jenny didn't want to hurt him. She didn't know what to say. She felt very confused.

Rick scowled and stared out the window.

Jenny started to say something but was interrupted by shouting from upstairs. "What was that?" she asked.

Claire and Eli seemed to be having some sort of an argument.

"No, you can't!" Eli was screaming. "I *said* no!"

"What's the little spaz carrying on about now?" Rick asked, still avoiding Jenny's glance.

Jenny started to the front stairs. She was halfway across the living room when she heard Claire scream.

Then she heard the *thud-thud-thud* of someone toppling down the steep staircase.

"Oh, no! Eli!" Jenny cried.

But it wasn't Eli.

She reached the stairs in time to see Claire hit the bottom step, then drop onto the floor.

"Claire — are you all right?"

Claire didn't reply. She lay on her back, her eyes opened wide, her face still locked in an expression of terror, her neck bent at an odd, unnatural angle.

"Claire? Claire?" Jenny cried.

Rick was right behind her now. "How did she fall?"

"I don't know," Jenny replied, bending over her unmoving friend. She grabbed Claire's shoulder. "Claire — are you okay? Can you hear me?"

Claire didn't move.

"She's unconscious," Rick said, on his knees next to Jenny. "She's knocked out."

"Claire?" Jenny looked for some kind of a response, *any* kind of response.

Then, suddenly remembering Eli, she turned her glance to the top of the stairs. Eli stood on the landing, leaning against the banister, staring down at them. Jenny gasped when she saw that he was grinning, his eyes twinkling merrily under the yellow hall light.

Chapter 15

"He was standing at the top of the stairs, just grinning down at us. Enjoying it. I think he was really enjoying it, Dr. Schindler," Jenny said, sitting up rigidly on the couch. She was much too worked up to lie back.

"Sometimes people laugh or smile when they're nervous or scared," Dr. Schindler said thoughtfully, sucking on the eraser end of a yellow pencil.

"What do you mean?" Jenny asked.

"I mean, Eli may have been very frightened. He may not have realized that he was grinning. It's very normal for people to have inappropriate facial expressions when they're under stress."

"Well, Eli didn't look too stressed out to me," Jenny insisted. "There was Claire lying at the bottom of the stairs, totally unconscious. And there was Eli grinning down at us like it was some kind of joke. Or one of those slasher movies that he loves so much."

"Go on with the story," Dr. Schindler said, putting down the pencil. "What happened next? Did you call an ambulance?"

"Yes. I called 911. They sent an ambulance and some paramedics. It didn't take long for them to get there. I don't know how long, exactly. But Claire woke up before they arrived."

"She was okay?" the psychiatrist asked.

"Yeah. Pretty much," Jenny told him, fiddling with the sleeve of her T-shirt, pulling it nervously up and down. "Her head hurt. She hit it pretty hard on the way down. And she pulled a muscle in her shoulder. That's what they said at the hospital. But aside from that, Claire was okay. I mean, she felt pretty shaky for a while. But she was okay."

"And how did the accident happen?" Dr. Schindler asked.

"I'm not so sure it *was* an accident," Jenny said, raising her eyes to see the doctor's reaction.

He waited for her to continue, his face as expressionless as always.

"I mean, Eli said it was an accident. He said Claire ran out of his room and just slipped and fell down the stairs," Jenny explained, still picturing the gleeful grin on Eli's face. "But when I talked to Claire after she got home from the hospital, Claire told me she thought she was pushed."

"By Eli?" the doctor asked, leaning back in his chair.

"Yes. She wasn't really sure. It happened so fast.

But Claire thinks that Eli pushed her down the stairs."

"She wasn't sure?"

"No." Jenny shook her head. "But if Eli didn't push her, why was he grinning like that?"

"What do you think?" Dr. Schindler asked.

"I don't know."

"Do you think Eli pushed your friend, Jenny?"

"I don't know. I don't know what to think, Dr. Schindler."

"Do you think this ten-year-old would deliberately try to hurt someone, maybe even kill someone?"

"I . . . I don't know."

"Well . . . do you think Eli is *evil*?"

Jenny thought hard about it. "Maybe . . ." she said.

"How is your friend doing?" Mr. Wexner asked, struggling to tie his necktie.

"She's fine," Jenny said, dropping her backpack on the hallway floor. She was wearing faded powder-blue denim cutoffs and a sleeveless green T-shirt. "It's sweltering out there," she said, trying to change the subject.

Mr. Wexner turned away from the hall mirror to look at her. "We didn't know you had planned to have some friends over." He tried to say it lightly, but it was obvious he was scolding her.

"I didn't plan it. They surprised me," Jenny said

defensively. And then she added, "It won't happen again."

Especially since your son is a demented *killer*, she thought.

She knew she was exaggerating, but she couldn't help it.

She wondered if she'd ever be able to look at Eli again without thinking of the way he grinned down at poor, unconscious Claire.

"Eli was pretty upset about what happened," Mr. Wexner said, giving up on the knot and starting all over again. "He didn't say anything, but — "

At that moment, Eli came charging into the hallway. He ran into Jenny, nearly knocking her over, and threw his arms around her in a tight, affectionate hug.

"Eli — " his father started, surprised.

Eli continued to hug Jenny, pressing his head into her waist. Jenny patted his head tenderly. Her terrible thoughts about him started to melt away.

He's just a little boy, she thought.

He's just a troubled, spoiled little boy.

How could I have thought he was some kind of evil monster?

"I want to give you a kiss," he said.

As Mr. Wexner looked on in obvious surprise, Jenny leaned down and Eli gave her a noisy kiss on the cheek. Then he let go of her and, without saying another word, ran up the stairs to his room.

"Eli has really taken to Jenny," Mr. Wexner said

to his wife as she entered the hallway from the back of the house.

"Really?" She couldn't hide her surprise.

"I've never seen him be so affectionate with anyone," Mr. Wexner said. And then he quickly added, "Outside the family, I mean."

"He's very sweet," Jenny said, still feeling Eli's warm lips on her cheek.

"He is!?" Mrs. Wexner exclaimed, staring at Jenny. "Eli?"

Mr. Wexner laughed. "You should've seen him. He's obviously nuts about her. What a display!"

A thought crossed Jenny's mind: Maybe Eli was being so affectionate because he felt guilty about the other night.

Jenny scolded herself for being so suspicious. Maybe he just *likes* you, she told herself.

The Wexners left a few minutes later, still talking about how affectionate Eli had been toward Jenny. Jenny went to the bottom of the stairs and, standing on the spot where Claire had lain so still, so lifeless, called up to Eli. "What are you doing up there?"

"Nothing," came the reply from somewhere deep in Eli's room.

"Want to play a game or watch a tape or something?" Jenny asked.

"No," was Eli's curt reply. "I'm busy."

Probably pounding away on his computer, Jenny thought. She took a book out of her backpack and plopped down on the couch to read. Outside the living room window, a light drizzle fell. The sky was darker than usual, the blackness interrupted by gray-yellow clouds lined up eerily in straight rows. The rain, tossed by gusting winds, pattered in waves against the window, receded, then pattered noisily again.

Jenny read for about half an hour, listening to the rain against the glass. She was reading *Wuthering Heights*, one of her summer reading books. Such a romantic book, she thought. Wish I lived back then. Wish I could go walking on the moors with a handsome young man dressed for the hunt. . . .

Suddenly realizing she hadn't heard a sound from Eli's room, she closed the book and headed toward the stairs to investigate. The phone rang just as she passed it.

Startled, she picked it up before the first ring had ended. "Hello?"

"Hi, Babes." The whispered voice. *"Are you all alone?"*

"Hey — " Jenny cried angrily.

"Company's coming, Babes. Company's coming."

Her heart pounding, Jenny slammed down the receiver. She pressed her head against the wall and shut her eyes tight.

Who was it?

Who was doing this to her?

People didn't come back from the dead. They just didn't.

She forced herself not to panic, remembering

294

that she was on her way to Eli's room.

What was Eli doing up there, anyway? Why was he so quiet?

She tried to shut the hoarse, whispering voice out of her mind, to think about Eli instead of the frightening phone call.

She reached the top of the stairs, took a few steps toward Eli's room — and then stopped.

And listened.

A voice. She heard a voice coming from the room. But not Eli's voice.

Someone was in Eli's room, talking very quickly in a low whisper.

A hoarse whisper.

Jenny leaned back hard against the wall to keep from falling.

Everything started to spin. The floor tilted, then appeared to float up toward her.

Jenny had to force herself to breathe. Her fear tightened her throat, pinned her against the wall.

It was him!

The whisperer.

He was there — in Eli's room!

Chapter 16

What has he done to Eli?

Is Eli okay?

Holding her breath, her back still against the wall, Jenny began to edge slowly toward Eli's room.

She could hear the hoarse, whispered voice but couldn't make out the words.

He's on the phone, she realized.

He's whispering to someone else.

She stopped just before the open doorway. Pale white light poured out into the hall. She could hear the whispered voice speaking haltingly now into the phone.

Who is it?

How did he get into the house?

Where is Eli?

She had to find out.

With a burst of courage, Jenny grabbed the door molding, leaned forward, and peered into the room.

Eli sat at his counter, his back to her.

He had the receiver of his homemade phone to his ear. He was whispering hoarsely into the receiver, disguising his voice.

"Eli!" Jenny screamed.

He dropped the receiver onto the phone and spun around to face her. His face filled with surprise at first, then reddened with guilt.

"Eli!" she repeated, looking frantically around the room to make sure no one else was there with him.

No. Eli was alone.

"You scared me!" he cried, his lower lip trembling.

"What were you doing?" Jenny demanded.

He didn't reply. "You scared me," he repeated, quieter this time, avoiding her accusing stare.

"Answer my question, Eli. What were you doing?"

"Nothing," he said defensively. "Playing."

"Eli — I saw you talking on the phone."

"So what? It's *my* phone."

"Who were you talking to?" Jenny demanded, walking up to him, standing over him, forcing him to look at her. "Who?"

"Why are you so angry?" he asked, his voice growing tiny and frightened. "I was just playing jokes."

"Jokes?"

"Yeah. You know. Calling people. Saying funny things."

"You whispered things?" He looked away. She repeated the question. There was no way she was going to let him off the hook.

"I just said funny things. That's all." He shrugged. His tone turned impatient, irritable.

"Who did you call?" Jenny asked, putting her hands firmly on the narrow shoulders of his T-shirt.

"Kids from school," he told her. "Just kids I know."

"Did you call *me*?" Jenny asked.

He stared into her eyes as if trying to decide which answer she wanted to hear.

"Did you?" she repeated, squeezing his shoulders. "Eli, did you call me?"

"Yes," he said, his face a blank.

Jenny took a deep breath and let it out.

Was this possible? The frightening calls? Was it really possible that this innocent-looking ten-year-old was responsible?

"Don't you remember?" Eli asked. "I called you late at night. You were the first person I called on my phone."

"Huh?" Jenny realized she had read too much into his answer. Eli wasn't confessing after all. "What about tonight? Eli, did you call me a few minutes ago?"

He stared at her. "I told you. I just called friends."

She stared back at him, but she couldn't tell if he was telling the truth or not. Suddenly he reached forward and hugged her again, wrapping his spindly arms around her waist. He held onto her for a long time. Jenny couldn't see his expression. She put a hand tenderly on his shoulder, wondering if she had misjudged him or not.

After a while, he let go and sat back in his desk chair. He looked up at her, his face bathed eerily in yellow light from his desk lamp, making him look pale, ghostlike, a strange smile on his face. "Jenny, tell me about your other baby-sitting job," he said.

The rain had stopped when she reached the parking lot at the Walker Mall. A steady stream of cars, pale beams of light from their headlights steaming in the wet night air, flowed out of the lot as Jenny pulled in.

For a moment she pictured the parking lot as a vast, dark ocean, and here she was struggling to move against the tide.

She eased the car past the closing stores, her tires splashing through the deep puddles on both sides of the lane. She slowed to a crawl as she passed by Mulligan's, the ice-cream store. The last customers were walking out with cones. She couldn't see Cal inside. The store lights dimmed. She pushed down on the gas and headed toward the spot where they had arranged to meet.

What was so familiar about those large, green, clothing bins? she wondered.

She parked the car, cut the headlights, and rolled

down the window. Such a steamy night. The air felt thick and soupy. Perspiring, Jenny opened the door and climbed out.

A few dark cars dotted the enormous lot. Employees' cars, most likely. Jenny suddenly felt chilled despite the steamy heat of the night.

Why did this all seem so familiar?

Lights shifted and flickered across the vast, dark ocean, making it look to Jenny like waves bobbing and tumbling as far as she could see. More stores darkened. The stream of cars exiting the parking lot slowed to a trickle.

Jenny paced between her car and the green clothing bins. She felt nervous, fluttery, and couldn't figure out why.

I should have met Cal at the ice-cream store, she thought, her eyes surveying the empty lot. I don't know why he wanted me to meet him in this remote corner.

She squeezed the sides of her hair. Wet from the humid air. I must look a mess, she thought.

Where *is* Cal?

He probably had to clean up after the store closed.

I could use an ice-cream cone right now, she thought. Or maybe a sundae.

"Cal — where are you?" she called aloud.

More store lights darkened. The waves of the parking lot seemed to toss as the light changed.

Footsteps.

Jenny heard the splash of shoes through the puddles, the thud of feet hurrying across the wet pavement.

Someone is running toward me.

And in that instant, the dream returned. She suddenly remembered it all. . . . Waiting in this corner of the parking lot. Pacing back and forth under the yellow street lamp. Peering out through the darkness. Waiting, waiting.

And then the hand reaching out from the clothing bin. The odorous, decayed form pulling itself out, slogging toward her. Mr. Hagen, back from the dead, back to get his revenge on her.

It all came back to her.

She could see it so vividly and feel the fear. Fresh fear.

Fresh, paralyzing fear.

Here she was again, in this very same parking lot, in this very same spot.

In the very same dream.

And the footsteps grew louder. Faster.

Wake up, Jenny. He's coming after you.

Wake up. Wake up. Wake up.

Only this time it wasn't a dream.

This time she couldn't wake up from it.

This time it was real.

She uttered a desperate cry and started to run.

Chapter 17

Cold rainwater splashed over her sneakers as she ran. The footsteps, steady, rhythmic, continued to come toward her.

Which way? Which way? she asked herself, her panic causing her to stop just beyond her car.

Which way out of this dream?

The parking lot seemed to roll and tumble. Wave after wave, and once again, she was struggling against the tide.

Which way? Which way?

Wake up, Jenny. Please — wake up safe and sound in your bed at home.

No.

She had to run. She had to get away.

The footsteps wouldn't go away.

This was real. Real danger.

Fresh fear.

I'll run toward the stores, she thought. I'll run toward the light.

So why wouldn't her legs cooperate?

Impulsively she spun around to face her pursuer.

He stepped slowly out of the shadows.

"Dr. Schindler!" she cried. Panic and surprise tightened her voice to a shrill whistle.

His face filled with surprise. He was balancing a bulging, brown-paper grocery bag awkwardly against one shoulder. He had a dark stain on one leg of his chinos. His white sneakers were wet and muddy.

"Jenny?"

"Dr. Schindler. You — you frightened me," Jenny stammered.

What is he doing here? she asked herself. Why does he look so nervous?

He glanced quickly around. "I never can find my car in these big parking lots," he said. "Are you . . . waiting for someone?"

"Yes. A friend. Here he comes now."

Dr. Schindler turned to see Cal crossing the lot, both hands stuffed in his pockets. He shifted the grocery bag onto his other shoulder. "Hey — there's my car. Way down there. I see it now." A smile crossed his face as he pointed.

Jenny waved to Cal.

I really am cracking up, she thought.

Why did I run from Dr. Schindler? Why didn't I wait to see who was approaching?

It was the dream, she told herself.

For a moment, I was back in the dream.

You're crazy. Crazy. Crazy. The word repeated in her mind, drowning out what Dr. Schindler was saying to her.

"What?" she asked.

"I said good night." He still looked very nervous and uncomfortable. "I'm sorry if I frightened you."

"Good night," Jenny said, looking over Dr. Schindler's shoulder at Cal, who started to jog toward her.

Struggling with the grocery bag, Dr. Schindler hurried off to his car. "Who was that?" Cal asked, running up to Jenny.

"My shrink," Jenny said and took Cal's arm.

"Huh? What's he doing here?"

"Buying groceries, I guess," Jenny said, watching Dr. Schindler's dark Saab glide away toward the exit.

"You okay?" Cal was studying her face intently.

"He scared me, that's all. I mean . . . I don't know," Jenny said, feeling frightened again, feeling not in control, feeling as if she might burst into tears or start screaming.

Crazy. Crazy. Crazy.

"I had a dream, and it sort of came true," she told Cal, realizing that it wasn't much of an explanation.

"Want to go somewhere and talk?" Cal asked tenderly, slipping his arm around her shoulder. He smelled of ice cream. Chocolate. Strawberry.

"Yes." She decided she wanted to tell him everything, everything that was happening to her, the threats, the cold, whispered threats from the man she had sent to the grave. "Yes," she said. "I — I'm in trouble, kind of."

He held the car door open for her. "I'm a good listener," he said softly. "I've been in trouble, too."

She turned and studied his face, shadowy in the dim yellow light. The scar on his chin suddenly seemed deep and dangerous. "What kind of trouble?" she asked.

He shrugged in reply and closed her car door.

They drove to a Wendy's on the south side, empty except for three sullen teenagers in a front booth and an old man sleeping over a cup of coffee. Jenny led Cal to a table against the back wall, and over french fries and Cokes, told him the story from the beginning, starting with the night she went to work baby-sitting for the Hagens.

She told him about the attacks on baby-sitters all over town. She told him about the frightening telephone threats she began to receive.

She told him how it was Mr. Hagen who made the threats, who attacked the baby-sitters.

She told him about the terrifying night when Mr. Hagen forced her to the rock quarry outside town where he had planned to kill her and had ended up dead himself, plunging over the side to the rocks below.

She told him about the new phone calls, about the whispered voice so filled with menace. The whispered threat: *"Jenny, I'm back. Jenny, company's coming."*

She told him about Chuck, about Chuck's violent temper, about how Chuck was the only other person who knew Mr. Hagen's exact words to her.

And she told him about Eli, what a strange boy he was, and how she had caught him making furtive, whispered phone calls.

She started to tell Cal about finding the dead tarantula in her bag when she realized who it was who was trying to terrify her.

It came to Jenny in a flash.

She stopped in midsentence, her mouth dropped open, her dark eyes growing wide.

She had solved the mystery.

Chapter 18

"Jenny — what's wrong?"

Jenny didn't reply. She was thinking too hard about her sudden inspiration.

"Jenny?" Cal reached across the table and took her hand. "Earth calling Jenny."

"Oh. Sorry." She smiled at him, but she still wasn't ready to talk.

Her mind felt super-charged, as if she could feel electricity coursing through her head, through her entire body.

Suddenly, everything — or almost every-thing — made sense.

She knew she was right. She knew she had just solved the mystery. But knowing the answer didn't solve the problem.

And knowing who was doing it didn't tell her why.

"Whoa. Jenny — you're a million miles away," Cal complained, still holding her hand.

"You've got ketchup on your arm," she said, pointing.

They both laughed. The laughter helped to bring her back to Cal. She pulled a napkin out of the dispenser and helped wipe the sticky ketchup off his arm.

"I just solved the mystery," she told him. "While I was talking to you."

"I *told* you I'm a great listener," he said.

"I know who's been calling me. I know who's been trying to frighten me."

He balled up the ketchup-stained napkin and tossed it into a glass ashtray. "Jenny — who?"

"Dr. Schindler."

Cal didn't react at all, just stared at her, expressionless.

"Didn't you hear me? It's Dr. Schindler," she repeated, pounding the table for emphasis.

Cal narrowed his blue eyes thoughtfully. But he still didn't say anything.

"You don't believe me — do you?" Jenny accused.

"Why Dr. Schindler?" he asked, finally finding his voice.

"I know it's him," Jenny said. "It has to be him."

"Why?" Cal repeated. He watched over her shoulder as the three teenagers got up and left, bumping each other as they made their way out the glass door.

"He's the only one who knows the whole story. Don't you see?" Jenny asked. There was a plea in her voice. Please believe me, she was saying to Cal.

"Yeah. But what does that prove?" Cal asked, staring hard at her as if trying to penetrate her mind, invade her thoughts.

"I've told him everything," Jenny said excitedly. "Every detail. Every word Mr. Hagen said to me. Dr. Schindler is the only other person besides Chuck who knows everything."

"So what makes you think it isn't Chuck?" Cal asked, rolling the plastic salt and pepper shakers in his hands.

"Chuck is angry at me because I broke up with him," Jenny explained. "But he isn't really a bad guy. He was with me all through that terrible time. He helped me a lot. He knows what a nightmare it was. He would never try to scare me about it. He would never pretend to be Mr. Hagen. I know Chuck. Even with his bad temper, he'd never do that to me. He just wouldn't."

Cal thought about it for a while, fiddling with the salt and pepper. "So we're back to my original question: Why Dr. Schindler?"

"I don't really know why," Jenny said thoughtfully. "I mean, I don't know why he's doing it to me. I just know he's the only one it could be. I've gone over the story about Mr. Hagen with him again and again. Dr. Schindler knows every detail, every dream I've had about it, every thought I've had, every fear."

"But, Jenny — "

"And he looked so nervous at the mall parking

lot tonight, so uncomfortable," Jenny continued, not giving Cal a chance to break her train of thought. "What was he doing there, Cal? His car wasn't even near mine. What was he doing there?"

Cal started to say something, but Jenny answered for him.

"It wasn't a coincidence. He was following me. I'm sure of it. He wanted to scare me. He knew about my dream that took place there. He knew. You know, I'm remembering more things about him now," Jenny said, thinking hard.

"Like what?" Cal asked, rubbing the scar on his chin.

"Like how he always asks me where I'm going and where I'm going to be."

"What do you mean, Jenny?"

"He always wants to know if I'll be baby-sitting at the Wexners or not. He's always so curious about where I'll be after my sessions with him. And why is that?"

"Because he's really interested in you?" Cal suggested.

"No. He's only interested in his clock. In finishing on time and getting on to the next session. He isn't really interested in me. It's just a job to him. But he asks me those questions about where I'm going to be because he wants to know where to call. He wants to know where I'll be so he can frighten me. It's so obvious!"

She looked at Cal, eager for him to agree with her. But his face was still filled with doubt.

"Why, Jenny?" he asked. "You have to answer that question. Why would Dr. Schindler do that to you? Why would he try to frighten you?"

"Maybe he's crazy," Jenny suggested. She flung up her arms in frustration. "I don't know! Maybe it's a new kind of shock therapy!"

Cal laughed. He stopped when he saw the irritated look on Jenny's face. "There's no motive," he said. "Dr. Schindler has no motive."

"But if it isn't Dr. Schindler, it has to be Mr. Hagen," Jenny said, fear tightening her features. "If it isn't Dr. Schindler, that means Mr. Hagen really is back. That means I'm being pursued by a dead man, a zombie, some kind of monster. I really don't want to believe that, Cal. I really don't."

"Maybe it's the little boy," Cal suggested quietly.

"No," Jenny insisted. "It's Dr. Schindler. I know it is. I should have known the second I saw that look on his face in the parking lot. I should've known." She grabbed Cal's hand. "I'm going to prove it, Cal."

His eyes narrowed as he studied her face, still trying to read her thoughts. "How? How are you going to prove it?"

"I'm going to set a trap for him," Jenny said. "You've got to help me, Cal. You've got to. Even if you don't believe me, you've got to help me."

Chapter 19

"The doctor is running a little late this morning," Miss Gurney said, looking up from her typewriter.

"That's unusual," Jenny replied, glancing around the empty waiting room. Her eyes stopped at the tropical fish tank built into the wall. The fish all seemed to be darting wildly up and down.

They're as nervous as I am today, Jenny thought.

"I just fed them," Miss Gurney said, following Jenny's glance. "I like your hair, dear. Did you do something new to it?"

"No. Just washed it this morning," Jenny said absently, fascinated by the frenzied fish. She walked up to the tank to get a better look.

"Such a lovely color," Miss Gurney continued. "I always wanted dark brown hair like yours. Mine was always such a mousey color. So washed-out."

The inner door opened, and Dr. Schindler poked his head out, looking all around the waiting room. "Good morning, Jenny. Admiring the fish?"

"Look at them. They're going crazy!" Jenny exclaimed.

"Crazy isn't a word we use in this office," Dr. Schindler said, pursing his lips.

Jenny realized he had just made a joke, so she forced a brief laugh.

"Shall we begin?" He dropped some files onto Miss Gurney's desk, then motioned for Jenny to follow him into the office.

Even the fish know something strange is going on here, Jenny thought. She took a seat on the leather couch.

Dr. Schindler slid into his chair and pulled it up to the desk. He looks tired, Jenny thought. He looks as if he were trying to look super-alert and energetic to hide the fact that he is tired.

You're hiding something, Jenny thought.

You're hiding something. But I'm going to get it out into the open.

I'm going to end all this so I can go on with my life.

She felt a sudden tremor of fear.

Here I am, closed up in this room with the man who has been threatening me.

He's a monster. A Jekyll and Hyde.

But not for much longer.

"You seem very pensive today," he said, leaning forward, elbows on the desk, propping his chin in his hands, concentrating all of his attention on her.

Jenny didn't know how to reply to that, so she waited for him to go on.

"What would you like to talk about today?" he asked.

"Well . . ." Jenny started, taking a deep breath, clasping her hands together tightly in her lap. "I have this idea."

"Idea?"

"Yeah. About how to stop my nightmares. You know. How to get this all behind me."

"I'd like to hear your idea," he said quietly, staring into her eyes.

"Well, it's just a feeling I have."

"A feeling? Can you describe it?"

"Well," Jenny said, pretending to be working it out in her mind even though she had rehearsed this carefully. "These nightmares. These fears. I just have the feeling I'm never going to leave them behind me unless I face them head-on."

She stopped and looked to see how he reacted.

"Go on," he said, his face a blank.

"Well," she continued, wondering what he was really thinking, "to cut right to the chase, my idea is to go back to the rock quarry."

His eyes blinked wide in surprise. Then he quickly resumed his blank expression.

"To go back to the quarry. At night. To face this thing down. To show myself that there's nothing there. That it's just a pile of rocks. That there's nothing in that rock quarry that's going to come after me. I know it sounds crazy. . . ."

He cleared his throat. "As I said, we don't use that word around here."

"I just have the feeling that if I face it again, face it one last time, I can put the whole dreadful experience behind me," Jenny said. "And then maybe the nightmares will stop, and the strange phone calls, the strange thoughts that flash through my mind. Everything will go away."

She watched him carefully to see if he'd react when she mentioned the phone calls. But he remained stone-faced.

"I can see you've given this a great deal of thought," he said finally, seeming to choose his words carefully. "And I think your idea is an interesting one, and one we should discuss." He cleared his throat again. "But I feel that it is my obligation to warn you, Jenny, that there is no quick solution to your problems. No easy answer. We should try everything we can. And mainly, we should continue to talk. But you've got to realize that this could be a very long process. Years, even. You've suffered quite a trauma, let's not forget. The kind of trauma that most people never experience in a lifetime. With time, I think you will find your life, your thoughts, your subconscious thoughts, all will return to what we could call normal."

She stared at him, trying to figure out what was going on in his mind while those smooth, professional words were coming out.

Are you thinking about your next whispered phone call, Dr. Schindler? Are you thinking about what threat you're going to whisper next time?

Jenny wondered if he had other patients he terrorized, or if she was the only one.

Why me? she wondered. Why me?

"So are you recommending that I *not* go back to the quarry?" she asked.

He picked up his desk clock and rolled it between his hands. "Not necessarily," he said. "It's hard to say. It might be beneficial in some ways. Or it might serve to deepen your anxieties."

"I'm going to do it," Jenny said decisively, sitting up straight. "I've made up my mind, Dr. Schindler. I just *know* it's going to help me."

"Well, if you feel so strongly . . ." he started.

"I'm going there tonight!" Jenny declared.

Dr. Schindler switched off his tape recorder.

"Good luck," he said.

Something about the way he said it gave Jenny the chills.

Chapter 20

"Jenny, I'm back."

Jenny, lost in thought, felt a jolt as she heard those words. She spun around to see Eli smiling at her.

"What did you say?" she asked.

"I said I'm back," Eli repeated impatiently. "I went out to get the mail. I put it on the kitchen table."

"Oh." Jenny realized she was breathing hard.

"Are you okay?" Eli asked.

"Yes. I'm fine. I was just thinking about something else," Jenny said, giving his hair a playful tug.

After her session with Dr. Schindler, she had been distracted all afternoon. She had barely paid any attention at all to Eli. And when Rick had called to apologize for acting like a jerk, she had cut him off quickly without really meaning to, leaving him thinking that she was still mad at him.

All she could think about was the rock quarry. She kept picturing it in her mind, seeing it at night the way she had seen it the first time. The flat, hard, barren ground leading up to the quarry. The enormous deep, dark pit. The sheer drop. The sharp rocks far down below, jutting up in the darkness.

Thinking about going there brought back all of the terror of that dreadful night last fall. But Jenny's mind was made up. She knew she had to do it. She had to make the nightmares stop.

She had to end the constant fear, all of the fear.

She had to expose Dr. Schindler.

Then she had to get on with her life. . . .

She was thinking about her dream for the millionth time — seeing Mr. Hagen, his dead flesh rotting away, climbing up from the quarry pit, coming after her — when Mrs. Wexner returned home.

"Oh. Hi," Jenny said, jumping up from the couch, shaking her head hard as if trying to shake her thoughts away.

"How was Eli today?" Mrs. Wexner asked, stepping out of her high heels, rubbing her feet through her sheer stockings.

"Fine," Jenny said. She realized she hadn't paid much attention to Eli. I'll make it up to him on Saturday, she thought.

Eli appeared in the living room doorway, chocolate stains around his mouth. "Eli, what have you been eating? It's almost dinnertime," Mrs. Wexner scolded.

"Nothing," Eli replied, unaware that the chocolate gave him away.

"Well, say good-bye to Jenny. She's leaving."

318

Without warning, Eli came rushing up to Jenny and gave her an enthusiastic hug. She hugged him back briefly, then started toward the door, but he wouldn't let go.

He clung tightly to her, pressing his head against her waist.

It's as if he knows something is going to happen, Jenny thought. It's as if he senses that I'm about to do something dangerous.

That he might never see me again.

She scolded herself for letting her imagination run away with her. Eli doesn't sense anything, she told herself. He's just trying to make it difficult for me to leave.

"I'll see you on Saturday," she told him, gently prying him off her. She made her way quickly to the front door and hurried out without looking back.

I *hope* I see you on Saturday, she thought.

I hope I'm still alive on Saturday.

As she walked home, a red sun lowering in a cloudless, darkening sky, she could see the quarry opening up in front of her, see the endlessly deep pit, the deadly rocks awaiting below.

She started to run along the curb and, lost in her dark, frightening thoughts, nearly ran past her house before she realized where she was.

She forced herself to be cheerful at dinner, making up funny anecdotes about Eli to tell her mother. She wondered if her mother could tell that she was putting on an act.

Cal picked her up in his little car a few minutes after seven-thirty. He seemed nervous and serious, his eyes flat and lusterless, without their usual sparkle.

"Why don't we just go to a movie?" he suggested, only half-kidding.

"After tonight, we can go to the movies every night," Jenny said, squeezing his arm.

They were out of town, driving through farmland now, the dark fields interrupted by occasional silos and low farmhouses.

"What do you think is going to happen?" Cal asked, his eyes on the road, both hands gripping the top of the wheel tightly.

The question took Jenny by surprise.

She had spent so much time thinking about the past, about what had happened at the quarry, about Mr. Hagen, about her dreams, her nightmares, that she hadn't given much thought to what would happen when she actually returned to the quarry.

"I don't know," she said edgily. "I guess I'll look around and remember everything."

"You already remember everything," Cal interrupted.

"You're not being helpful," Jenny said sharply. "Don't give me a hard time."

He quickly apologized, his eyes on the road.

"I know this seems crazy to you, Cal, but you haven't lived inside my skin for the past six months. You haven't had my nightmares."

The farms gave way to barren flatlands. Theirs

was the only car on the narrow road.

"Dr. Schindler will be there," Jenny continued. "I know he will. He'll try to frighten me. But he won't be counting on you being there."

"What am I supposed to do?" Cal asked, trying to sound calm and businesslike but unable to keep the worry from his voice.

"Just be there," Jenny said. "I think that'll be enough. Once Dr. Schindler sees that he's been found out, he'll give up. He'll run."

"What if he wants to fight or something?" Cal demanded.

"He's a shrink. He won't fight," Jenny said. "He'll be afraid of you, Cal. You look tough. He's probably never been in an actual fight in his life."

"Are you telling me the truth?" Cal asked, following the road as it curved through the dark, flat countryside.

"Of course I am," Jenny told him. "Don't worry. He won't fight. When he sees you, he'll run."

"Maybe he won't show up," Cal said.

"Right," Jenny said sarcastically. "Maybe Mr. Hagen will show up instead. Maybe my nightmare will come true and Mr. Hagen will leap up out of the quarry with his skin falling off and his skull showing, and he'll grab us both and take us back to his grave with him."

Cal didn't reply.

"I'm sorry," Jenny said quickly. "Don't pay any attention to me. I'm just nervous."

"Don't worry," Cal said softly. His face, caught

in the bright headlights of an oncoming car, looked hard as if set for trouble. She had never seen that expression before. "I'll be right here," he said through gritted teeth.

For some reason, those words, meant to comfort her, gave her a sudden chill.

Cal hit the brakes hard, startling her, and turned off the road. The small car bounced onto a bumpy dirt road.

"Cal — what are you doing?" Jenny cried.

"I almost missed the turnoff," he said. "It isn't very clearly marked. Guess they don't expect many visitors at night."

"We're here," Jenny said, thinking aloud.

"Afraid?" he asked.

She wanted to answer, but her reply caught in her throat.

Chapter 21

Cal cut the engine and switched off the headlights. The world went completely black for a moment. Then Jenny began to make out dark shapes and shades of black and gray.

She pushed open the car door, took a deep breath of the hot, humid air, and stepped out onto the hard rock ground. Cal took her hand as they walked toward the quarry edge.

"It's different," Jenny said, whispering, squeezing his hand tightly. Her hand was ice-cold. His felt warm and dry. "Those piles of gravel," she whispered, pointing to the tall, dark mountain shapes around them, "they weren't here last fall."

"Guess they've been working here," Cal whispered back.

"Strange," Jenny whispered as they walked closer to the edge. "This place was deserted for years."

"How do you feel? Are you okay?" Cal asked. He put an arm heavily around her shoulder.

Straight ahead, about twenty yards away, lay the enormous pit. Jenny couldn't see it. She could just make out where the ground stopped and gave way to total blackness.

"I'm frightened, but I'm okay," Jenny whispered.

"Can we leave now?" Cal asked.

She couldn't tell if he was serious or not. "Go hide over there," she said, pointing to the nearest mound of gravel.

"Maybe I should just stay here with you," he insisted, his arm around her tightly.

"No," she said. "I want to stand here alone. I want to face this alone. And — "

She stopped.

They both saw the flash of light in the trees. Car headlights.

They could hear a car bumping along the dirt road.

The lights went out. Then the car sounds stopped. Far down the road.

"Dr. Schindler. I knew it," Jenny whispered excitedly. Her heart pounded in her chest. She gave Cal a soft shove. "Quick. Hide. Behind that gravel."

"But, Jenny — " He started to protest, but changed his mind and jogged off to the gravel pile. "I'll be right here," he called back in a loud whisper. He disappeared behind the dark mound of stones.

Jenny stood alone, breathing hard, her eyes surveying the dark mounds around the quarry. Behind her lay the open pit, black and silent.

No ghosts here tonight, she thought, reassuring herself.

No one back from the grave.

Just me. And Cal. And a visitor. A living, human visitor.

She stood still as a statue. Watching. Listening.

She could hear the crunch of footsteps approaching, hurrying over the hard ground.

I hear you, Dr. Schindler, she thought.

I hear you. I'm waiting for you.

I'm ready for you. . . .

Her senses seemed to be heightened by her fear. She could smell the rocks. She could hear each approaching footstep. She felt as if she could see the *air*.

I'm ready. I'm ready. . . .

And then suddenly, the dark figure loomed in front of her.

"*Jenny, I'm here.*" The hoarse, whispered voice.

Closer, closer. Until Jenny could see her pursuer perfectly.

"You!" Jenny cried in astonishment. "What are *you* doing here?!"

Chapter 22

"Jenny, I'm here."

"But — why?" Jenny cried, taking a step back as the figure moved closer.

"Company's coming."

"I don't believe it!" Jenny cried. "Why *you?*"

Miss Gurney took another step toward Jenny. Her hair, usually tied tightly behind her head, dropped wildly about her face. She wore baggy black slacks and a black blouse, long-sleeved despite the heat.

"Why?" Jenny cried, still stunned at the identity of her pursuer. "Why have you been doing this to me?"

"You can't have him," Miss Gurney said in her hoarse voice. She stopped advancing on Jenny and put her hands on her wide hips.

"What? I don't understand," Jenny exclaimed.

"You can't have him," Miss Gurney repeated. "You can't have Dr. Schindler."

"But — but — I don't — "

326

"You have boyfriends. Lots of boyfriends," Miss Gurney continued, spitting out her words scornfully. "You have everything, don't you! The pretty hair. The nice clothes. And the boyfriends. I know. I know everything about you, Jenny. I listen to the tapes. They tell me everything."

"Miss Gurney, I really don't know why — "

"Shut up!" the woman screamed, moving forward in a rage. "Shut up! Shut up! Shut up! You can't have him! I've seen the doctor with his hand on your shoulder. I've seen how he talks to you. He hardly says a word to me."

"I'm just a patient!" Jenny screamed.

"I was a patient, too!" Miss Gurney shouted back. "But now he ignores me. Day after day, he ignores me. While you get all the attention. He spends hours listening to your tapes. He spends hours talking with you. Why should you have everything? Why can't I have *anything*?"

"Please — calm down," Jenny pleaded. "Let's talk, okay?"

I've got to keep her talking, Jenny thought. Maybe I can make her see that this is all crazy. Crazy!

"Calm down," she said. "Let's have a nice, quiet talk about Dr. Schindler. Just you and me."

"I *won't* calm down!" Miss Gurney screamed, backing Jenny closer to the quarry edge. "Why should I calm down? The doctor doesn't even look at me anymore. But he looks at you. At your pretty, clean hair. At your pretty, dark eyes. Oh, he looks at you, all right. With your nice clothes. And all of your nightmares. All those nightmares to talk about. To talk about with *my* doctor for hours and hours. All those nightmares I listened to on your tapes."

Miss Gurney paused to take a breath. "Well, guess what, Jenny? Guess what? *I'm* your nightmare now. *I'm* your nightmare. And there's no Dr. Schindler to tell it to. There's just you and me, dear."

"I don't understand. Let's just talk," Jenny begged as Miss Gurney drew closer. "You made those frightening phone calls? You put the dead tarantula in my bag while I was in seeing the doctor?"

"I just wanted you to notice me," Miss Gurney said, lowering her voice ominously. "I just wanted you to know that I knew what you were up to. That I wouldn't let you get away with it. *And I won't!* You can't have him! You can't have him!"

"What are you going to do?" Jenny asked, backing away from the steadily approaching woman.

"You're going to die like that poor Mr. Hagen died," Miss Gurney said.

Without further warning, she rushed at Jenny, her arms outstretched, ready to push Jenny over the quarry edge.

"No!" Jenny screamed. "Cal! Help!"

She saw Cal leap out from behind the mound of gravel, running at full speed.

Startled by the unexpected sound of someone

328

behind her, Miss Gurney turned. "What?" she cried. "Who's there?"

With a loud groan, Cal leaped at her, intent on tackling her, bringing her to the ground.

But Miss Gurney dived to the ground just as he leaped.

Cal sailed over the startled woman.

And as Jenny watched in horror and disbelief, Cal plunged over the edge, headfirst into the quarry.

Chapter 23

He's gone, Jenny thought.

Cal is gone.

I've killed him. Just as I killed Mr. Hagen.

Killed my own friend.

Jenny saw Miss Gurney climbing slowly to her feet, a pleased smile on her face, her hair flying wildly about her head.

And then Jenny saw the hand reach up over the quarry side.

My dream, she thought in horror. My dream is coming true.

A second hand appeared on the edge of the pit. And then two arms.

It's Mr. Hagen, Jenny thought. He really has come back.

She stood, frozen to the spot, paralyzed as in the dream. And she waited to see the decaying flesh, the empty eye socket, the grinning, evil face of the dead man.

But the face that appeared at the edge of the pit wasn't Mr. Hagen's. It was Cal's.

Soaking wet, Cal pulled himself up onto the ground.

The quarry — it's been filled with water! Jenny realized.

She had screamed so loudly when Cal plunged over the side that she didn't hear the splash.

"Cal — are you okay?"

She started toward him, but Miss Gurney grabbed her around the waist.

"Let go!" Jenny cried, struggling to free herself.

"You can't have him! You can't!" Miss Gurney shrieked, squeezing Jenny's waist, trying to wrestle her over the edge.

"Let go!" Jenny repeated.

The big woman was surprisingly strong.

"You can't have him! You can't have him!"

She gave Jenny a hard push, then toppled on top of her.

Jenny felt the ground disappear, saw the dark water loom up.

Both of them plunged into the cold, still quarry water.

Down, down. Miss Gurney held tightly, wouldn't let go.

Jenny flailed her arms and legs. She tried to kick the big woman away with her knees.

But Miss Gurney held Jenny's waist in an ever-tightening grip.

So cold. So heavy.

So dark in this water.

Dark as death.

They floated to the surface, their heads popping above the water.

Both gulped in mouthfuls of air.

"Let go!" Jenny managed to cry.

She pushed Miss Gurney hard, and the woman lost her grip on Jenny for a moment.

Sputtering, kicking, Jenny tried to swim to the edge.

But Miss Gurney grabbed her arm, pulled her back, then pushed her head under the water.

She's too strong, Jenny thought.

Her rage makes her strong.

She kicked at the woman and pulled with all her strength.

But Miss Gurney had a tight grip on Jenny's head, pushing down with both hands now.

Dark. Then darker.

Dark as death.

Cold as death.

Jenny flailed frantically but couldn't free herself.

Her lungs felt about to burst.

Miss Gurney pushed her down, down, holding her head below the surface.

I'm going to drown, Jenny realized.

I'm starting to drown.

I can't hold my breath any longer, Jenny thought, as everything turned bright red.

Chapter 24

Up, up.

She was floating up. Up through the water. Still red.

Everything was still red.

Flashing on and off. Red then black. Red then black.

Where was Miss Gurney?

Gone.

Lost in the red. Everything so red.

Have I drowned?

No. Jenny realized she was breathing.

Someone was holding onto her. Pulling her up.

Cal.

"Cal — it's you?"

He was pulling her out of the water. She felt so heavy. So tired and so heavy. Like a rock.

Like a rock from the quarry.

"Cal — why is everything so red?"

He pulled her up and held her close. The world started to come back into focus.

There were cars all around. And men. Flashing red then black. Red then black.

Jenny realized that the flashing red lights were on top of cars. Police cars.

Several police officers were trying to fish Miss Gurney out of the water. She splashed and screamed. She wasn't cooperating. She was refusing to come out.

"Cal, we're okay," Jenny said, resting her head against his soaked shirt.

"Yeah. We're okay," Cal said quietly. "I got her off you just in time."

"You're okay!" a man's voice cried.

He stepped out of the shadows, into the blinking red light.

"Dr. Schindler!" Jenny cried, holding tightly to Cal. "How? I mean — why?"

"I brought the police," Dr. Schindler said. "You're okay? You're both okay?"

"Just wet," Jenny said. "But how did you know?"

"I couldn't find your tapes this evening. They were missing. Completely gone. Then I figured out what was going on," Dr. Schindler said. "I should have figured it out when you first told me about the phone calls. I just didn't think."

"Miss Gurney — " Jenny said pointing toward the water, where the frantic woman was still screaming at the police, still splashing in the water.

"She had violent, jealous episodes before," Dr. Schindler said. "That's what I treated her for. She was doing reasonably well, I thought. She had worked for me for three years without incident. But when I saw that she had taken your tapes, I knew she had to be the one who was frightening you. And I knew that she would come here tonight after listening to today's tape. I'm just so glad you're okay."

Apologizing again for not figuring it out sooner, Dr. Schindler hurried down to the quarry edge to try to help persuade Miss Gurney out of the water.

"You two can leave," a policeman said quietly. "Get into some dry clothes. We'll get a statement from you later."

Jenny thanked the policeman.

Cal, his arm around Jenny's shoulder, gently led her toward the car. "Had enough of the quarry?" he asked.

"Yes," she nodded, shivering. "I don't think I'll ever need to see this horrid place again."

"Good," he said, holding open the car door for her. "Does this mean we can go to the movies instead?"

She stood facing him, one hand on the car door, one hand on the soggy front of his shirt. "Yes. From now on. The movies," she said. "What would you like to see?"

"Well . . ." — his laughing eyes sparkled in the

darkness — "*Return of the Living Dead* is playing at the sixplex."

"Cal," she said, shaking her head, "you have a sick sense of humor."

She kissed him.

"Thanks," he said.

THE
BABY-SITTER
III

Jenny pushed open the glass door and escaped into the crowded mall. As she walked past The Doughnut Hole, she glanced back through the glass in time to see Mr. Larson stuff an entire chocolate cruller into his mouth.

Jenny had to laugh. No wonder Mr. Larson was beginning to resemble a doughnut!

Still chuckling, she walked away quickly, dodging a baby stroller, nearly colliding with a boy on Rollerblades.

Jenny's thoughts were on the summer. It won't be a lot of fun, she thought. But at least I've got a job. Mom will be happy.

She sighed as she continued down the crowded mall corridor. The job, she realized, didn't pay much better than baby-sitting.

Baby-sitting.

The word still made Jenny shudder and feel cold all over.

She'd had such horrifying experiences as a baby-sitter. She knew she'd never baby-sit again.

It was nearly two years later, and she still thought about it all the time. Two years later, and she still thought about Mr. Hagen, the man who hated baby-sitters. Jenny was the baby-sitter for the Hagens. Until Mr. Hagen had tried to kill her.

But she had lived. And he had died.

Died because of her.

Dr. Schindler — he was Jenny's psychiatrist — said she was doing really well.

But Jenny wasn't so sure.

Why did she still think about Mr. Hagen so much? Why did she still dream about him? About the night he tried to push her over the edge of the rock quarry and instead went hurtling to his own death? Why did every blond little boy remind her of Donny Hagen, his son?

Wasn't it time she forgot all that had happened?

"Jenny! Hey — Jenny!" A hand grabbed Jenny's shoulder.

Startled, she spun around to find her best

friends Claire and Rick grinning at her. "Didn't you hear us calling you?" Claire asked.

"No. I . . . uh . . . was thinking about something," Jenny replied. "How's it going? What are you guys doing?"

"Just hanging out," Rick said, placing a hand on Claire's shoulder. He shrugged. his broad shoulders and flashed Jenny his goofy grin.

Rick was a big, good-looking, teddy bear of a guy, with dark eyes that always seemed to be laughing and curly black hair that he seldom brushed. He was wearing faded-jeans, torn at both knees, and a red-and-black T-shirt with the words *METAL MANIACS* emblazoned across the chest.

Claire was tall and thin, an inch or two taller than Rick, with straight brown hair swept back in a ponytail and serious brown eyes. She wasn't really pretty, but would be some day. She was wearing an enormous yellow T-shirt over black leggings.

"We were too late for the movie, so we're wandering around," Claire said. "You shopping?"

"No." Jenny shook her head. "I just had a summer job interview. At The Doughnut Hole."

"Are you going to be a doughnut?" Rick joked.

Claire shoved him away. "That was really lame, you know?"

Rick laughed. "Yeah. I know."

"I got the job," Jenny said without enthusiasm.

"Hey, that's great," Claire started. Then seeing Jenny's downcast expression, she added, "Isn't it?"

"Well . . . I need a job," Jenny replied, shoving her hands into her jeans pockets. "Dr. Schindler thinks it's a good idea for me to get out of the house and do something different this summer. And, of course, with Mom being laid off, we really need the money."

"And the free doughnuts!" Rick added with a grin.

Jenny shook her head. "No free samples," she said, imitating Mr. Larson's stem voice.

"No free samples? You should quit!" Rick declared.

Claire glared at him. "Give Jenny a break."

Claire didn't like to kid around. She was a serious, caring person, and seldom made jokes. Rick was an unlikely boyfriend for Claire. He was always cracking jokes, seldom serious.

Claire turned to Jenny. "You're lucky to get a job. Most places aren't hiring this summer."

"Yeah, I know," Jenny replied quietly. She tugged a strand of dark hair off her forehead.

"I'm working the morning shift, so at least I'll be free at night to see Cal."

"Does Cal have a job yet?" Rick asked.

Jenny shook her head. "Not yet."

Claire glanced at the clock over the entrance to Sutton's, the largest department store at the mall. "We have time before the next show. Come on — walk around with us."

"Okay. Good," Jenny replied, smiling. "I promised Mom I'd get the car home. But I have a little time."

"I'm just going to grab a cone at Mulligan's," Rick said, starting across the aisle toward the ice cream parlor. "Can I get you anything?"

"No thanks," Claire and Jenny replied in unison.

Claire stopped to stare at the display in a shoe store window.

A bathing suit in Sutton's window caught Jenny's eye, and she moved close to admire it.

I won't be needing a bathing suit this summer, she thought wistfully. Not at The Doughnut Hole.

When she turned away from the window, she saw him.

And froze.

He was walking toward her. A large man in a yellow windbreaker.

She saw the red face. The close-cropped brown hair.

And those eyes. Those steel-gray eyes.

Mr. Hagen.

It's Mr. Hagen, Jenny realized, gaping at the approaching figure in horror.

But he's *dead.*

I know he's *dead.*

He's dead, and he's here, walking toward me.

And what was that in his hands?

Jenny pressed her, back against the window glass and stared open-mouthed.

He was carrying a baby.

Mr. Hagen — dead Mr. Hagen — was carrying a baby in his arms.

And as he drew near, he raised his steel-gray eyes to Jenny's.

His expression was blank, as blank as death.

And with a quick, simple motion, he grabbed the baby's head with one hand, twisted it, and pulled it off.

About the Author

R. L. STINE is the author of the series *Fear Street*, *Nightmare Room*, *Give Yourself Goosebumps*, and the phenomenally successful *Goosebumps*. His thrilling teen titles have sold more than 250 million copies internationally — enough to earn him a spot in the *Guinness Book of World Records*! Mr. Stine lives in New York City with his wife, Jane, and his son, Matt.